The Songs of Manolo Escobar

The Songs of Manolo Escobar

Carlos Alba

First published in Great Britain in 2011 by Polygon,
an imprint of Birlinn Ltd
West Newington House
10 Newington Road
Edinburgh EH9 1QS
www.birlinn.co.uk

ISBN 978 1 84697 173 0

British Library Cataloguing-in-Publication Data
A catalogue record for this book is available on request from the British Library.

The publishers acknowledge subsidy from

Typeset by Hewer Text UK Ltd, Edinburgh
Printed and bound in Great Britain by Bell & Bain Ltd., Glasgow

For my mum and dad

Acknowledgments

I'd like to thank several people for helping with the research for this book: Emilio Silva at the Association for the Recovery of Historical Memory; Valentina Montoya Martinez for sharing her experiences of coming to Britain from Chile as a child, following her country's military coup in 1973; staff at La Biblioteca del Casino de Manresa; staff at the Rif Hotel and El Minzah Hotel in Tangier; and Dr Nathanial Gardner at the Glasgow University School of Modern Languages and Cultures.

I

I was five years old when I learned I was Spanish. I came home from school and told Mama I'd been pushed to the ground by a classmate for being a Paki.

'You're not a Pakistani, you're a Spaniard,' she informed me indignantly.

I returned to school the following day and proudly announced that I was from Spain. I was pushed to the ground by the same classmate for being a Dago.

Even so young, I'd suspected for some time that our family was different. Why, for example, were Pablito, my elder brother, and I dark-haired and tanned when the rest of my classmates had hair the colour of sand, with pale skin and freckles? Why did our family have a second way of speaking, which I didn't understand? Why was ours the only home I knew where the walls were full of pictures of serious-faced men in waistcoats and tight trousers?

'We come from another country, another culture,' Mama told me, which at least helped to explain why my parents were a mama and a papa and not a ma and a da, why they sat glued to the BBC World Service every night with expectant looks on their faces and left in their wake the faint whiff of garlic and Aqua Velva.

Ours was not a neighbourhood that celebrated diversity. Difference was tolerated only if it conformed to expectations: Pakistanis were poor and they ran shops; Italians were well off and they ran cafés; Spaniards slept in the afternoons and lived in Spain. There was no reason for them to be in Mosspark, where there was no afternoon sun to be slept through and where the retail sector had already been sewn up by the Pakistanis and the Italians.

At primary school the teachers, all of them floral-frock-wearing spinsters, insisted on anglicising my name.

'His name's Antonio,' Mama pointed out.

'We prefer Anthony,' my Primary One teacher replied with a dismissive tilt of her nose.

'But his name's Antonio,' Mama insisted, a note of exasperation creeping into her voice.

Mosspark's ignorance of all things Iberian was reflected in the unwanted nicknames that followed me around throughout my childhood – like Greaser or Dago, and, inevitably, Manuel, after the fictional waiter. At least he was actually Spanish. I was also likened to Speedy Gonzalez, the sombrero-wearing Mexican cartoon mouse; Rangi Ram, the Indian lackey from *It Ain't Half Hot Mum*; and Idi Amin, the president of Uganda.

Coming to terms with being an outsider in my own country was hard, and the worst of it was I seemed to be alone. Pablito was happy enough to flaunt his foreignness, correcting friends when they mispronounced his name, peppering his sentences with Spanish words and eating Mama's cooking without complaint.

But I didn't want to be different. When I was about seven, I made a conscious effort not to learn any more Spanish, and I used that ignorance as a weapon against my parents. Although Mama was trying to learn English and was happy to practise with me, my stubborn refusal to speak or even allow myself to understand Spanish at home provoked a series of angry exchanges with Papa.

'*Habla español*,' he constantly ordered.

'I don't want to speak in Spanish,' I replied.

'*En ese caso, no dicen nada*,' he said. 'Then don't say anything.'

I didn't care. I wanted to be like my friends. I *wanted* to be Anthony, not Antonio. I wanted to eat sausages and fish suppers, not *chorizo* and *pescaíto frito*. I wanted to be normal.

One wet Monday morning in the playground, Bobby Miller – known to all as Max – told me that I'd never be able to play football for Scotland.

'But I was born here – that makes me Scottish,' I protested.

'Disnae work like that. It's yer da that decides who you can play fur,' Max Miller insisted. 'Y'ill huv tae play fur the Dagos.'

It didn't seem fair. I wanted to play for Scotland. I'd seen the footage of the oily, moustachioed Atlético Madrid players kicking wee Jimmy Johnstone up and down the park when they played Celtic in the European Cup, and, along with every other Scottish supporter, I was appalled.

When I consulted Mama on the matter, she said I could play for either country because I had dual nationality. This sounded like a disease. But if it meant I could play for Scotland, I was prepared to accept it.

'I *can* play for Scotland. I have *dual nationality*,' I told Max Miller the next day, enunciating the words slowly and deliberately.

This seemed to silence him, but worse was to come. The following week, he appeared in school brandishing a copy of *The Victor* which included a strip where Matt Braddock, VC and bar – the valiant British Second World War flying ace – single-handedly foiled a Nazi plot to smuggle arms to beastly Irish collaborators through the Iberian peninsula, assisted by equally beastly Spanish fascists. Braddock's swashbuckling heroics were accompanied by speech bubbles containing imperatives such as 'Take that, snivelling Nazi Quislings!' and 'Eat lead, Hitler-loving swine!'

'You helped the Jerries in the war,' Max Miller spat at me accusingly. 'You cannae be on Britain's side any more.'

'What are you talking about? I always fight on Britain's side,' I protested. I didn't want to be banished to fight alongside the friendless dunces who made up the German forces in our daily breaktime game of Commandos.

'We cannae take the chance,' he said through grinning teeth. 'How dae we know you willnae give away secrets tae the Nazis?'

Max Miller had done his homework. He'd consulted with his Uncle Eddie, who'd informed him that thousands of Spanish soldiers and workers had flooded into Germany to help with the Nazi war effort.

I couldn't believe what I was hearing. Surely it couldn't be true? Was I really descended from a nation of Nazi sympathisers? All the stiff-upper-lip values of straight-batted, battling-Jerry-for-Blighty honesty ingrained in my psyche from years of watching the on-screen exploits of Trevor Howard and Jack Hawkins seemed like a sick joke. I may have been a British subject, but I was a second-class British subject, I now realised – and, if Max Miller's playground straw poll was anything to go by, I was only in Britain under sufferance.

'Why you wanna know about the bloody war?' Papa demanded angrily that evening as we ate dinner.

'A boy in my class says Spain was on the same side as the Jerries.'

'You tell yer friend tae mind his bloody business.'

'But is it true?' I asked desperately.

Papa stopped eating. He put down his fork and looked into my eyes. His face broke into a warm, reassuring smile.

'Na, is nae true,' he said, ruffling my hair. 'You tell yer friend he talk a load a bloody rubbish.'

I made my way down an impossibly steep and narrow wooden staircase. On either side, walls were plastered with posters advertising obscure musical acts like Chainsaw Armageddon and Satan's Rampant Fuckstick.

At the foot of the stairs a stiff door opened into a darkened, smoke-filled room where the unmistakable, musky stench of dope hung heavy in the air. A few shabby, wooden tables were populated by pale, gaunt men dressed mainly in black leather. Thumping, primal rhythms boomed from large speakers. If hell had bars, I felt sure they looked like this.

Is this what I'd spent five years at university and journalism college preparing for? I'd been asking myself this with increasing frequency of late. Earlier in the day I'd been in Bournemouth to interview Britain's youngest mother, a sullen eleven-year-old who chain-smoked through our exchange while her lumpy-faced mother pored over the details of their contract with the paper. The putative father whom they'd promised I could meet failed to materialise. Why, as a political editor, I should be despatched on such a mission was beyond me. But then job titles didn't seem to mean anything any more in our ever-dwindling pool of talent. You did what you had to do.

'It's got social repercussions,' Kevin the so-called news editor had insisted. 'It's all about Broken Britain. That's politics, isn't it?'

After leaving the family to prepare for their imminent infamy, I was making my way back up to London to catch a train to Scotland to visit my parents when Kevin rang again. A reader had been in touch, claiming to have mobile-phone footage of Nigel Piers, the junior environment minister, fellating a Somali rent boy in a public toilet in Clapton. That was hardly news, I pointed out, but Kevin assured me that wasn't the real story. Piers, the rent boy claimed, had later taken him to Petrus and told him to order what he liked as he'd be claiming the meal on expenses.

The rent boy had demonstrated admirable resourcefulness in snapping the receipt with his phone while Piers was taking a piss, and he was willing to hand over all of the evidence for a price to be negotiated. I was told to meet him in this fetid dungeon in Canning Town and to go no higher than five grand.

A wall of lifeless eyes locked on to me, and I felt myself sweating coldly. I slipped open the top button of my shirt and loosened my tie. I became aware of someone standing in the doorway, immediately behind me, a little too close for comfort. It was the same figure I'd caught sight of outside in the street, minutes earlier. I'd only seen him from behind, but it had been enough for me to make a mental note that this was someone to avoid in a dark alley. He was tall, with greasy black hair tied in a ponytail. Daubed in white paint on the back of his leather biker's jacket were the words 'Cradle of Filth'. Dirty, ripped jeans hung loosely around his shapeless arse, their legs tucked into knee-length motorcycle boots. On each wrist he wore a black leather cuff, studded with chrome spikes.

It flashed through my mind that perhaps he'd followed me in. I looked away, trying to ignore him. He moved closer. I tensed as I felt his hand rest on my shoulder.

'Dad, I thought it was you.'

'Shit, what are you doing here?' I demanded, overcome with relief and a less familiar sensation – genuine pleasure at seeing my teenage son.

'I hang out here sometimes. What are *you* doing here?'

'Work, believe it or not. Where the hell did you get these clothes?' I asked.

'Camden Market, mostly.'

'I meant where did you get the money to pay for them?'

'Gran gave me a couple of hundred for my birthday and Mum bought me the boots.'

'Jesus, what are they thinking of, letting you walk the streets like that?'

'I've had them for ages. You must have seen them before.'

I decided we should leave. I had no desire to spend another moment of what was supposed to be my free time seeking out the rent boy, least of all in the company of Ben. I'd tell Kevin he hadn't shown up. If he was that desperate to land the story, he could send one of the bottom-feeders to do it. They were on little more than the minimum wage and, unlike me, had no professional dignity to sacrifice. Whereas I remembered a time when I actually enjoyed going to work in the morning. I thought about quitting the job most days now, but I knew that the way things were going, I'd never find another.

We moved out into the daylight and found a burger bar across the road. I ordered two coffees and carried them to a table where Ben was seated, fiddling with his iPhone. I couldn't recall the last time I'd witnessed him conscious and vertical. Even when I was at home I barely saw him. He was never out of bed before midday, and in the evenings he was God knows where when he should have been locked away, studying for his A-levels.

'So how are things?' I asked.

'Fine.'

'Would you care to elaborate?'

He shrugged as he tore open a sachet of sugar, spilling the contents on to the table. He reached for another one, ripped off a corner and deposited the contents into his polystyrene cup.

'What do you want me to say? Things are fine.'

'Well, given that I haven't seen you for over a week, I thought you might have some conversation. Why don't we start with what you've been doing?'

He lifted a plastic stirrer and lethargically dragged it around the inside of his cup.

'Oh, you know, the usual.'

7

I resisted the impulse to raise my voice. 'No, I don't know. What's the usual?'

'The usual – eating, sleeping, studying.'

'So you *are* studying?'

'Yes, I'm studying,' he said, irritated.

'Okay, don't lose your temper.'

'Well, how would you know whether I have nor not? You're never around.'

I couldn't think of a decent retort.

'So are you and Mum getting a divorce?' he asked casually.

Actually, it seemed more like a statement than a question, and I felt suddenly disengaged from my surroundings, as though I was coming round after a blow to the head. I was taken aback, not just by his comment, but how blithely he'd made it. I tried to say something, but I was lost, my mind filled with random abstractions – like how much we'd get for the house, who'd take the cat and whether I'd ever have sex again. I placed my hands on the table to steady myself. The bitter smell of cheap coffee was abhorrent, and a wave of nausea washed over me.

'Is that what your mother said? Did she say that?'

'No, I managed to figure it by myself.'

I couldn't abide his cockiness – this was a new thing.

'Well, don't figure. Do you hear me? Don't figure things that you know nothing about.' I found myself jabbing a finger at his face, and my voice was loud enough to attract the attention of the cleaner at the opposite side of the restaurant.

'Okay, chill out, you can't blame me for thinking that. You and Mum hardly talk any more. And when you do, you're at each other's throats.'

I felt a strong desire to see Cheryl right then, to have it out with her, to hear her take on what was going on between us, to know precisely where I stood. I wished I hadn't agreed to go to Glasgow that afternoon, but Mama's voice on the phone had sounded so insistent, panicked even.

'So what kind of work were you doing in that place, anyway?' Ben asked. 'You never said.'

'Oh, it's not important.'

He nodded unintererertedly and looked away.

'Will you be home tonight?'

'I'm going to visit Abuela and Abuelo for a day or two,' I explained.

'Christ, what do they want?'

'Don't speak about them like that, they're your grandparents.'

'Sorry, it's just that . . . well, there's always something with them. What's the crisis this time?'

'There's no crisis, they just want to see me, that's all.'

As the train pulled away, I watched Ben grow smaller and smaller until he was little more than a gothic dot on the platform. I slumped into my seat and sighed, exhausted. I needed to relax. Everything seemed so frenzied and urgent all the time. I was glad I'd decided against flying to Glasgow, finally taking Cheryl's advice and using the train. I had to admit it was an agreeable change. There was no queuing, no check-in, no security frisking, no X-ray machines.

Cheryl travelled everywhere by train that she couldn't get to by bike or on foot. She was so infuriatingly virtuous and didn't seem to understand that not everyone could be as socially responsible as her. What did she know about the demands of the real world, sitting in her municipal ivory tower, sniffily disapproving of my job as though it was some grubby, morally reprehensible pursuit? I agreed with her that global warming was a bad thing. I just didn't see why it had to occupy such an increasing proportion of the decreasing number of conversations we had together. In our most recent exchange, I'd managed to drive her from the room simply by pointing out that I didn't have time to worry about composting every time I peeled a banana. She was less than sympathetic. I seemed to have developed a knack of annoying her without trying. We'd lost the ability to talk without each sentence being unpicked for the slightest hint of ulterior motive. We didn't converse any more, we negotiated emotional territory.

As the train swept through the countryside, my mind gradually emptied, and I succumbed to the hypnotic pull of the fleeting landscape and the rhythm of the train's wheels rolling over the tracks. I fell into a deep, comforting sleep and, for the first time in ages, I had a proper dream.

I dreamed I was a child again, on one of our regular train journeys to sort out my parents' immigration papers in Manchester, the closest city to Scotland that had a Spanish consulate. We were packed into a hot, smoky compartment. Mama had packed a *tortilla*, wrapped in tinfoil, and there was a crusty white loaf and a flask of coffee. She looked dowdy in a patterned print dress. She never had taken as much interest in her appearance as Papa, but then, as she pointed out, she was in the house all day, so who was going to see her? Her job, she said, was to make Papa look presentable to the outside world because he was the family's ambassador in public. She was cutting into the omelette with a crucifix that normally stood in pride of place on our living-room mantelpiece, and then handing slices to everyone. Pablito was there too, but he was an adult, drinking whisky straight from a half-bottle and bragging about a girl he'd slept with the night before. Mama was pretending not to listen, but Papa was laughing and egging him on. He was sitting nearest the window, with shards of sunlight reflecting off his lustrous black, curly hair, and was dressed smartly in a dark, pure wool suit with a crisply starched white shirt, shiny cufflinks and a sober silk tie. In his right hand was an untipped Chesterfield.

I woke with a fright, groping helplessly through the fug of mid-dream state as the conductor stood over me, waiting for my ticket. From the dirty urban landscape I guessed we were somewhere in the West Midlands. As I searched my pockets, I suddenly felt gripped by panic and wondered if Ben was right. Were Cheryl and I really heading for a divorce? Even if neither of us had uttered the word, it was clearly something he'd picked up on.

There was no doubt she and I were going through a rocky patch, but I always felt the best way to tackle these problems was to ignore them. Marriages often hit on testing times, but that didn't mean you gave up on them. You simply waited for the difficulties to fade in importance, as they inevitably did, and the irresistible grind of routine would reassert itself. I felt strongly about the importance of marriage – not that I was religious in any way, but it was one of the few values that had stayed with me from childhood. Mama and Papa believed family was everything. You supported it and stuck by it, no matter what. And that's why they were still together.

It was also, I supposed, the reason why I was now heading north, responding to a cry for help from my beleaguered mother. She hadn't told me what the problem was, but I knew it would have something to do with Papa. From previous experience I guessed it would involve some internecine dispute of baffling Iberian complexity. I also knew that my role, like that of a priest, would be pastoral and mediatory. There was every reason to believe I'd come and go with the substantial question still unresolved, but that my sober, *anglosajón* rationality would provide a calming influence.

I dozed intermittently, and, in no time it seemed, the train was crossing the border into Scotland. We pulled through the barren hills of the southern uplands and entered the post-industrial wasteland of South Lanarkshire, passing through the drab continuum of high-rises, chaotic undergrowth and deserted goods yards. Gone were the steelworks and the mines that had peppered the countryside of my childhood; in their place sat a few modern housing estates and the occasional recently built factory, now closed, that had, for a spell, churned out mobile phones and semiconductors. Mostly it was just acres of nothingness, and I felt the first pangs of anxiety that I knew would increase exponentially the closer I got to my father.

As I stepped on to the platform at Glasgow Central Station he was the first person I saw, standing on the concourse. In the monochrome photographs from my youth, he'd had the flawless, sculpted profile of a matinée idol, but his looks had faded, and he no longer turned heads. He was simply conspicuous rather than striking. As a child I'd thought he was tall, but now I towered over him – and it didn't help that he was beginning to stoop. His hair was still thick, but it had turned a metallic grey, and it sat on his head like a clump of fraying wire wool.

We embraced and exchanged a fleeting brush of lips on cheeks. It was an involuntary gesture to him, as instinctive as breathing, but it never felt natural to me, kissing another man – even my father – in public.

'You like da cheapskin?' he asked.

His accent threw me. It always happened when I'd been away for a long time and my ears weren't tuned properly to his lazy, pidgin diction of short Spanish vowels mugged by a flat Glaswegian drawl. I knew from his reaction to my hesitation that he was irritated. He liked to think he was clearly understood.

'Da cheapskin? Dae you like da cheapskin?'

'I know what you said. Yes, I like your coat, it's very nice.'

I didn't tell him I was trying to ignore it – this fur-trimmed, other-era garment, with its cash-up-front showiness.

'How much cost?' he demanded.

I hated it when he did that.

'You tell me, how much cost?'

'I don't know, Papa.'

He threw up his hands dismissively.

'I know you nae know, I ask you guess. You guess how much.'

'I really have no idea. Four hundred,' I ventured, deliberately high.

A look of unalloyed triumph washed over his face.

'Nae four hundred, nae even close. One hundred thirty. Only one hundred thirty quid. I get from this guy in, wha you call it?'

'Land of Leather,' I said.

He'd been buying his coats from the same Bangladeshi supplier for years.

'*Si*, in Land a Leather, in Barrhead. I get you one. You give me your size, I get you one.'

'I don't want one.'

'Wha you mean, you nae want? Only one hundred thirty quid, you nae get cheaper nowhere.'

'Really Papa, I don't want one. I've got plenty of coats.'

'Ach, I nae understand you, this is bargain, this cheapskin,' he said as he turned on his heel and marched off.

As winter's early darkness fell, we chugged along Mosspark Drive to the reassuringly benign putt-putt sound of Papa's Volkswagon Beetle, past the shops and the achingly familiar sight of the old swingpark, where I learned to ride a bike and smoked my first cigarette.

I noticed how the passage of time had taken its toll on the neighbourhood, whose council-estate uniformity had been replaced with a surfeit of satellite dishes, stone-cladding and driveways populated with garish customised cars. The family-run shops were gone, closed and shuttered, replaced by a single mini-market with grilled windows covered in adverts for low-cost energy drinks and cigarettes.

The car pulled up outside the compact, two-bedroom house in which I'd grown up. It hadn't changed in any significant way since my youth. My parents were among the few residents who still rented from the council. 'Why I wanna buy a bloody house?' Papa demanded testily whenever I tried to point out the financial benefits of owning property. 'If I wanna fix roof or windows, I phone the council. If I buy a house, I dae myself.'

Mama had heard the car's rasping engine and was standing on the doorstep, ready with a smile and a needy embrace.

'How is my boy?' she asked, her accent as much Glaswegian as it was Spanish.

'I'm doing fine, Mama.'

She eyed me sceptically. 'You don't look fine, are you eating?'

'I'm eating.'

13

'But are you eating properly?'

There was pathos in her concern that made me feel slightly sad – that I was in my mid-forties, with a family of my own, that I earned in a month what she and Papa lived on for a year, and yet she still felt responsible for my welfare.

I stepped into the hallway and was met by the smell of lambs' kidneys braising in sherry. I made my way upstairs to my old bedroom, which hadn't changed since I'd shared it with Pablito thirty years before.

I'd kept urging Mama to redecorate it, even offering her the money, but she said she didn't have the heart. It retained the imprint of teenage boyhood, with fading posters of rock bands hanging limply from the walls, along with occasional cut-outs of footballers from Spanish magazines, with their 1970s mullets and sideburns. Neither Pablito nor I ever saw them play, but we pretended we idolised them to humour Papa.

Other than twin single beds, the only item of furniture was a cheap mock-pine chest of drawers purchased from an industrial estate in Renfrew. On top of it sat a couple of well-thumbed Alistair MacLean novels and a clutch of dusty, scratched cassette cases.

I dumped my holdall on the floor and collapsed on to the bed, lurching precariously to one side as the loosely-sprung mattress sagged beneath my weight. I felt a sudden urge to speak to Cheryl. I pulled out my mobile phone and dialled our home number, but the moment I heard it click on to voicemail, I wished I hadn't.

'Hi, I'm just checking in, to see if you're all right,' I said, trying to sound casual and breezy. 'Just thought I'd touch base.'

Touch base? What the hell did that mean? I hated making these phone calls, but I couldn't seem to stop myself. Even if she'd answered, we'd have had a few moments of unsatisfying, directionless conversation, then I'd probably have spent the rest of the night worrying, rehearsing in my head every syllable she'd spoken, every pause, searching for clues as to what she was really thinking.

I felt trapped inside my aching body. I changed into a sweat-shirt and a pair of jeans. I trudged into the bathroom and threw some cold water over my face, rubbing my eyes to dislodge the crumbs of sleep that had built up on the train journey.

At the bottom of the staircase was a large bag of dirty laundry. Mama had told me on the phone that Pablito might be eating with us, although she wasn't certain he'd definitely make it because of his work schedule. He'd promised to 'pull some strings', she said. He'd recently switched jobs – again – his latest designation being in what he referred to as 'petroleum retail'.

I entered the living room and found him and Papa kneeling in front of the television set, crouched over some sort of electrical item.

'Hey *hermano*, how's it going?' I asked nonchalantly.

Pablito looked up and managed a less than convincing smile, then continued his conversation with Papa.

'. . . so I said, "Don't be an arsehole, Brian. You may be senior retail executive but I've got a lifetime of experience in sales, and I know the consumer mindset."'

Papa watched him transfixed.

'Brian said, "Don't talk to me like that, Pablito, I am your boss, remember." So I looked at him, and I said, "Well, behave like a boss and don't talk such fucking shite."'

They both laughed.

'How *is* the petrol station, Pablito?' I asked.

He eyed me uncertainly.

'It's fine.'

There was a short silence before Papa intervened.

'This is just temporary job for Pablito. He go work for big firm to sell, how you say, conservations?'

'Conservatories,' Pablito said.

'Oh right, conservatories' I said more cynically than I'd intended. 'What, you mean like for a double-glazing firm?'

'They do double-glazing as well, but I'll be focusing more on the conservatory side of the business,' he replied defensively. 'It's a growth industry.'

'This is good job. He earn two thousand pound every week,' Papa said enthusiastically. 'Two thousand pound,' he repeated, to emphasise the vastness of the figure.

Pablito looked embarrassed.

'Two grand, wow. Is that basic?' I asked him.

'Eh, no, that's with commission, but that would mean only having to sell a couple of conservatories a week.'

They continued with their technical collusion, holding up the ends of wires, speculating where they might go. I took a proper look at the item. It was a crude metal box with a series of red and green lights on the fascia, with wires protruding from the back. There appeared to be no writing on it to indicate who had produced it or what it was for.

'What is that?' I asked.

Neither of them answered.

'Okay, ignore me, I don't want to know.'

'Is satellite TV,' Papa said without looking up.

'Satellite TV?'

'Si.'

'And where's the satellite dish?' I asked.

'Is in garden.'

I went into the kitchen, where Mama was cooking, and looked out of the window. The dish occupied my entire field of vision – a large, battleship-grey installation, supported on either side by two rusting metal poles.

'Where the fuck did you get that thing?' I shouted.

Papa looked up.

'Eh, you nae swear in front of your Mama. You show some respect.'

'Sorry, I didn't mean to. It's just that . . . Christ, where did you get that thing? It looks like it fell off a Soviet space station in 1972 and landed in the garden. You could use it as a paddling pool.'

'Pablito. He get it from one of his clients,' Papa explained.

'One of his clients?' I said, trying not to laugh. 'What, you mean one of the dodgy customers at the petrol station?'

'It's not stolen, if that's what you're getting at,' Pablito said. 'It's perfectly legitimate.'

'I'm not worried about it being stolen, I'm worried about it bringing down a 747 while you're trying to get *Blackadder* on UK Gold.'

I left them to it and remained in the kitchen with Mama to help her prepare the meal. I wanted to get her on her own so that I could quiz her on the supposed emergency that had hastened my journey north. I closed the door so that Papa couldn't hear what we were saying.

I remembered the kitchen from my youth as a pristine beacon of technology, but it hadn't aged well. Paint was flaking from the walls, and the cupboard doors were scratched and fading. Its surfaces were cluttered with freakishly large electric juicers, peelers, dicers and mixers like props from an old episode of *Dr Who*. A tarnished chrome microwave dominated, with its giant clockwork dials and luminous green LEDs. All of these things that Papa had bought Mama as Christmas presents through advertisements on the back page of the *Daily Express* had simply gathered dust. She only ever seemed to use three kitchen items – her pressure cooker, her ageing, blackened griddle pan and a large terracotta *cazuela*.

She handed me a large Cos lettuce to wash and separate while she got on with other things.

'So what's the crisis?' I asked.

She stopped chopping a large onion and looked at me.

'It's your Papa.'

'Who else would it be?'

'He's decided he wants to go back to Spain.'

I stopped what I was doing and laughed. Papa hadn't been to Spain for almost seventy years.

'You mean for a holiday?'

She nodded.

'Well, that's good news, isn't it? It's what we've been pressing him to do for years, to visit the places where he grew up, see old friends.'

17

'It's not as simple as that. He's been writing to the Ajuntamente in Lerida.'

'To the what?'

'The local council.'

Lerida was the town in Catalonia where his family came from. That much I knew about his background. That was pretty much all I knew. None of his family had survived the Civil War, and he'd always insisted Spain was a part of his life that was behind him. The last time he'd even come close to returning was more than twenty-five years before, when he and Mama had thought about going there to live, but there was an attempted *coup d'état* and everything changed. It was then that Mama resolved they would end their days in Britain. She was, she said, tired of feeling rootless and uncertain, and Glasgow was to be their home.

'What does he want with the local council?' I asked.

'Oh, he has a bee in his bonnet about something or other and he's got into an argument with them over it.'

'Why is he arguing with officials in a country he hasn't visited for so long?'

'He won't tell me. His writing is very poor, which is making him frustrated, but he won't let me help.'

Papa and Pablito came in, and we took our places at the table. Papa began with a starter of lettuce leaves sprinkled with a little salt, eating with a knife and fork as we watched. This was the ritual with which we'd started every family meal since I could remember. I never understood why it existed. I had once asked Mama about it as a child, and she simply said 'Papa likes his lettuce.'

When I asked why I couldn't have any, she laughed. 'You think I can afford lettuce every day for a whole family?' she asked.

I'd bought a bottle of Rioja at the train station but I knew I'd have to wait until later to open it. Papa wouldn't allow anyone to drink alcohol in his presence, and he became infuriated if he caught the smell of it. Even now, middle-aged, I didn't want to risk his disapproval.

'So, how's Carlitos?' I asked Pablito breezily as Papa munched through his lettuce.

I was the only member of the family who still asked my brother about his son, principally because I knew it annoyed him so much. If I'd really wanted to know about my nephew's welfare, the last person I'd have asked was his father. He eyed me guardedly and his bottom lip quivered, as though he wanted desperately to reply with something caustic but his brain couldn't keep up. He couldn't be certain I was inquiring out of anything but genuine concern, and that's what riled him so much.

'He's good,' he snapped.

'He must have left university by now,' I said. 'What's he going to do?'

'Eh, I don't know, I think he's looking for a job. His mother never answers her phone.'

Mama served up plates of plump kidney pieces in a rich brown sauce, served on a bed of fluffy rice flavoured with saffron. There was a tension in the air, an implicit sense that everyone knew why we were there and that we had things to discuss, but that no one was willing to break the silence. I decided it would have to be me.

'So, Mama tells me you want to go to Spain.'

Papa looked up from his plate.

'*Si*, I go Spain,' he said quietly.

Silence resumed. I was waiting for him to elaborate but he continued eating.

'Do you want to explain why?' I asked.

'I nae explain. I go, this is all.'

'And you don't think that suddenly deciding to return, at the age of eighty-three, to a country you've spent the past seventy-odd years avoiding deserves a bit more explanation than that?'

'I think it's a good idea for him to go,' Pablito chipped in.

'Oh, Christ, that's all we need,' I said.

Pablito threw his fork down on his plate.

'Well, why not, if that's what he wants to do. I've said for a long time he should go back.'

'We've all said for a long time he should go back, and he's always refused, so what's changed?'

'Well, he's decided he wants to go, and I think he needs our support, not your negativity.'

'He's eighty-fucking-three years old.'

'Hey, you watcha yer mouth,' Papa growled.

'He's eighty-three. Mama's seventy-nine, and he suddenly wants to jet off to sip sangria on the Costas. Don't you think that's a bit strange?'

I turned to Papa.

'What about the dangers?'

He ignored me and carried on eating.

'What about the army generals waiting to seize power, the old scores waiting to be settled, the murderers still walking the streets, the Falangist agents in the Guardia Civil – all the things that have stopped you going back for most of your life?'

Still he ignored me.

'Have you asked Mama what she thinks of the idea?'

'She is okay,' he whispered defiantly.

'Have you asked her if she's okay?'

Mama had been sitting silently, her reddened face following the conversation back and forth as though she was watching a tennis match.

'That's just so like you, Papa, to assume that Mama will do whatever you say.'

I put my cutlery down but Papa continued to eat.

'She is my wife, she dae wha I say,' he said blithely, chewing on a piece of kidney.

Mama shifted uncomfortably.

'Let's just drop it,' she implored. 'We can discuss it another time.'

We finished eating in silence. After the meal, Papa and Pablito returned to the living room where, I was astonished to see, they had managed to tune in their satellite contraption to a Spanish football match. Mama prepared a pot of tea for them and laid out a plate of toasted, sugar-glazed almonds before returning to me in the kitchen.

I couldn't help noticing how tired she looked. She'd always appeared older than her years, but she'd lost weight recently, and her hair had turned silvery white. A network of lines had appeared, pinched around her mouth, making her face look like it was drawing in on itself.

We washed and dried the dishes and then sat down at the table, chatting about a number of peripheral issues, all except the important matter at hand.

When the football match ended, Pablito said his goodbyes and left to return to the studio flat in Docklands where he'd lived since his divorce eight years before. Papa walked slowly upstairs and retired to bed.

I needed a drink, so I retrieved the wine from my holdall and opened it, promising Mama I'd put the empty bottle out with the rubbish. She looked on uneasily, but when she was sure Papa was in bed and asleep, she joined me in a glass and immediately appeared more relaxed.

Although Pablito was older than me, I was the one in whom Mama confided. There were always certain areas where we never ventured, principally her relationship with Papa. I knew how devoted to him she was and how much loyalty she gave him.

'Well, whatever it is that he's up to, and clearly he's not saying, at least you'll get a holiday out of it,' I said.

'It's not as simple as that,' she replied.

'Whatever it is, it's manageable. If he wants to write to town clerks, let him do it. Go on holiday, enjoy it, and keep him away from Lerida.'

'No, you don't understand. He's dying,' she said.

It was said almost as an aside, and I had to get her to repeat it to make sure I hadn't misheard.

'It's true, he is dying.'

I was increasingly aware of my parents' mortality, and I'd often wondered how I would learn that either of them was dying or had died. I reached for a packet of cigarettes Papa had left lying on the kitchen table. I hadn't smoked for years, and the moment I lit one I realised it wasn't going to help. I stubbed it out.

'What is it?'

'Cancer,' Mama said.

It wasn't a complete surprise. He'd experienced severe back pain the previous year, which he'd put down to a slipped disc until it had spread to his stomach. I'd been getting regular updates on his health from Mama until about six months before, when they'd stopped. I hadn't pressed her for details because I'd figured that, if the news was positive, she'd have volunteered it.

'He doesn't know,' Mama said, doing her best to hold back the tears.

'How can he not know?'

'The doctor thought it would be best coming from me but I don't have the strength to tell him.'

'Does he suspect?'

'Yes, he must.'

'Hence the sudden desire to return to Spain?'

'I've said too much. I promised him I wouldn't talk to you about it.'

'To me?' I asked, surprised that I'd been singled out for such censorship.

'To anyone.'

I knew she wouldn't say any more. She never willingly spoke about Papa behind his back. She had no choice but to tell me he was dying, but I could see that the pain was almost unbearable for her. Anything more would be a betrayal too far.

'Does Pablito know?'

'No, he'll take it very badly.'

I wondered whether to be offended at the implication that I'd take the news less badly, but I forgave her. We both knew things were more complicated than that. I also knew that Pablito would have to be told.

'How long has Papa got?' I asked her.

'Not long,' she replied.

3

For most of my childhood Mama and Papa were the only Spanish people I'd ever met. We couldn't afford to visit Spain and our relatives couldn't afford to come to us. Mama kept in touch with her mother and sisters by writing to them, and I'd seen the photographs they frequently sent with their letters.

Papa had no surviving family – all we knew about his past was that he'd been raised in an orphanage near Barcelona before he went to Morocco, where he had met Mama. In a tattered leather suitcase that he kept stashed under his bed were a few reminders of his earlier life – pathetic items, vague with age, whose alien images and crude textures spoke of a distant past. When my parents weren't around, I would creep into their room and open the suitcase, trying to weigh its contents against what I knew of my father's life. There was a fragile cigarette packet with a barely legible motif, made up of the initials of what I guessed was the tobacco company – Compania Appendattaria de Tabacos – and a small booklet with a blood-red fabric cover, bearing a gold-crested image of a muscular factory worker and the words Confederación Nacional del Trabajo Espana. Inside were a few bible-thin pages of official verbiage and, on one of them, my father's name and date of birth written with a fountain pen. There was also a postcard with a strange picture unlike those on any of the smiling holiday cards I was used to seeing. A red, yellow and purple flag gave way to an eerie ink etching of factories and smoking chimneys. Emblazoned across the bottom were the words '*Viva La Republica*'.

Then there was Papa's collection of Manolo Escobar LPs. They sat next to the gramophone, under the television in the living room, and were brought out and played with religious regularity every Saturday night. Each time the singer had a new record out, Mama's sisters would send it through the post. Papa had all of them, beginning with a recording of Manolo's legendary break-through performance at the Teatro Duque de Rivas in Cordoba in 1961. On the earliest black-and-white covers he had slicked-back hair and marply-pressed suits. He was handsome, like a film star, but he also seemed slightly scary, as though he had a temper that you wouldn't want to test. As the years passed, his portraits became mellower, his face fuller and more lined, and slowly I lost my fear.

I couldn't understand the words he sang, though I began to believe they were directed at me, that he knew about the problems I faced, with Max Miller and my dual nationality, that he was telling me, through his songs, how to deal with them. I used to wonder what it would be like if Manolo Escobar was my father. His life seemed to have run in parallel with Papa's, and often I would imagine that my father was a famous singer and that Manolo Escobar packed bags on to aeroplanes at Glasgow Airport.

Over breakfast one morning, Mama announced we were to meet our Spanish grandmother for the first time. Her mother, Abuela, as we were instructed to call her, had won a few thousand pesetas in the Spanish lottery, and she was coming to spend the summer with us.

I was curious to see what a real, authentic Spaniard from Spain looked like in the flesh. At the same time, the last thing I needed was a further reminder of my differentness.

Abuela had written to say she'd be arriving at Glasgow Airport on an Iberia flight from Madrid. She couldn't be precise about a time, or even a date, because she'd been told that, to qualify for a cheap ticket, she'd be required to fly at short notice in the event of a late cancellation. All she could tell us was that she'd be arriving on a Sunday evening some time soon.

Papa didn't want to spend the money on telephone calls to Spain to find out whether she'd secured a seat, so it was decided that we'd all wait at the airport every Sunday until she stepped off the plane. We were able to sit in the staff common-room with Papa and his bag-handler colleagues and drink tea while he chatted and joked with them. After the first couple of Sundays, when Abuela failed to show up, Mama and Pablito decided they would rather stay at home, and it was left to Papa and me to make the trips. It was one of the few occasions I remember spending any proper time alone with him. We fell into a routine where I would tell him jokes I'd learned at school and he would laugh, though I could tell he didn't understand half of them. He seemed happy and relaxed, and that was enough to satisfy me.

During one such trip, I asked him to tell *me* a joke. He said he couldn't think of one, but he offered to tell me a funny story instead about something that had happened to him when he was a child. I was intrigued – anecdotes about his past were rare. He told me how, when he was very small, his mama regularly sent him to the local shop to buy a tiny amount of salt for cooking. It was the first time I could remember him mentioning either of his parents.

'I thought your mama and papa died,' I said.

'*Si*, they die.'

'But you remember them?'

'A little.'

'So what age were you when they died?'

He became agitated at my questioning.

'You nae ask questions, you listen,' he ordered.

He continued with his story. He would usually be playing with his friends when his mama asked him to go to the local shop, and he hated the chore of having to walk to the end of the street. Then one day he asked her why she didn't give him money to buy a week's worth of salt so that he wouldn't have to go to the shop every day.

'She laugh and laugh, and she say tae me, I nae afford tae gie you money to buy salt for one day, never mind for a week.'

He stopped talking, and I studied his face, expecting him to continue, waiting for the punchline, before the realisation dawned that it had already been delivered.

'You nae think this is funny?' he asked with a hurt expression.

I fought for the right response so as not to disappoint him.

'So you said, "Why don't you give me money for more salt?" and she said –'

He interrupted, his voice cut with irritation. 'We have very little money, my family, you understand?'

'Yes, I got that bit, it's just . . .' I stuttered.

'My Papa, he work in the olive fields, and he get paid every day only a very small amount.' His voice grew louder and more agitated.

'Oh, right, I see,' I said with a laugh, trying my best to rescue the situation. 'So you didn't know that you were so poor you couldn't buy more than a day's worth of salt?'

He looked at me sceptically, sizing me up, then his lips curled reluctantly into a smile.

'Yes, we were poor,' he said slowly and quietly. 'Very poor.'

After four more abortive trips to the airport, Abuela finally arrived. She waddled through the international arrivals gate like a squat, grandmother-shaped blancmange, dressed all in black, with thinning white hair and the teeth as large as a thoroughbred's.

After spotting Papa, she swept over to him and they embraced in a swirl of mutual cheek-kissing and voluble, indecipherable lingo. Their animated blabbering continued for several minutes until the other passengers had filed past to the baggage reclaim area. Then Papa pointed in my direction and she came homing towards me, wielding a walking stick in one hand and a large black handbag in the other. She eyed me up and down, making several comments in Spanish, before gathering me into her fleshy arms and pulling me into a tight embrace.

I'd never been this close to an old person before. She had an acrid, unfamiliar smell, part days-old sweat, part cheap perfume.

Her aged skin looked cracked and leathery, but was pillow-soft to the touch. When I kissed her face, my lips left a deep divot which remained for several moments before the skin regained its fullness.

At the baggage carousel Papa collected two large, battered trunks that looked like relics from another age and lifted them on to a trolley. We made our way to the car park at an agonisingly slow pace, dictated by Abuela, whose rickety, banana-shaped legs struggled to cope with the pressure of her weight. As I followed behind, I noticed her baggy black tights sagging around her knees.

We arrived home to an emotional reunion with Mama on the doorstep. There were tears and loud cries of joy that set curtains twitching on the other side of the street. They exchanged bursts of guttural, rapid-fire conversation, their dialogue so strident and lively, and accompanied by such expansive, arm-waving gestures, that several times I thought they were on the verge of coming to blows. However, as I was to learn, that was just the natural level at which they conversed.

They talked and talked and talked, well into the night. At some point Abuela opened one of her trunks, amid considerable fanfare from Mama and Papa. On top of the piles of black clothing was a horde of food – colourful, exotic and unfamiliar. There were packets of biscuits and sweets; tins of assorted fish and seafood – *almejas, mejillónes, calamari, boquerones* and *pescaditos*; jars of plump green olives, stuffed with peppers and anchovies; a thick red *chorizo* the size of a baseball bat with white streaky veins, and small, shiny *morcilla* black puddings.

Every item was held aloft, squeezed and sniffed, unscrewed, uncorked, kissed and caressed as Mama and Papa delivered an emotional eulogy to its merits. I couldn't understand what they were saying, but I recognised the sentiment. Every sight and smell, every occasion on which these items had played a central role – at lunches, dinners, parties, weddings and baptisms – carried with it an eloquent testimonial. Through food, they relived a past about which I knew nothing.

Mama and Papa might have been Spanish, but they'd lived in Britain long enough to be more or less accepted. They spoke English, though heavily accented, they dressed like natives, and their demeanour was, for the most part, naturalised. Abuela, in contrast, stood out like a manzanillo olive in a fish supper.

She was loud, aggressive and opinionated. She spent her days splayed across our sofa, eating compulsively and holding forth on issues of pressing Mediterranean importance. Despite having carried two giant trunks of clothing all the way from Madrid, she wore the same black nylon housecoat and slippers every day. According to Mama, she had worn black since the death of her husband a decade before, as a mark of respect, the only exception being her giant, baggy, dishwater-grey knickers.

Her laundered underwear became a neighbourhood landmark. Three pairs of giant pants, hung in a row, occupied the entire washing line, flapping in the summer breeze like parachutes caught in a tree. Word spread and Mossparkers came from far and near, from the outermost reaches of the estate, to point and stare, to gasp and snigger, to marvel at their gargantuan vastness.

Grandmothers weren't supposed to be like this. They were supposed to be petite, demure and withdrawn. They committed themselves to acts of domestic industry, slaving over pots of soup. They sucked boiled sweets, did the *Evening Citizen* crossword and collected their pensions from the Post Office. They kept themselves to themselves and they never knowingly expressed an opinion that post-dated 1945 or was more controversial than the apparent shrinkage of Fry's Peppermint Cream bars.

Abuela, it seemed, had something to say on every subject. Most of her opinions were directed at Papa. She was loud, angry and unceasing, her voice throaty and rasping like the sound of a holed exhaust pipe on a second-hand car. In the seclusion of our home, I wondered what the neighbours would think of her trumpeting tones, heard through the insubstantial dividing walls. Outdoors, in shops, cafés and restaurants, I shuddered at the attention of onlookers, captivated by this voluble foreign side-show, all dressed in black.

Lengthy conversations between Papa and Abuela started at breakfast and meandered through the day, reaching a dizzying crescendo late at night. They were largely one-sided, Papa occasionally lobbing in a word or two and prompting another verbal battering from Abuela. Mama and Pablito generally remained silent on the sidelines.

Occasionally I caught a word or two that I thought I understood, or at least recognised. *España*, I knew, was Spain – that came up a lot. So did *politico*, which had something to do with politics, and *militar*, which was to do with the army and fighting. Papa said *Republicano* a lot.

But these were minor snatches of meaning in what to me was a blank. I asked Pablito what they were talking about, but he just brushed me aside, saying I wouldn't be interested. No doubt he was right. Nothing held my attention for long.

And I had more pressing concerns. Max Miller had caught wind of Abuela's knickers and led a delegation to our house to witness them. They all stood at the gate, peering through until they caught sight of the garments on the line, and then they collapsed on the pavement, laughing uproariously, slapping their thighs. Whatever derogatory nickname I had borne in the past was nothing compared to my new one, Spanish Granny Pants.

But Max Miller's vendetta didn't end there. He arrived at school clutching a pocket encyclopaedia with a page dog-eared at the appropriate section, and proudly read aloud to everyone:

Although Spain was formally neutral throughout the Second World War, it remained ideologically aligned with the Nazis in Germany and the Fascists in Italy. When Germany invaded the Soviet Union, Spain, pressured by the Germans, offered manpower to help in civilian war work and military volunteers to fight against the Bolsheviks. This was accepted by Hitler and, within two weeks, there were more than enough volunteers to form a division – the Blue Division or División Azul under Agustín Muñoz Grandes – including an air force squadron – the Blue Squadron . . .

I'd heard enough. The words burned deep into my head, fuelling a raging, pulsating hatred towards Spain and all things Spanish. I wished I'd never heard of the blasted place. I grabbed the book from Max Miller and threw it to the ground, grinding its pages beneath the sole of my muddy shoe.

Our eyes met and a smile of satisfaction danced around his mouth – I'd just ruined his encyclopedia but, clearly, this was the reaction he was seeking. I punched him squarely on the face, unleashing a torrent of blood from his nose. A stunned expression registered in his eyes, and he began to cry. I punched him again, bursting his upper lip, and felt a sharp prick from one of his teeth piercing the skin over my knuckle. There were gasps of astonishment from the crowd as they waited for Max Miller to react.

I willed him to respond. I was pumped full of hateful aggression, and I needed an excuse to punch him again. Max Miller's face was puffy and bloody, but he was only a proxy for the real object of my anger – Papa. This is what I would be doing to him if only I was big enough and brave enough. I detested his weak, horrible lies – I'd rather he'd been honest about Spain and the war. I hated the country and everything it stood for, but I'd rather know the truth than have to face this humiliation.

Max Miller wailed through trails of blood-streaked tears and snot. 'You're fucking mental, Antonio Noguera. D'you know that?'

I tried to punch him again, but he was expecting it, and he pulled away. My fist missed his head and swung through the air, flailing aimlessly.

'Ha ha, missed, Spanish Granny Pants,' he hissed as he turned and ran in the direction of the school nurse's room. Later the headmaster put the squeeze on him to divulge who had messed up his face, but he refused to rat on me. That only made me feel angrier and more stupid.

4

Papa leant on Mama as if she was a crutch. He'd always depended on her because she spoke better English than him, but now it seemed he'd surrendered all responsibility for his life to her. As we queued at the airport check-in I tried to recall the last time I'd been out of the house with them together. It must have been years, and it was shocking to see how reluctant he was to engage with the world when she was there to do it for him.

His sole concession to independence was occasionally picking up or dropping off someone in his car, but only if he knew the route in advance and there was no deviation from it. Otherwise his every move was guided and facilitated by his wife: she told him when to walk and when to stop, she opened doors for him and answered questions on his behalf. Though he'd never properly integrated into his adopted homeland, he used to at least make an effort to understand, but now he appeared to have stopped trying.

'The lady wants to know if anyone could have interfered with your suitcase,' Mama said with exaggerated patience, as though she was talking to a child.

'Wha you talk, interfere?'

She sighed.

'It's a standard question.'

'You nae ask question, you nae tell me interfere,' he said to the woman harshly.

'They ask the same question to everyone who's going to fly,' Mama explained.

'I work here thirty year, you nae ask me interfere.'

33

'No one has interfered with his bag,' I said curtly.

The woman behind the desk smiled.

I was exhausted from several days of travelling, juggling diary dates and dealing with Kevin's baffled irritation at my insistence that I needed, suddenly, to take a fortnight's annual leave a few days before the start of the party conference season. Attending the conferences was one of the few concessions to my post that he tolerated, largely because he acknowledged the possibility that someone senior might get pissed or be caught shagging.

I'd been riding a taxi through central London, on my way to the daily lobby briefing at Westminster, when Mama had called in a state of panic. Pablito, she related breathlessly, had booked a last-minute package holiday for the three of them in what I knew to be a tits, chips and beer tourist resort on the Costa Brava.

'It is only a couple of hours drive from Lerida,' she said, panicked.

She wouldn't elaborate, but the implication was clear; she was worried about the responsibility of chaperoning abroad her fatally ill husband, who was apparently intent on some kind of misadventure involving the local council, with no one but her dysfunctional elder son for support. The result was that the next day, I was standing with them in the departures terminal of Glasgow Airport, preparing to depart on a two-week holiday.

This was a momentous day for Papa. He had spent most of his life packing and unpacking aircraft, but he'd never flown. His arrival in Scotland from Tangier fifty years earlier had followed a protracted and complicated journey by sea and rail involving changes at Lisbon, Southampton and London. Air travel had clearly undergone a paradigm shift since he'd last worked here. Back then, the airport had been a place of smiling, liberating possibilities. Now it was characterised by grim-faced paranoia, little more than a functional space for airlines whose sole purpose was to get their clients to a destination without allowing them to be killed.

Papa looked nervy and self-conscious, obviously seeking a toehold of recognition on a wall of unfamiliar sights – X-ray machines, metal detectors and armed policemen talking into two-way radios.

He'd dressed for summer, in a short-sleeved shirt and a pair of loose-fitting trousers. It only occurred to me after his suitcase had been checked in that he wasn't wearing a jacket. I warned him the temperature in a pressurised cabin could be cold, but he waved me aside.

'What about when you get off the plane? It's not going to be tropical in northern Spain at this time of year,' I said.

'Wha you tell me about Spain?' he demanded testily. 'I know better than you about Spain.'

'Leave him alone,' Pablito ordered. 'If he says he won't be cold, he won't be cold.'

I'd long ago developed a sense that alerted me to impending problems involving my father or brother, problems that I knew I'd end up having to deal with. While they queued for passport control, I stopped by one of the chintzy tourist boutiques and bought Papa an overpriced sweatshirt emblazoned with a picture of Highland cattle. When I caught up with them Papa snorted dismissively, refusing to take it.

As we passed through the various checks, he complained about the length of the queues, at having to remove his shoes and at being frisked by a security guard. But as we entered the duty-free area, his eyes lit up at the sight of all the cigarettes. He shuffled from aisle to aisle, picking up boxes of increasing size, giddy with excitement. As he and Pablito discussed the best deals, Mama and I moved to the café area. She sank into a chair, exhausted, while I ordered coffees.

'I'm worried about him,' she said the moment I returned. 'He's on a fairly high dose of morphine, and his mood is unpredictable.'

Over in duty-free Papa was holding a carton of three hundred Benson & Hedges, engaged in a loud argument with Pablito, who evidently wanted to buy a large packet of rolling tobacco instead.

'I think he sees the trip as a pilgrimage. He realises this will be his last chance to visit Spain.'

'That's understandable. It's his homeland, no matter how long he's been away,' I said.

She stared intently at Papa and Pablito quarrelling. 'I hope he doesn't do anything silly.'

'What do you mean?'

She sighed. 'Oh, nothing.'

'You mean regarding this argument he's been having with the local council?'

She nodded silently.

'Come on Mama, tell me. What's the argument about? You can't continue to keep everything to yourself. It's not fair.'

She sighed again, continuing to stare at Papa.

'Mama, tell me.'

'It's just that he had some bad news that has made him very angry.'

'From the Ajuntamente? What kind of bad news?'

Papa and Pablito had decided against buying anything and were walking towards us. Mama went silent, and I knew I'd have to wait until I was alone with her again before I could pursue the matter further.

'We get cheaper in Spain,' Papa announced confidently.

As we boarded the aircraft he had clearly started to flag, and any semblance of tolerance had evaporated. He complained about the steepness of the steps, the air stewardess's failure to smile, and the lack of leg-room. Once airborne, he complained about the speed of the take-off, the effect of the air pressure on his ears, the no-smoking policy, the queue for the toilet, the excessive price of refreshments and the failure of the other stewardess to smile. Forty minutes into the flight he was complaining exclusively about the cold. I remained silent.

'Hey, you give me jumper with cow,' he demanded without a hint of contrition.

Despite the time of year the temperature in Girona was high, and we were met with a blast of hot air as we emerged from the aircraft. By the time we'd cleared Customs and reclaimed our bags, Papa's legs were threatening to buckle. There was a long queue for the charter bus that was to drop us at our resort. Papa sat on his upended suitcase and stared into the distance. I offered to hire a car.

'I was going to suggest that,' Pablito said, hastily rising to his feet. 'I'll go and book it. You stay here.'

After a short conversation with a clerk at the car rental desk, he returned, red-faced. 'Antonio, did you remember to bring your driving licence?'

As we drove along the dual carriageway towards the coast, the piercing afternoon sun illuminated a constellation of white, flat-roofed villas dotted randomly across the rugged, pine-covered hills. We entered a small village and Papa's head moved from side to side, his eyes alighting on every item of interest – a bread shop, a charcuterie, a small café with a table outside at which several old men sat smoking, a group of bronzed youngsters gathered around a fountain, holding upended skateboards.

Occasionally he turned around to Mama, who was sitting in the back with Pablito, to pass comment on this or that. It occurred to me that, when he'd left Spain, this area would have been virtually unchanged since medieval times. While I guessed it had retained some of its character, it was now well-equipped and evidently affluent. For Papa it must have been like watching an old friend he hadn't seen since childhood grown up and made good.

As we drove further along the road the natural terrain gave way, abruptly, to a chaotic collage of bars, restaurants and skyline-breaking apartment blocks. Despite it being off-season, the streets crawled with pink-fleshed tourists clad in replica football shirts and nightclub touts clutching bundles of fliers.

I'd been to a resort similar to this with Cheryl when we were first married and remembered enough of it to know the form. From early evening the streets thrummed with the noise of riotous single-mindedness; strobe lights flashed, music pumped and drinks arrived by the jug. Revellers whooped, clacked, staggered and fell. Beer spilled and, intermittently, fights erupted. By midnight, I knew, the party would be in full swing with inhibitions freely surrendered, and by morning the streets would resemble the aftermath of a battle, a casualty-strewn stretch littered with broken glass, half-eaten hamburgers and spatterings of vomit. The revellers would emerge blinkingly and contritely around lunchtime before the first mid-day drink squared the whole debauched, self-gratifying circle again

As we pulled away from the traffic lights, Papa laughed dismissively. A few blocks further on, the satellite navigation system instructed me to turn left, further into the town, and his head swung instantly to face me.

'We stay here?' he asked, his voice infused with mild panic.

'So it would seem,' I said calmly.

We parked, and I helped Papa out of the car. Pablito bustled forward and took responsibility for ushering him inside, despatching me to retrieve the suitcases from the boot. Our hotel looked cheap and seedy, located in what appeared to be the centre of a bar and nightclub complex, at least a mile from the beach, I guessed.

We were checked in by a kindly old lady who directed us to the seventh floor. We emerged on to a landing and Mama put her hand to her mouth, too late to stifle an intake of breath. Vast and echoing, it was like a prison hall, with walls and floor of bare stone, coated with dirty salmon-coloured paint. The roof was made of transparent corrugated plastic and was comprehensively spattered with seagull droppings. We inched along the landing, which was punctuated with large plant-pots full of discarded cigarette butts.

If Papa and Pablito held any immediate opinions about their surroundings, they didn't make them known. We arrived at our rooms and entered the double that had been booked for Mama and Papa. It was small and serviceable, equipped with a bed, a sofa, a small dining table, a cooker hob and a fridge. Pablito and I were in an adjoining twin room.

After we'd unpacked, we decided to go for a drive to explore some of the small fishing villages and resorts crammed into the craggy turns of the coastline. We stopped at a beach bar and Papa ordered a *horchata de chufa*, a sweet milky drink made from tiger nuts, which he hadn't drunk since his childhood. With his first sip, a warm smile of recognition washed over his face.

The wind was low and the sun's malevolence was waning, agreeably temperate conditions in which to watch the crisp, azure waves lap against the rugged shoreline. The combined scents of spicy acorns and black, toasted tobacco appeared to have a calming effect on Papa, who smiled indulgently, apparently reassured that there were some things about his country that never changed.

When we returned to the resort, Pablito suggested we change and meet in the restaurant for dinner.

'There is no restaurant,' I pointed out.

'Of course there's a restaurant, it's a hotel, isn't it?'

'No, it's an apartment hotel, which means it's self-catering. The clue's in the title.'

His expression hardened and his eyes shifted unsteadily. It was obvious he hadn't properly understood what he had signed up for. 'Well, they didn't make that clear to me. They gave me the impression meals would be included.'

'Look, don't worry, there are plenty of restaurants here in the resort. My treat,' I said smiling.

Immediately Papa intervened.

'We nae eat in restaurant, we have kitchen here. Your Mama she cook.'

Her face fell.

'We're on holiday, Papa. Mama's not cooking, she's here to enjoy herself.'

Papa waved a hand in my direction and began to unzip his suitcase.

'That's what people do when they come to places like this,' I continued. 'They eat out in restaurants. The kitchenettes are there to make breakfast. No one ever uses them to cook dinner.'

'Wha you know wha people dae? We eat here.'

My chest tightened. As a child I'd felt belittled and powerless at his ready discard of reason, but at least then I had the consolation of knowing I'd grow up and he'd grow old. Now I was an adult, stronger and smarter than him, more affluent, more successful and more articulate, and yet still his will prevailed.

Mama and I went to the local supermarket, which, as I'd antici-pated, turned out to be little more than a convenience store for tourists to purchase breakfast staples and other essentials they'd forgotten to bring with them from home. We came back with some bread and a few tins of sardines and olives. Mama turned them out on to the cheap white crockery that was stashed in the cupboards under the hob.

It was barely eight o'clock when we'd finished eating, but Mama insisted Papa should have an early night because he was tired from the journey. He didn't complain. She'd brought a book with her, and she offered to sit with him, suggesting Pablito and I should go out for a drink. He seemed keen to get out of the hotel, so I agreed, though I felt sure it must have been twenty years since Pablito and I had done anything together. He was ten years older than me, and there had been no stage when we were growing up at which our interests had converged. The gap in our ages seemed to justify our lack of closeness.

We ambled along some empty side streets until we came to a boulevard with a few bars and restaurants. It had just turned dark, but the air was still warm enough to sit outside, and there was a pleasing mix of cooking smells in the sea air. A handful of tourists had started early at some of the gaudier bars, but we managed to find a small pavement café that was empty apart from a couple of young local women sitting on bar stools, drink-ing coffee and smoking. I ordered two beers and we sat at a table.

I feared we'd have nothing to talk about, but the events of the day provided enough material to allow the conversation to meander along without us settling on anything in particular, far less any issues that might provoke contention. Pablito sat slumped in his seat and took a long draught of beer.

'The old man's in great nick for his age, isn't he? He'll go on forever,' he said cheerily.

'You think so?'

'Yeah, I mean, he's got a very positive attitude, and coming back here will be a tremendous boost for him. That's why I insisted he should come. If I'd left it to him he'd have put if off for months, so I just thought, hell, book it, and he'll have no choice but to come.'

'You don't think it might stir up bad memories he'd sooner forget?'

'What do you mean?' he asked, genuinely perplexed.

I didn't really know what I meant. Papa's rare recollections of Spain always seemed so doom-laden, but he spoke in such generalised terms I was never entirely clear why he should feel personally threatened.

'Well, you know the way he used to go on about Franco and the Civil War and all of that stuff,' I said, unintentionally belittling my argument.

'Yeah, but that was years ago, and I've always told him he can't live in the past. These times are dead and long gone.'

Pablito offered to buy us both another drink, and as I watched his hunched frame draped over the front of the bar, I felt a sudden, sad pain. He'd inherited more of Papa's magnetism than I had, but he'd been a reckless guardian of his looks and now he was stooped and beaten. His youthful gameness was gone, and his face looked shrunken and deep-lined.

It was after eleven o'clock when we returned to the hotel, by which time an orgy of merriment was in full swing in the adjoining bars and nightclubs. Flashing strobe lights and the spine-jolting boom of dance music followed us through the complex. Several touts tried to coax us into their establishments with the promise of deals on lethal-sounding drinks.

41

I pressed ahead, flushed and harassed, but Pablito allowed himself to be detained by a couple of tall, blonde girls no older than Ben, dressed in teetering high heels and skimpy lingerie. I was too far away to hear their conversation, but the forced laughter of the girls was clearly enough to manipulate Pablito's gossamer-thin ego, and he decided to go off with them.

When he finally arrived back in our hotel room, it was almost four a.m. I'd long since abandoned any hope of sleeping. The metronomic beat of the music was loud and constant, interrupted sporadically by soprano howls of giddiness and aggressive alpha-male exchanges. When the music finally stopped it was light outside, and I felt like a punch-drunk boxer.

I came to with a start mid-morning. Pablito was still asleep, so I made my way through to Mama and Papa's room. Mama was sitting outside on the verandah. Papa had gone out to look for a British newspaper, she said, so I made myself a cup of coffee.

'He never reads newspapers,' I pointed out.

'I think he's missing home already,' she said smiling. 'He wants to know what's going on.'

I sat down with my coffee and closed my eyes. For a few moments I basked silently in the rejuvenating morning sun. It was the first time Mama and I had been alone since we had arrived, so I decided it was a good time to quiz her again about Papa's letters to the Ajuntamente in Lerida. But her anxieties appeared to have dissipated, because she no longer felt willing to discuss or explain it.

'It's not important,' she said dismissively.

I felt angry. It was clearly something that had troubled her to the extent that she'd taken me into her confidence, forcing me to drop everything and leave my work at a critical time, because she'd felt so concerned about it. Now she'd decided it wasn't even worth mentioning.

'You can't do that to me, Mama. I have a right to know.'

She shuffled irritably. 'You don't need to know.'

'I know I don't need to but I want to know.'

She looked pained. 'I'm sorry, I can't tell you.'

By the time Pablito wandered through, looking hungover and dishevelled, it was almost one o'clock. Papa hadn't yet returned from his mission to buy a newspaper. We'd made plans to drive into Girona and wander around the shops in the afternoon, so Pablito agreed to go to look for him while Mama and I cleared away the breakfast dishes. He returned half an hour later, having failed to find Papa.

'He'll be fine, Mama, you know what he's like. He'll have gone for a walk and discovered something that has grabbed his interest,' Pablito said, trying to calm her down.

Judging by Mama's reaction, I wasn't so sure. Pablito and I agreed to search a bigger area together. As he'd gone out to buy a paper, we planned to take one side of the town each and visit all the tourist shops. We were about to set off when I noticed the car was missing from its parking space. I told Mama and she sat down slowly.

'We should call the police,' she said.

'The police? What are you talking about?' Pablito demanded.

'We need to call the police. We need to stop him. He's going to Lerida.'

'What's he going to do in Lerida?' I asked calmly.

She didn't answer.

'Talk to me. Why is he going to Lerida?'

She dropped her head and gazed at the floor.

'We can't call the police if you're not willing to be open, Mama. What are we going to tell them – that we're concerned for the safety of an 83-year-old man driving an uninsured car, hell-bent on a mission to settle a score that you'd rather not talk about?'

She blushed. I suggested we had two options – we could sit and wait for him to return, or we could follow him to Lerida and hope we arrived in time to stop him doing whatever it was he'd gone there for.

'Let's go,' she said with a sudden burst of determination.

By the time we were on the road it was late afternoon. I'd had to track down a different car-hire firm from the one we'd used previously, to avoid questions about why I needed a second vehicle, and then I had to persuade the clerk to serve me before the office closed for the siesta.

Navigating an unknown route and driving on the right in an attempt to find my lost father would have been stressful enough without the presence of Mama, sitting in the back and continually asking if I was sure we were going the right way. We took the motorway to the north of Barcelona and from there we drove through the mountains, where the temperature dropped and the terrain changed from brown to a lush green. The hills were cloaked in mature fir trees, and for a while my mind was lost in their stillness.

By late afternoon we were approaching Lerida on the main trunk road, and Mama said we should look for an area called Alguaire. I reprogrammed the satnav and followed the instructions to a hamlet about fifteen kilometres north of the centre of Lerida.

The roads leading into it were flanked by peach and fig groves, vineyards and olive fields, and the centre was a bustle of activity, with narrow cobbled streets, lofty stucco apartments and sloping terracotta roofs. Small Juliet balconies were framed with bushes of purple bougainvillea and potted orange carnations. This was where Papa was born, Mama told us – this was our home village.

The main square was lined by rows of horse-chestnut trees whose thick foliage provided a canopy against the late-afternoon sun. There were a few small shops and a bar with a couple of pavement tables. A small group of black men, I guessed migrant workers servicing the local farms, gathered around the door of a telegraph office that offered cheap international calls.

I parked the car and we found the Ajuntamente, a small modern building at the corner of the square. Inside its reception area was low-ceilinged, sparsely furnished with a pair of desks and some filing cabinets. We arrived just as it was about to close and an elderly cleaner, wearing a sky-blue housecoat and carrying a damp cloth, looked at us, wide-eyed and edgy, as we entered. Mama took a photograph of Papa out of her handbag and mentioned him by name. The woman immediately became animated, speaking loudly and pointing at the picture repeatedly before throwing her head back and her hands in the air. I couldn't make out most of what she said, but two words I did understand were 'Guardia Civil'.

We left and walked quickly along the narrow streets towards the other side of town, where the cleaner had told Mama the village police station was located. It was a single-storey building with nothing to distinguish it as a hub of law enforcement other than a small silver plaque on the door, and we would have walked past it had Pablito not spotted our first hire car parked around the side.

Inside, two uniformed officers sat languidly in a stale, smoky fug, their feet resting on adjacent desks. A couple of yellowing computer terminals were located amid a jungle of paperwork, overflowing ashtrays and dirty cups. The scene resembled Ben's bedroom, though with the addition of a pair of utility belts to which handcuffs and pistols were attached.

The men were fixated on a basketball game playing on a small television set attached high on a wall on the far side of the room. The game had reached a critical juncture, and we had to wait until the team in red had missed a penalty shot before we were afforded the attention of one of the officers.

'Si,' he said curtly, without standing up.

Mama went through the same routine she had gone through with the cleaner in the Ajuntamente, handing him the photo-graph, which he held and scrutinised before throwing it down on his desk next to a plate of olive stones. He looked too old to still be working: his clothes hung off his skinny frame, and large, protruding gums dominated his mouth. His hair was pitch black, greasy and thinning, and he hadn't shaved for several days.

He talked slowly and unenthusiastically, frequently shrugging and pouting. He struck me as a time-server, seeing out the dog-end of his career in a backwater town. From his tone I might have deduced that he didn't know anything about Papa, if it hadn't been for the fact that his car was parked outside the building.

'What's going on, Mama?' I asked.

She ignored me, continuing to address the policeman in a tone that became sharper and firmer the more she spoke. The mood changed quickly and the policeman exploded in anger. He stood up and gesticulated, presenting his upturned hands to Mama, jutting his head forward in a gesture of rebuke. He spoke for around a minute, apparently building a concise, empirical case. As he neared the end of his diatribe, Mama interrupted.

'¿Dónde está mi marido?' she asked slowly and deliberately. 'Where is my husband?'

The policeman ignored her question and continued with his rhetoric. She asked the question a second time, louder and more forcefully.

'¿Dónde está mi marido?'

Again he ignored the question and raised his voice to compensate. Suddenly Mama snapped, her face reddened, and she began to shout at the top of her voice.

'¿Dónde está mi marido?' she screamed. 'Quiero ver mi marido.' 'I want to see my husband.'

The other policeman, who until now had remained silent, stood up, white-faced, and intervened. He was clearly the good cop – younger than his colleague, and apparently the junior partner, but more eager to help. He turned down the sound on the television set with the remote control and offered Mama a glass of water, which she accepted. The bad cop sat down slowly and sheepishly concerned himself with something on his computer.

'Mi marido está muy enfermo,' Mama said. 'My husband is very ill.'

She reached into her handbag and pulled out a strip of tablets.

'*Él tiene cáncer. Si él no toma su morfina regularmente, los efectos de su tumor serán muy dolorosos,*' she explained. 'He has cancer. If he doesn't take his morphine regularly the effects of his tumour will be very painful.'

'What did you say?' Pablito asked.

Mama put her hand over her mouth.

'I'm sorry Pablito,' she said. 'I didn't mean for you to find out like this.'

My brother rocked on his feet and I moved forward to steady him, then I lowered him on to a seat. He slumped down and stared at the floor.

The good cop spoke to Mama at length. She nodded appreciatively, occasionally mouthing '*claro*', a term of understanding and conciliation. He took the pills from her and lifted a bottle of water from his desk, then he turned and unlocked a door immediately behind him, below the television set, that led into another room. Mama tried to follow him, but he closed the door behind him and locked it from the other side. He was gone only for a couple of minutes, and when he returned he picked up the telephone and dialled a number.

'What's going on, Mama?' I asked.

'Let's go outside,' she said. 'I need some air.'

It was dark and cool and perfectly silent, and the sky was peppered with golden bright stars. It was at times like this I wished I smoked.

'Your papa's in trouble,' Mama said tremulously.

'I guessed that. What's he done?'

'He went to the Ajuntamente and threatened the staff unless they told him who in the village had objected to his request.'

'What request?'

'He submitted an official request to dig a piece of ground but he was refused because several of the villagers objected.'

'What?'

'And when they refused to tell him who the objectors were, he went to the place, which is on a farm that grows olives on the edge of the town, and he started to dig, and when the farmer moved to stop him he tried to hit him with the shovel and now . . .'

'Wait a minute, I'm lost – start again,' I pleaded. 'Papa was digging in an olive field, and he tried to hit a farmer with a shovel? Mama, what the . . .'

'. . . and now the police want to charge him with violent behaviour and trespassing on to someone's property and criminal damage.'

She began to cry.

'Stop crying, Mama, and explain to me what this is about. Why did Papa travel halfway across Spain to dig a hole in the middle of the countryside?'

'He was looking for bodies. He wanted to exhume them and give them a proper . . .'

'Bodies? What bodies?'

'His parents,' she said calmly. 'He was looking for the bodies of his parents.'

I felt shocked but not surprised. Deep within me, I'd always imagined a day like this would come.

5

The good cop emerged from the police station and beckoned Mama over. They spoke for a few moments, his expression earnest throughout, but I could tell from the easing of tension across Mama's face that he had good news.

'What's happening?' I asked after he'd returned inside.

'The policeman has spoken to his superiors in Lerida, and, because of your papa's age and his illness, they will release him. The farmer he threatened doesn't want to press charges, no one wants to . . . what's the English expression? . . . pick old sores.'

'So he's free to go?'

'On the condition that he leaves Alguaire and returns to the resort, where he must stay until we leave Spain.'

We were made to wait until Papa had signed some forms. I needed some time alone, so I decided to go for a walk, wandering the deserted streets until I found myself back in the main square where the Ajuntamente was located. Opposite it was a tall building with a bell tower I hadn't noticed earlier in the day. It was the only structure in the village that looked anything like it might pre-date the last century. It had obviously been badly damaged at some point and only a small proportion – a gable end and part of the facing wall – remained of the original yellow sandstone structure, which dated, I guessed, from the eighteenth or early nineteenth century. There had been a restoration attempt, but it looked rushed and unsympathetic, with cheap red house-bricks replacing the damaged parts.

It was possible to imagine the building in a previous incarnation, handsome and impressive, perhaps municipal chambers, or even a church, but now it had the disfigured look of a poorly healed burns victim, an ill-considered hybrid of old and new, principle and compromise.

A figure emerged from the darkness, crossing the square, and on impulse I stopped him and asked him if he spoke English.

'Of course,' he said, as though I had insulted his family.

He was young, perhaps in his late twenties, with thin rimmed glasses and a neatly cropped beard.

'I was wondering about that building over there. Why is it like that?'

'It was damaged during the Civil War, I believe,' he said.

'Was it shelled by the Nationalists?'

He gestured across the road to the Ajuntamente. 'Why don't you ask at the town hall? They'll be able to help.'

I explained to him that I'd be leaving the village that night and wouldn't be returning. 'I'd really like to know what happened to this building.'

He smiled. 'I'm sorry, I don't know.'

'Is this your hometown?' I asked.

The smile dropped from his face, and he eyed me suspiciously. 'Yes it is. Where are you from?' he asked, suddenly disconcerted.

'I'm from Britain.'

'What are you doing here?'

'I'm half Spanish. My family is from Alguaire.'

His expression softened. 'Oh. Well, good luck with your inquiries.'

Papa was guided from the police station by the good cop, with Mama's coat draped over his shoulders. He crouched in the back seat of the car, head bowed like a prisoner under escort, and Pablito followed close behind him, dazed and robotic.

Despite telling the police that we would return to the resort immediately, Mama and I agreed Papa was too tired to endure a two-hour drive back that night, so we decided to stay in Lerida. We drove the short distance in silence and circled the centre for a few minutes before settling on a smart-looking hotel on the edge of the old town.

Pablito seemed close to tears and said he was going straight to bed. Mama didn't want him to be alone, so she volunteered to sit with him. Neither Papa nor I had eaten all day and we were both hungry. I suggested we dine in the hotel restaurant, which was almost empty, but he wanted to go into the town.

The narrow lanes were bustling with people shopping before closing time. Elegant boutiques hawked expensive jewellery, designer clothes and handbags, and in the windows of smart *dulcerías* and *pastelerías* there were elaborate displays of hand-made sweets and pastries. We strolled across the main plaza, which sat in the shadow of a baroque cathedral. The night was pleasantly mild without a hint of a breeze, and chic couples and students sat at café terraces, nursing glasses of wine, chattering loudly in hypnotic, quickfire Catalan. It was a modern, affluent centre, difficult to reconcile with Papa's impoverished background.

His progress was slow, but he looked relaxed as he breathed the sweet, balmy air. We settled on a small back-street café and sat at one of a handful of pavement tables. The waiter arrived and I deferred to Papa, who ordered tapas. It was the usual selection of *gambas, calamares, albóndigas, chipirones* and *tortillas*, served in small terracotta dishes, nothing that wasn't available in any number of the tapas bars that had sprung up in London in recent years, but Papa knew little of that world, and he marvelled at the authenticity it all.

He was starving, and he ate voraciously. I was keen to quiz him about his behaviour in Alguaire, but I was prepared to wait until there were no distractions. After a few minutes all the dishes were empty.

'So, do you want to tell me what all that was about back there?' I asked.

He sat back in his chair, looking small and hunted.

'Come on, Papa, you didn't think you could get away with something like that without at least an effort at explaining what it was all about?'

He raised his head slightly and his eyes turned upwards, white with defiance.

'Wha you say explain? I nae explain nothin.'

My body tensed. I leaned across the table and grabbed hold of his arm. He winced and tried to pull away from me, but I grabbed it tighter. He scowled.

'Do you hear what I'm saying?'

'*Si*, I hear,' he said through the pain.

The waiter came over to collect the empty dishes, so I let go of Papa's arm and ordered two *carajillos* – small glasses of coffee fortified with harsh country brandy. Papa protested – he hadn't touched alcohol for years.

'Come on, Papa. It will do you good.'

The waiter stood by patiently until Papa backed down.

The drinks arrived and Papa ventured a sip, wincing, but he continued to drink, a small amount at a time, until it was finished. When the waiter passed our table, I ordered another two. After a while Papa's shoulders relaxed, and his face acquired an opiated grin.

'Any time you're ready,' I said.

We sat in silence for another few minutes, and I was beginning to doubt whether the message had got through to him, whether he understood that I was serious, but then suddenly he spoke.

'Is cold – 1937 is coldest winter ever in Alguaire,' he said airily.

This wasn't what I had been expecting, but I kept quiet and let him continue.

'The *gasolina* in trucks it freeze, and the ground is so hard we use dynamite tae dig trenches. The Fascist bombs they grow louder. All the time the German planes they fly over and cause explosion but all we can think is tae keep warm and eat.'

'Who's we?' I asked.

He looked at me impatiently.

'My mama, my papa and my two brothers.'

'So you had a family?' I asked.

He nodded.

'What were their names?'

'Your grandfather, he is called Antonio, this is how you get your name.' He smiled warmly. 'And your grandmother, she is called Josefa.'

'And your brothers?'

'Paco and Josepe, who we call Pepe.'

'What were they like?'

He smiled. 'Paco is good shot. In fields he shoot rabbits. Very quick.'

'How old was Paco in 1937?'

He waved a hand dismissively in my direction.

'Ach, I nae remember this,' he said irritably.

I felt anxious, determined to get as much information from him as I could during this brief opportunity when he was feeling relaxed.

'Come on, Papa, try to remember.'

'Pepe, he is oldest.'

'How old was he, then?'

He reclined and arched his neck, staring at the sky, which was peppered with millions of dots, as though he was contemplating an issue of great importance. Then he looked at me with a grin. 'He is very handsome. Very good-looking. All the girls, they like Pepe.'

My gentle approach wasn't getting me anywhere, so I decided to be more direct. 'Why were you digging in a field today?'

The grin dropped from his face.

'Why did you come here today, Papa, what did you think you were going to achieve?'

He said nothing.

'Even if you had come across the remains of your parents, what did you plan to do with them – pack them in your suitcase and take them home?'

He looked at me with a hard, accusing stare.

'How you know this?'

'Mama told me. How else would I know?'

'She have nae right.'

'Well, she didn't have much option. How else was she to explain the fact that you were in a police cell after threatening to brain a farmer whose land you were trying to dig up?'

He squirmed and flapped a hand, as though he was trying to get rid of me. 'What else she tell you?'

'Nothing, she didn't tell me anything else, other than that you were looking for the bodies of your parents. You're lucky you have such a loyal wife.'

'You nae tell me this. I know how lucky I am.' He bowed his head and his shoulders dropped. He looked frail.

'What did your father do?' I asked.

'He work in olive fields, for a how you say, *latifundista*.'

'A landowner.'

'*Si*, landowner. But when war start, this landowner he disappear because Anarchists they say they will kill him. So my father he have nae job and we are hungry. We have small house, only two rooms, with no water.'

'So how did your parents end up dead and buried on a farm?'

'They are kill by Falange, by soldiers of Franco,' he said bluntly.

Finally I felt as though I was getting somewhere.

'Why were they killed? Did they fight for the other side, for the Republicans?'

'*Si*, they fight. We all fight. Even my mama, she learn to use Mauser.'

'A rifle?'

'*Si*, she use a rifle with no training. My brothers and me, we go to Lerida to fight with Anarchist militia.'

I made a quick mental calculation and established that my father would have been thirteen.

'We stay in old building that is used to store grain with rats and mice. We fight in trenches outside to town. On one day the *Franquistas*, they plan big attack, aeroplanes they come low over trenches, lots of bullets and bombs . . . boom, boom . . . I no know wha happen. Everyone around is dead, and I nae even know how tae work gun. I nae see Pepe. He is with me but then I nae see him and everywhere is smoke and blood on ground. The soldiers, they scream and cry, and I am pull tae ground by my friend who say we must go. I say I nae go, I look for Pepe, but one soldier say "I see him, and he is shot. Your brother is dead".'

There was a look of incredulity on his face, as though even after all of this time he was still unable to believe what had happened. I wanted to comfort him.

'I'm sorry, Papa, I had no idea.'

'I run intae town and everyone they look for shelter but I go tae look for Paco. After two hours I find him in centre, nae far from here.'

He pointed to the end of the lane in which we were sitting.

'He is injure but he can walk, and I say we go tae Alguaire tae find Mama and Papa.'

'So what happened, did you find them?' I asked.

'We find two bicycles and we ride but when we are near to village we meet neighbour, a friend of my papa, who say "You nae go, the Falange they are there and they kill all *rojos* and *anarchistas*." I say, "Where is our parents?" and he say, "Your parents, they are dead."'

A tear trembled in the corner of his eye and tumbled out over the creases of his red face. I lifted a napkin from the table and handed it to him.

'How did they die?'

'The *Franquistas*, they line up everyone in village and they say you take off shirt, even women. Everyone who have bruise on neck and shoulders, they say "You use rifle tae shoot us because of, how you say . . ."' He mimed the force of a rifle recoiling.

'The kickback."

'*Si*, kickback. They shoot both my parents in back of head and they bury them in ground.'

'In the olive field?'

He nodded.

'Why did you try to dig them up today? What did you expect?'

'I nae expect nothin. I dae it tae say tae people who wanna leave my mama and papa in ground, I say "You look at me, you watch me dig, you cannae ignore me, I will make noise until you listen tae me."'

'But there are ways of protesting, Papa, and that's not one of them. You have to go through the proper channels, and, if you come up against resistance, you argue your case. That's how you get things done.'

He laughed out loud, but not in anger; it was a laugh of despair.

'You nae know wha you talk about. This is nae Britain, this is Spain, they nae wanna know about wha is done in history. They wanna forget.'

There was a perceptiveness about his comment, a reminder that, although he rarely talked about this country, he never stopped thinking about it.

'What happened to your brother Paco?'

'He die,' Papa said curtly.

'How did he die?'

'I nae say. He die, this is all.'

I thought about pressing him, but I felt he'd been put through enough for one day. He'd told me more over two *carajillos* than he had in the past forty years, so I figured it could wait.

I paid the bill and we wandered back along a narrow street with shops and upper-storey apartments crowded in on either side. After a few yards Papa stopped at a cloistered passage to the right that climbed steeply before disappearing into the darkness.

'You wait here,' he ordered as he turned.

He took a few steps and then his pace quickened. After several minutes, when he hadn't returned, I began to worry. I was about to go after him when I heard him calling me. I turned around and saw him approaching from the other direction at a canter.

'I remember this,' he said laughing. 'I play here as boy, and I remember where it come out. I nae here for seventy years, but I remember this road.'

We returned to our hotel rooms and I lay on the bed, restless and alert well into the early hours. Every time I tried to force myself to sleep, events resurfaced and unnerved me. So many things had happened, even before the previous day, that I felt overwhelmed. I was also troubled by a recurring idea that had entered my mind immediately after learning about Papa's illness. It was fleeting, almost negligible, and even referring to it as a fully formulated thought wasn't quite right: *Perhaps it's a good thing he's dying. At least when he dies he won't be able to cause us any more heartache.*

In the morning I found Mama, Papa and Pablito in the hotel restaurant, eating breakfast. Together they'd agreed that they didn't want to stay in Spain any longer. I offered to book us all into a nicer hotel in a quieter resort, but Pablito became agitated at the suggestion, insisting he wanted to go home.

Mama asked if I could book us all on to the next available flight back to Britain. I went into the hotel lobby to use one of the computers. There were no charter flights until the end of the week, so I booked us all on a scheduled flight from Barcelona to Gatwick for early the following morning, and then bought tickets for the three of them to fly on to Glasgow.

Then I decided to phone Cheryl. I'd been putting off the call since I'd arrived in Spain. My intention had been to delay it until after I'd returned to London, to leave her with the impression I'd only just got round to squeezing her into my tight schedule, but I couldn't wait until then. By the fourth ring I knew she wasn't going to answer. I hung up and dialled our home number. My heart raced in anticipation and I had difficulty breathing. Still clutching the phone tightly against my ear, I paced back and forward. After eight rings, the familiar answer-machine message clicked in.

'Hello, I'm afraid that neither Cheryl, Antonio nor Ben can come to the phone at the moment. Please leave a message and one of us will get back to you.'

It pained me to hear her voice and not to be able to speak to her. I remembered when she'd recorded the message. I wasn't happy with her first attempt – she'd said none of us was in, which, I pointed out, would let potential burglars know the house was empty. I'd made her change it, which led to a fight. She said I was being ridiculous.

I thought about leaving a message, but I couldn't trust that my voice wouldn't have a note of desperation. I hung up when I heard the beep. Then it occurred to me that I could phone Connie. Not that I expected Cheryl to be with her, but I hoped she might know where her sister was. She answered after a couple of rings, but when I spoke she seemed surprised and nervous.

'I'm really sorry, Tony,' she said.

I liked it when Connie called me Tony. When other people used it, they made me feel like an Italian chip-shop owner, but with her it sounded clannish and familiar.

'What about?' I asked.

There was another silence.

'What are you sorry about, Connie?'

'Where are you?' she asked.

'I'm in Spain, with my parents.'

'You haven't been home?'

'No, not for a couple of days. I had to come away at short notice.'

There was another lengthy silence.

'What's going on, Connie? I phoned to see if you knew where Cheryl was. I can't get hold of her.'

'Oh, right, no, I don't know where she is.'

I was becoming agitated at her cryptic tone.

'What's going on, Connie? Why did you ask me if I'd been home?'

'There's nothing going on, I just wanted to know where you were.'

I felt tears well up, and I wanted to ask her straight out the question that had been nagging at me for weeks, that I could have put to Cheryl countless times but had avoided. Perhaps it would be easier for me if it came from Connie. And if anyone was likely to know, it was her. She and Cheryl were stiflingly close and told one another everything.

'Are you all right, Tony?'

I fought to hold back the tears. 'Yes, I'm fine.'

'Are you sure?'

I closed my eyes tight and pinched the bridge of my nose. 'Yes, I'm sure.'

6

Mama and Papa were arguing loudly in Spanish when I asked her to write a letter to Mr McKendry, my music teacher. I wanted to take clarinet lessons. Sandy Bryson had got clarinet lessons after his dad sent a long letter to McKendry, saying how he'd had to stop work because of his asbestosis and how they couldn't afford to pay for private tuition and how Sandy had a musical gift and how it would really mean a lot to them. I asked Mama to do the same thing for me. She always took care of important things like writing letters to teachers or signing forms or helping with homework. But she looked past me, as though she was preoccupied, and I thought she hadn't heard me. 'Your father will write it for you,' she said scathingly.

Papa scrambled around the house for a notepad, but he couldn't find one, so he ended up tearing a page out of my arithmetic jotter. I knew it was inappropriate to write a formal letter on squared paper, but I decided not to make a fuss – better to have a substandard letter than none at all, I reasoned. He spent ages thinking about what he was going to write, with the Biro hovering a couple of inches above the page. Several times he appealed to Mama for help, but she told him to do it himself. That only made him angrier and more frustrated. When finally he'd finished, he folded the page into quarters and said I would just have to deliver it like that because he didn't have an envelope.

On the way to school the next day I took out the letter and read it. The writing was thin and spidery and covered no more than a single line, which tailed off in a downward curve as it neared the edge of the page.

Dir Mr Mikenri, I wil lik my sun to ply in the clarinet. from Pablo Noguera.

I wanted to cry. I tore the letter into pieces and shoved them through the bars of a drain cover at the end of our street.

After school, I didn't feel like going home. I hung around the playground for a bit until it emptied, then I sat on a bench at a bus stop, avoiding the gaze of anyone walking past. I thought about catching the first bus that came along and staying on it as far as it went, then walking and walking until it was dark, but I didn't have any money for the fare, and it was cold and getting dark, so I decided to go home. Besides, I was starving, and it was fried fish for tea.

When I got home, Mama was on the telephone, speaking Spanish. '¿Franco ha muerto?' She said with a look of incredulity. I guessed that whatever these words meant, they were important, because the colour drained from her face, and her arms dropped to her sides, the receiver still clutched tightly in her hand.

'What's going on?' I asked Papa and Pablito.

They remained silent.

'What does that mean, Franco ha mawerto?' I demanded.

'It means Franco's dead,' Pablito murmured.

'Who's Franco?'

No one responded. Everyone sat down as though the responsibility of standing had suddenly become unbearable, and they stared ahead, silent and open-mouthed.

'What's going on? Who's Franco? How did he die?'

Still no one spoke. It reminded me of a scene from a black-and-white horror film of the 1930s when all you could hear was the crackling of the soundtrack. Mama began to sob, and I sat next to her, laying my arm gently around her shoulder. Papa started to talk in Spanish, slowly at first, but then his words arrived quicker and more fluidly, as though he was delivering a speech, setting forth the components of an argument, the pitch of his voice rising incrementally, his delivery booming ever louder as he built towards an angry, impassioned climax.

Though I couldn't make out the full content of his speech, it was clear this was an issue about which he felt strongly. He was in full flight when Mama rose to her feet, her face red with anger.

'*Poco de respeto*,' she said quietly but sternly.

He stopped. It was one of the few times I witnessed her challenge him so directly, halting him in his tracks. I knew what she'd said, it was a phrase he often directed towards me. 'Show some respect.'

Later I asked him who Franco was and why his death was so important.

'He was a very bad man,' Papa replied.

'Don't teach the child disrespect,' she said, in that same stern tone. She looked at me, her eyes reddened and damp.

'Franco was the leader of our country,' she said measuredly. 'He kept order on the streets when there was none.'

I was confused, not knowing what to think or how to feel, whether to be pro- or anti-Franco, to be happy that he was dead, as Papa appeared to be, or sad, like Mama. I couldn't understand how two people could have such wildly differing opinions about the same person. They even called him by different names. Papa spat his name out like it was a term of abuse, while Mama called him *el Caudillo*, which she said was his proper title. Pablito was firmly anti-Franco, but then he agreed with everything Papa said, and I was sure he didn't know any more about the ruler than I did.

A pall descended over the house, where it remained for several days. Mama wore black, and she had a permanently concerned look on her face as she monitored the World Service for updates. A large bundle of Spanish magazines arrived through the post from Abuela, all dominated by pictures of important-looking men, dressed in formal suits with black ties, looking solemn. Papa did his best to appear unintererted, but he listened out for the news on the radio and he pored over the magazine coverage.

From the pictures Franco looked friendly enough, particularly in his younger days, with his bushy eyebrows like Denis Healey's, his thin, neatly trimmed moustache and his warm, reassuring smile. I guessed he was a jolly man, the sort you'd like to have as your uncle, who would buy you presents at Christmas and lead the singing at a family party.

His clothes were militaristic and dashing. In some of the more recent shots, when he was ageing and balder, he wore a black uniform with gold epaulettes and a red sash, a ceremonial hat with a white feathered plume and white gloves. In older pictures, he favoured a beret and what looked remarkably like the uniform of the SS. He appeared to be giving a Nazi salute to a convoy of trucks carrying troops. I also heard him described on the radio as the 'former Fascist dictator of Spain'. And I knew that Hitler had been a Fascist.

It hadn't occurred to me until then that Franco was the same bloke who'd been the leader of the country during the war, all those years ago, when Spain supported Germany, but from his pictures he looked pretty old, so I guessed he might well have been. If that was the case, I couldn't understand why Mama was so upset. Surely she wouldn't cry over someone who had been friends with the filthy Hun, would she? I considered asking Papa but thought better of it, remembering our previous run-in over Spain's military history that had ended with Max Miller's face being pummelled to a bloody pulp.

The worst of it was that no one else in Mosspark seemed to know anything about Franco's death. Nothing had changed, and the world beyond our front gate was oblivious to Mama's grief, to Papa's passionate displays of enmity, to the story that appeared to be dominating newspapers in Spain.

I didn't like bringing friends home, but around that time Bobby Watson persuaded me to let him come back to my place after school to watch *Magpie*. It started at four-thirty, and his ma and da didn't get home from work until five. Reluctantly I agreed, but the moment I saw Mama, dressed all in black, seated next to the radio, with a box of tissues on her lap, I knew I had some explaining to do.

'How come yer ma's greetin?' Bobby Watson inquired as we settled down on the settee.

'Cos Franco died,' I explained.

'Franko Baxter died?'

'No, not Franko Baxter. General Franco.'

'Who's General Franco?'

'The Spanish head of state.'

'Never heard ay him.'

Papa changed after Franco's death. Until then he'd barely mentioned Spain, only ever expressing ownership of his nationality when pressed to do so, when it was raised in conversation with strangers, or if it became an issue because of his poor English. His silence on the subject suited me – the less attention drawn to my foreignness the better, as far as I was concerned.

But now he referred to it unprompted, talking about the country in proprietorial terms, referring to the Spanish as 'we' and to Spain as 'my country'. There was clearly a reawakening of his interest, not just in Spain, but in Catalonia, the region of his birth. He spoke glowingly about its architecture and scenery, its history and culture and the artistry and industry of its people. He told us that many people regarded themselves as Catalan rather than Spanish, in the same way many people in this country saw themselves as Scottish rather than British.

Over dinner, he declared as a statement of fact that Gaudi's Temple Expiatori de la Sagrada Família in Barcelona was the most beautiful building in the world. He recalled, as a young man, watching Gypsy dancers in the Plaça de Sant Jaume and how he'd stood transfixed by their elegance and the rhythmic, erotic aggression of their movements. He spoke with passion of a bullfight he'd attended, of the primal beauty of the muscular, majestic bull pitted against the bold matador.

Long after we finished eating he was still talking, telling us about the breathtaking sweep of the Catalan landscape, from the hiking trails in the verdant hillsides of Val d'Aran, across the rich growing areas of the region known as *las cartas del paisaje* – literally the letters of the landscape – famed for its almonds and olive oil, to the coastal areas of Aigua Blava, Calella de Palafrugell and Tamariu, with their tiny, bobbing fishing boats nestling in craggy coves, cast in his memory as forever sunkissed, idyllic and untouched by modernity.

In this new spirit of openness, I discovered important things about Papa's past – how he'd left the orphanage where he grew up when he was eighteen and moved to Tangier. I asked him why he'd moved to another country, and he said it was something to do with the Civil War. I asked him what a civil war was. He said it was when people in the same country fight each other, when friends and brothers are often enemies. He said the war was started by Franco, then a military general, who used the army to overthrow the government and kill all the Spaniards who didn't agree with him.

'Why would an army kill its own people?' I asked, but Mama interrupted and said angrily, 'Pablo. You shouldn't be talking to him about these things.'

I knew that Morocco was in Africa, on the other side of the Strait of Gibraltar from Spain, because we'd done it in Geography and I'd read about the Moors in the *National Geographic* in the school library.

'This is where I meet your Mama and where Pablito is born,' Papa announced blithely.

I reeled from the force of this bombshell. If what he said was true, it meant I had a brother who was African. As soon as we got up from the table I headed straight for my bedroom, put my head between my legs and forced myself to breathe deeply. Being Spanish was bad enough, but at least Spain was in Europe. Morocco wasn't just another country, it was another continent, full of Arabs who smelled and didn't believe in Jesus, according to Shitebag Shearer, our gym teacher. If that got out at school, my life wouldn't be worth living.

*   *   *

As well as being more overt about his Spanish heritage, Papa became more cynical about his adopted homeland. He'd never particularly liked Britain, but his complaints became bitter and more frequent. He talked scathingly of its people and their fondness for drink, of the drab cities, the thick accents and the poor, joyless food.

He saw petty discrimination everywhere – in newspapers, on the television news, in football commentaries, in supermarket queues, in traffic jams – and every setback was seen as part of a conspiracy to debase and discredit him by arrogant *anglosájones*.

Mama, in contrast, loved Britain, with its expansive countryside, its temperate climate, its friendly, warm-hearted people and, above all, the opportunities it afforded families like us to better ourselves. She accused Papa of deriding the country which had accepted him so welcomingly and had given him such a good standard of living compared with what he could have expected back in Spain.

Her position relative to his hardened, and, while he'd always appeared to be the dominant force, I became aware of a creeping acceptance that she now set the ground rules. She served him devotedly and industriously, but if she decided to take a stand on an issue, like when he lost a month's wages gambling on cards with his fellow baggage handlers, she imposed her will, and he accepted it uncomplainingly.

He began to seek out fellow Spaniards to socialise with. Opportunities were few, given the sparseness of the Spanish population in Scotland, but the consulate in Manchester put him in touch with an expatriate group that met weekly in a community centre in Edinburgh. He started attending their Tuesday meetings, where they swapped items of news and gossip from the old country, along with newspaper cuttings and magazine articles and items of Spanish food and drink they'd acquired.

Mama was sceptical. He'd never expressed any interest in meeting Spanish people before, and she pointed out that if he really wanted to do so, Spain was full of them. Why drive a hundred-mile round trip to meet a group of strangers with nothing in common but the geographical accident of their birth, to talk about a country he'd chosen not to set foot in for forty years?

Papa brushed aside her criticisms. On the nights the meetings took place he'd arrive home from work early, change, bathe, shave and dress in his finest clothes before setting off in a cloud of Aqua Velva.

He'd return home late at night, and over breakfast the following morning, buoyed and energised, he'd breathlessly recount the people he'd met and the things they'd discussed. Salvador, a chicken-sexer from Valladolid now living in Broxburn, knew a shop where you could buy authentic *turrón*. Jose, from Valencia, now running a Toyota dealership in Haddington, knew a restaurant in London where you could watch Spanish football matches from last season on videotape.

'So, you're going to travel all the way to London to watch a football game that's a year old?' Mama asked scornfully.

'I nae go, I only say is possible,' Papa said defensively.

'Did anyone have anything important to say, like what is happening politically back in Spain?'

Papa waved his hand dismissively. '*Politicamente? Si*, I tell you wha is happen, nothing, tha's wha is happen.'

'What about the move towards democracy that we keep hearing so much about on the World Service?'

'I tell you, there is no *democracia* while this *burro* Suárez is in charge.'

The ineffectiveness of Adolfo Suárez, the new Spanish prime minister, had become a source of vocal grievance for Papa, who regarded him as a stooge of King Juan Carlos, the new head of state, who in turn was a stooge of Franco.

Most of the Spaniards he encountered at his meetings had settled here with wives or husbands from Scotland whom they'd met while they were holidaying in Spain. There were others from Spanish-speaking countries, living in Scotland for an assortment of reasons, like Maria Cristina – or Dr Maria Cristina Carvajal to give her full title – from Chile, who taught South American history at Edinburgh University, and who seemed to occupy a greater proportion of Papa's conversation with every passing week.

His take on continuing developments in Spain became infused with her opinions and observations, and his every sentence seemed to begin with 'Maria Cristina says', or 'Maria Cristina thinks', or 'According to Maria Cristina'. He also began to share her interest in what was happening in Chile, where, I managed to surmise from the snippets of conversation I understood, something important had just happened. I wasn't altogether clear on the detail, but I knew that a lot of people were leaving the country because they didn't like its new leader – who must have been a real ogre, because Papa hated him even more than Franco.

'Maria Cristina, she say Spain is, how you say, full a corruption. She say it is soon like Chile unless all the old *Franquistas*, they are kick out.'

Mama, who had dubbed Maria Cristina 'Santa Maria', threw up her hands in exasperation every time her name was mentioned.

'Ah, Santa Maria knows everything. Why don't you go and live with her if she is so clever?'

Papa flushed and slammed his coffee mug down on the table.

'Wha you talk, woman? She talk more sense than you, I tell you this.'

Then one day when I returned home from school, Mama and Papa were involved in a blazing row. Papa was getting ready to attend his weekly meeting, and I figured their argument must have had something to do with that. I heard Maria Cristina's name mentioned several times, but this was more than Mama's usual gibes about Santa Maria. As he was leaving she followed him to the front door, screaming in Spanish, before slamming it behind him.

The atmosphere in the house for the rest of the evening was tense. Pablito arrived late home from school because he'd been given detention for failing to hand in his homework on time. This made Mama's mood even sourer. They had a heated conversation in Spanish, and I couldn't make out whether she was reprimanding him for his detention or continuing the argument she'd had with Papa. I tried asking her what was wrong, but she just said 'nothing' and told me to tidy my bedroom.

After we'd eaten dinner in silence, we sat down to watch television, but I could tell Mama wasn't paying attention. Every time she heard a car in the street outside she got up from her seat to peer through the gap in the curtains. Usually we were all in bed asleep by the time Papa returned from the meetings, but on this occasion it was clear she was determined to stay up. I was sent to bed at nine o'clock as usual but forced myself to stay awake, resolved that I wasn't going to miss out on whatever excitement was due to take place upon Papa's return.

It was around eleven-thirty when I heard the front door open and the sound of Spanish voices in the hallway. I waited until they moved into the living-room before climbing out of bed, and tentatively making my way downstairs. The hallway was dark and as cold as snow. Any residual heat that had built up through the evening had dissipated into the night when the door had opened, replaced by an icy swirl of air suffused with the acrid smell of coal smoke from neighbours' chimneys.

Gently, I pushed open the door to the living-room and peered inside. A woman and two children stood between Mama and Papa. Pablito was seated on the settee with his fist trapped under his chin, his eyes darting back and forth between our parents.

The strangers looked cold and hunted. The children – a boy of about eight and a younger girl – stood close to the woman, as though they were hiding behind her, each holding on to a leg. The boy clutched a dirty, brown, slickly matted cuddly toy close to his face with his thumb secreted inside his mouth, hard against his cheek. Their look was a world away from the people I was used to seeing in Mosspark. With their black hair and swarthy complexions, they more closely resembled us, but they were even darker, and with thin, almond-shaped eyes they appeared almost oriental.

After a tense stand-off the woman spoke, cautiously. Although she was speaking in Spanish, I was able to deduce that she was apologising. Mama interrupted, addressing her directly, then midway through her speech she turned to Papa and switched from Spanish to English.

'I told you I don't want them here. Why have you put me in this position?'

Papa opened his palms entreatingly. 'Wha you want me dae, put them out on the street? They have nowhere tae go.'

'That's not my problem, Pablo, I've told you a dozen times. What do I have to say to make you understand?'

'These people, they are lucky tae be alive. They come thousands a miles tae be safe and wha we dae, throw them out?' he asked.

'Why don't you send them to stay with Santa Maria? She is a rich college lecturer. She has plenty of room.'

'She already have a family stay with her.'

Mama laughed. The three strangers watched the exchange in silence, wincing as each contribution was delivered.

'Does she know where we live?' Mama asked. 'Does she know how many rooms we have? Have you told her, Mister Big Shot, in your tailored suit and your handmade shoes? Does she know that we live in a two-bedroom council house?'

The little girl began to cry and Mama stepped forward and lifted her into her arms, kissing her on the side of the head.

'Está bien, querido, no hay necesidad de llorar,' she said. 'It's all right, my darling, there's no need to cry.'

She saw me standing in the doorway and her expression hardened. 'You, get up to your bed,' she ordered sternly. 'This has nothing to do with you.'

I left and returned to the top of the stairs, from where I tried to listen to the rest of proceedings, but the door to the living-room had been closed and the voices were muffled and indistinct. What snatches of conversation I did catch were in Spanish, so, defeated, I went to bed and fell asleep.

I was woken by Mama ordering me from my bed. I guessed from the breaking light outside it was the early hours of the morning. She ushered me downstairs to the living-room, where two makeshift beds had been prepared using cushions from the settee and sleeping bags. She told me I was to sleep in one of them alongside Pablito. The family of odd, frightened-looking strangers was to have our bedroom.

7

There was a holiday feel about waking in a room that wasn't my bedroom, finding the hallway populated by strangers and having to queue for the bathroom. The children huddled, unblinking, under the protective arms of their mother, and they moved around as a unit.

Papa had already left for work. I'd heard him and Mama arguing in their bedroom earlier in the morning, in English. That was the one good thing about having the Chileans to stay – my parents couldn't say anything private in Spanish.

Finally it was my turn for the bathroom, which was just as well, because I was running late for school. I brushed my teeth, washed my face and ran downstairs to find the Chileans perched together on the sofa, looking painfully self-conscious, like animals in a zoo. They wore shabby, ill-fitting clothes – heavy-knit sweaters several sizes too big, with frayed shirt collars and baggy, threadbare trousers that extended below their feet.

The boy gripped his cuddly toy, which on closer inspection appeared to be a lion, close to his chest, and the little girl sang quietly to herself. She stood up and paced back and forth along the length of the window bay, running her hand along the sill. The mother had an unnerving, fixed smile on her face, though I could tell that underneath she was anxious and exhausted.

Mama appeared in the kitchen doorway looking harassed, an apron tied around her dressing-gown, and she said something to me in Spanish. I stared at her blankly and asked her to speak in English.

'I said you'd better leave, you don't have time for breakfast because you were made to wait so long to get into the toilet.'

I knew Mama had spoken in Spanish so the Chileans would know what she was saying. The woman stared at the floor. I said goodbye to everyone and forced a smile. I felt sorry for the Chileans, but I agreed with Mama: they had to go.

When I arrived at the school gates Max Miller was standing with Jim Sweeney, playing with a set of clackers that Sweeney's big sister had brought back from a holiday in Benidorm. I felt Max Miller's gaze follow me as I walked by.

'Hey, Speedy, why don't you show us how these things work?' he shouted.

It was the first time he'd spoken to me since I'd pummelled his face, and it unnerved me that he was being so cocksure. I panicked – perhaps he knew about the Chileans and was toying with me? But that wasn't possible, the Chileans hadn't arrived until late the previous evening, after dark. He couldn't have seen them, could he? His ma would never have let him out on the streets at that time. Perhaps his da had seen them when he was walking home from the bowling club; but they lived on the other side of Mosspark, he'd have had to take a lengthy detour to pass our house.

'Shove it up your arse, Miller,' I ventured, monitoring his face closely for any reaction.

He walked away. It was a good sign. If he had known about the Chileans, he'd certainly have said something then – he wouldn't have been able to help himself. I began to relax, but I wasn't taking anything for granted. It was morning, and I didn't know for sure that no one else had seen them. If I could just make it until the end of the day I'd be safe, because by then they'd be gone.

When I returned home, not only were they still there, but the children were now dressed in my old clothes. I protested to Mama, but she shot me an angry stare.

'They arrived here with nothing,' she said quietly, so they wouldn't hear. 'They stepped off the plane with only the clothes they were dressed in. They had to buy jumpers and trousers from a charity shop. Surely you wouldn't deny them old clothes that don't even fit you now?'

When she put it like that, how could I refuse? Actually, I had no real objection to them wearing my old clothes. I hated them anyway – greying, too-tight vests, scratchy shirts, and grimly functional hand-knitted sweaters in assorted ugly hues. And I didn't even mind sleeping in the living-room again. What troubled me was the apparent shift in Mama's attitude. When I'd left for school that morning, she was determined that they'd be away by evening. Now she seemed to be mellowing, and there was no sign of them departing any time soon. The threat was clear to me – the longer they stayed, the greater the possibility I'd be tainted by association with them. All it would take was for someone to recognise they were wearing my old clothes, and the connection would be made.

Two nights stretched into three and three into four. Still there was no sign of them leaving. Emilia, the mother, helped Mama with the laundry and the shopping, and they spent long hours sitting at the kitchen table, drinking endless cups of coffee made with the strong Colombian beans that the cabin crews brought back from Spain for Papa.

Then, after a week, Mama suddenly announced they'd be moving to the other side of the estate. A friend of hers who was a cleaner for an official in the housing department had managed to wangle them temporary accommodation until they could be assessed properly by the council. I was so relieved that I even allowed myself a moment of sympathy for them. In spite of myself I actually quite liked the boy, Jorge, who was quiet and good-natured, and a skilled footballer. His little sister Alejandra was a bit annoying, always trying to play with us, but she was also very sweet, the way she lost her temper and scolded me in Spanish if she thought I wasn't paying her enough attention.

Despite her early opposition, Mama had become friendly with Emilia, and I knew she'd miss having her around.

74

'Don't worry, Mama,' I told her. 'She'll only be ten minutes away. You can still meet up with her.'

'And of course you'll see Jorge at school,' Mama added cheerfully.

My heart thumped. It hadn't occurred to me the Chileans would have to go to school, far less my school. Alejandra was still of nursery age, but Jorge was only a few months younger than me, so he'd be in the same year, perhaps even the same class. To make matters worse, Mama wanted me to walk with him to school until he got settled in. I felt sick. This was my worst nightmare come true. Max Miller would have a field day.

The goodwill I'd felt towards the Chileans suddenly evaporated. I didn't want anything to do with them, with Jorge and his weird accent, his stupid Beatles haircut and his hand-me-down clothes.

The day he was due to start school I was despatched early to collect him from his house, to accompany him to the school gates. I'd barely slept the night before, worrying about what would happen if I was seen in his company. I came up with a dozen reasons why I couldn't do it – I'd be late for school; I had a stomach bug; the traffic was too dangerous on that side of the estate; I didn't even like him; there was no reason why he couldn't make his own way to school; he'd have to learn to stand on his own feet sooner or later; it wasn't fair.

For every argument, Mama had an answer. It was still only half-past seven, I had plenty of time; I could take cod liver oil for my stomach; I could walk on the pavements, that way I'd avoid the traffic; I didn't have to like Jorge, I just had to collect him; he was eight years old, he didn't speak English, and he didn't know the way to the school; he could start standing on his own two feet tomorrow; life wasn't fair.

I trudged down Mosspark Avenue as though I was on my way to the dentist. I could already imagine the scornful jeers of my classmates. It all seemed so unfair. There was nothing I could do about my family. It wasn't my fault my background distinguished me so conspicuously from my Scottish classmates. I had no control over the fact that that we had neither a family tartan nor a surname that began with Mac. I was different, but over the years I'd learned to live with it. Now, it seemed, all that was in danger of being washed away. I wasn't going to stand for it. I was Spanish, that much was incontestable, but I wouldn't be answerable for a family of Chilean refugees.

Jorge was a decent enough boy, but I'd paid my dues for being foreign, and I'd done it alone. By the time I'd started at primary school, Pablito had already moved on to the secondary school, so I'd had no one to stand up for me. I'd fought my own battles, and Jorge would have to do the same. Why should I provide him with support that had been denied to me? If he was coming to my school, he'd have to take care of himself.

When I got to Alcaig Road, a couple of hundred yards from his house, I turned right and doubled back. I arrived at the school gates and looked up at the full horror of what I knew would greet him on his arrival. Mama had told me about the tiny, rural schoolhouse Jorge had attended back in Chile – it apparently had clematis growing round the door and mandarin trees in the playground. Our school was a joyless, functional four-storey structure of grey concrete, built on stilts, surrounded by a running track and a high perimeter fence. Its main catchment areas were the badlands of Pollok and Govan, whose residents regarded Mosspark as an oasis of privilege – we had gardens and cars, and some of our parents even worked in offices. I cringed thinking about what the Pollok boys would make of Jorge.

Among their members was Joey Adams, whose brother had done time at Barlinnie following an incident at The Cart Bar. The details were shrouded in mystery, but rumours involved a ceremonial sword and a cut-off ear. Then there was Jerry Chaney, who wore a silver hooped earring that Mad Dog Murison made him remove before class every morning. Chaney was also made to wear a glove on his right hand because he had an Indian-ink tattoo across his knuckles that said 'FUCK'.

At nine o'clock the sound of the bell drowned out the deafening chorus of voices as hundreds of pupils slowly stopped their games of football and marbles, skipping and hopscotch, and trudged across the playground to their class lines.

A few moments later Mad Dog appeared, red and impatient, and he began to usher the first of the classes through the large double doors. Mad Dog was a bad-tempered pipe-smoker who wore Black Watch tartan trousers and a pale green herringbone tweed jacket over his short, sinewy frame. He had a bushy, nicotine-stained moustache, which drooped at the ends, and an ill-fitting grey toupee.

He'd served in one of the forces – no one knew for sure which one – before becoming a teacher, and he spent all of his spare time on manoeuvres with the Territorial Army in the Cairngorms. He was unmarried, and it was rumoured he had a lead-lined underground bunker in his garden that he kept stocked with bottles of water and tins of corned beef in case of a nuclear attack.

He took us for gym lessons when Dickhead Docherty was off, and he would make us march up and down the playground, square-bashing, as he breathlessly barked orders in between puffs of Condor Ready Rubbed. Afterwards he would come into the changing rooms and warn, with chin-stroking gravity, that if we didn't wash behind our foreskins we risked contracting cancer of the penis.

Everyone hated Mad Dog, but I had a grudging respect for him. He was the only member of staff whom the Pollok boys genuinely feared. On one occasion, Joey Adams told him to cock off or he'd get his brother to do his kneecaps. Mad Dog ordered him to the front of the classroom and stood toe-to-toe with him, staring into his eyes, screaming at him with such deranged ferocity that if his vocal cords had snapped, they'd surely have taken Joey Adams's eye out.

Mad Dog told him that he was a vile piece of human scum who didn't deserve an education, that all he'd ever amount to was a thieving junkie dropout, just like his brother, whom he'd taught, and how he was *more* useless than dog shit because at least dog shit made your roses grow. By the time he'd finished Joey Adams stood silent and quivering, and he spent the rest of the morning sitting at his desk, wiping tears from his eyes.

I hated everything about school, from the wire-reinforced windows to the bolted-down desks and chairs. That no one wanted to be there, least of all the teachers, was evident from the poor physical condition of the building, the curling flakes of paint that clung stubbornly to the dirty, crumbling walls and ceilings, the threadbare carpets with their smell of decay. No one was prepared to take responsibility for its upkeep. It was an unspoken dirty protest.

During the morning break I locked myself in a cubicle in the boys' toilets. The stench, as ever, made me gag, but I wanted to be alone, to gather my thoughts. I was dreading the row I knew I'd get from Mama when I got home for abandoning Jorge. What disturbed me even more was the certain knowledge that, at some stage today, Jorge was certain to arrive at the school.

Sure enough, halfway through a spelling test before lunch, there was a knock on the door, and Mrs Briggs, the school secretary, came into our classroom. She whispered something in Mad Dog's ear, and they left the room together before returning with Jorge trailing limply behind. My stomach lurched.

'This is Horgay,' Mad Dog said in his clipped accent. 'He's from Chile, a country in South America, and he will be part of our class from now on.'

Jorge looked terrified. I could see him scanning the rows of white faces, looking for me, so I dipped my head below the desk and pretended to tie my shoelace. The only free seat was at the end of the front row, next to Joey Adams, so Mad Dog led him by the arm and signalled for him to sit down.

Jorge turned around and, as I raised my head, he looked me straight in the eye and smiled. I stared at my desk, willing him to look away, praying he wouldn't call out my name or wave.

I gripped my forehead between my thumb and my index finger, using my hand to shield my eyes, as though that might offer some protection. My chest felt tight and my head faint, and I clenched my teeth, praying for the moment to pass. Mad Dog resumed the spelling test, and Jorge turned around to face the front of the class. I was safe, at least for now.

When the bell rang for lunchtime, I bolted from my seat and was out of the classroom and halfway down the stairs before he had the chance to approach me. Standing at the front of the queue for the dinner hall, I heard the distant footsteps and animated voices of my classmates approaching, making their way along the corridor. I willed the doors to open. As the first feet landed on the top step I heard the bolt released from the inside and I launched myself against the door, forcing my way into the hall and nearly knocking over the dinner lady on the other side.

I collected my lunch tray and moved to the furthest corner, hoping that by the time Jorge had managed to find his way down-stairs the room would be full, and I'd be able to hide among the sea of bodies.

I spent the rest of the lunchbreak hiding in the toilets to avoid him until it was time to return to our classroom. When the bell rang for home time I hung back, on the pretext of wanting to ask Mad Dog about the long-division homework he'd set, but really I was hoping that everyone, Jorge included, would disappear. Mad Dog eyed me suspiciously, wondering about my sudden interest. I strung out our exchange for as long as I could while the class emptied.

The playground was deserted as I made my way through the gates, but as I turned on to Mosspark Boulevard I spotted a group of boys gathered further ahead – Chaney and Adams, as well as two of their pie-faced henchmen, Benny Lugton and Barra McCann. At the centre of the group was Jorge, looking confused and scared. They circled him like leery cavemen inspecting an intruder and began to push him, laughing and whooping as he bounced between them.

He saw me standing in the distance. I held his gaze briefly and looked away. At that moment I hated him. I turned and headed back the way I'd come, round the corner, past the bookie's and out of sight.

When I returned home Mama was on the phone. I dumped my schoolbag in the kitchen and was about to run outside to play when she warned me not to go far.

'Your papa wants to speak with you when he comes home,' she said quietly.

I knew I was in big trouble – Mama rarely delegated discipline to Papa unless it was for something serious. I decided to go to my bedroom to start my homework early and perhaps lessen my inevitable punishment.

My throat tightened when I heard the front door open. I lay on the floor, trying to concentrate on my homework. I heard the familiar sounds of Papa's afternoon routine as he washed and changed, and then his footsteps as he walked out of the bathroom and stopped outside my room. The door opened slowly. He wandered in and sat down on the edge of my bed.

'Wha you dae?' he asked.

'Long division,' I said.

'Wha this?'

'It's maths. You know, sums?'

'*Si*, I know, *matemáticas*.'

He lit a cigarette. I braced myself for the expected onslaught, but his body was relaxed, and he seemed thoughtful.

'Wha is this sum?'

I looked down at my jotter.

'Eh, six hundred and seventy-five divided by twenty-five.

'*Veintisiete*,' he responded instantly.

I stared at him.

'Twenty-seven,' he said.

I hesitated, my pencil hovering above the page, unsure whether to write. It was obvious I didn't trust his answer, but he didn't lose his temper.

'You write, this correct answer, twenty-seven. I nae good with words but with numbers yes.'

He stood up slowly from the bed and arched his back. He let out a groan as he stretched, his muscles weary after spending the day lugging suitcases. He opened the window a few inches and flicked the ash of his cigarette into the back garden. Then he sat back down on the bed.

'Why you nae take Jorge tae school?'

I began a long-winded explanation I'd already rehearsed about losing the way and being late, and how, although I'd meant to take him, in the end I didn't have time, and . . . even as I was delivering my epic story, I realised how unconvincing it sounded.

'You think you have tough life?'

He leaned forward and rested his elbows on his knees so that our faces were only a couple of inches apart. His eyes were uncharacteristically warm.

'Pardon?' I asked, not sure what he was getting at.

'You think you have tough life?'

'Eh, not really, no,' I said defensively.

'You know wha these children, they go through in their country?'

His voice was quiet and husky, and the sharp smell of tobacco on his breath at close quarters made me want to pull away.

'You know wha happen tae them?'

I shook my head.

'In their country they have leader who is very bad man, who torture and beat up the people he nae like.'

'Why?'

'Because he is bastard.'

I'd never heard Papa swear before.

'This man, he send police tae house of Jorge and Alejandra in night with guns and sticks and they drag their papa from bed. Then they beat him with this sticks until he is near dead and they throw him in jail.'

His voice didn't waver as he continued with his story.

81

'The last thing Jorge see of his Papa is his blood in street outside house. He cry all night, then he nae speak for two months.'

'What, not even one word?' I asked.

'Nae, he nae speak a word. His mama she is very upset. She think he never speak again.'

'Why didn't he speak?' I asked.

Papa shrugged and stared at the floor, then he lifted his head, and his eyes were glazed.

'These people they come in night and this is terrible thing. You nae see them in dark, but they smell bad with wine in their mouth and they stagger, drunk and they laugh, they make joke, they throw you at wall and table and they laugh.'

I sat transfixed, unsure whether he was still talking about Alejandra and Jorge.

'They call you name. They say you are *hijo bastardo de una puta anarquista*. Bastard son of an anarchist whore.'

He stopped talking and looked at me.

'Some people they nae speak because they is afraid. Some people they cry all time. Emilia have, how you say . . . nightmare . . . she wake up crying. Some people, they run away and they nae stop, even when they think is safe. They hear man speak or they see someone they nae know and they think might be dangerous, then they run again. They never stop run.'

He placed his warm palm gently on the top of my head and held it there.

'You be good tae Jorge. You treat him well, you understand?'

I nodded. He stood up and left the room.

The first person I saw when I walked through the school gates the following morning was Jorge, clutching his schoolbag close to his chest.

Summoning up courage, I began to make my way towards him, but I saw I was too late – the Pollok boys had got there first.

'Will ye check thae strides?' Chaney said, laughing. 'What happened pal, did yer budgie die?'

I glanced at my old school trousers on Jorge's long legs, half-mast and pathetic. A few yards away stood a trio of primary seven girls, who looked disapprovingly at Chaney's bullying behaviour but did nothing to intervene. Jorge stared back at his tormentors, wide-eyed and confused.

'¿*Qué*?' he said, when it finally dawned on him that he had been asked a question.

'Kay?' repeated Chaney sneeringly. 'What the fuck does kay mean?'

'¿*Qué*?' Jorge repeated.

They laughed uproariously.

'It's fucking Manuel from *Fawlty Towers*,' Lugton announced loudly, and they laughed some more. This time even the girls joined in. Jorge made to move, but Chaney blocked his path.

'Wherr dae ye think yer gaun, ya wee fanny?'

Chaney grabbed Jorge's schoolbag, a dated item with shoulder straps that I guessed Emilia had picked up at a charity shop.

'Wherr did ye get this, oot an Enid Blyton book?'

Jorge said something in Spanish and they all looked at one another, puzzled. Chaney opened the bag and emptied the contents on to the ground. There were a couple of jotters that Mad Dog had handed him for spelling and sums, a pencil case and his cuddly brown lion. Jorge lunged for the lion, but Lugton got there first and pulled it out of his reach.

'What's this then, Manuel, yer bedtime pal?'

'*Démelo*,' Jorge said, 'give it to me.'

'What the fuck does that mean?' Lugton asked.

'*Démelo!*' Jorge shouted angrily, tears welling in his eyes.

'Oooh,' the group cooed in unison, before bursting into laughter.

'We don't know what it means,' Chaney said, with a wide grin.

'It means he wants it back.'

Everyone turned around and looked at me. My words hung in the air, and for a moment I doubted whether I had actually spoken them.

'Aw, look who it isnae,' said Chaney. 'Speedy Gonzalez. Ah might huv guessed you'd be somewhere aboot tae stick up fur a greaser.'

'Give him back the lion,' I heard myself say.

I suddenly felt faint and my legs trembled. I was going to get battered. I felt as though I'd been thrust on to a stage and told to perform without knowing the lines. Chaney and Lugton eyed one another and smiled, as though they couldn't believe their luck.

'Aw priceless, man,' Lugton said. 'This is gonnae be brilliant, getting tae kick seven shades a shite oot ay two dagos.'

They both laughed.

'Haw, Chaney, geez yer strikes,' Lugton demanded.

Chaney dipped into the pocket of his trousers for a box of matches. He lobbed it towards Lugton, who caught it with one hand, opened it and pulled out a match. Jorge's face was scarlet and tears trickled down his cheeks. Lugton held the lion and dangled it provocatively a few inches from Jorge's face, but when he reached out to grab it, pulled it away again.

Lugton struck the match and held the flame under the lion. Jorge screamed as the flame singed its matted surface. A gust of wind extinguished the match and Jorge made another lunge for the toy, but Chaney grabbed him from behind. Jorge let out an anguished cry as his arm was forced up his back and held there. He struggled, but Chaney applied extra pressure and Jorge screamed, his body going limp.

Lugton dropped the lion on the ground and crouched over it. He lit another match and cupped his hand around the flame to protect it from the wind. Slowly, as the flame gathered, he lowered it under the toy. I knew I couldn't stand by and do nothing, but I was terrified.

'Cut it out, Benny, enough's enough,' I said in as authoritative a voice as I could manage.

'Fuck off, Noguera,' he said.

A figure emerged from behind and marched past me towards Lugton, who didn't have time to look up before he felt the full weight of a kick hard against his shin. There was a sickening crack and then another kick before Lugton had time to let out a scream. He rolled over on to the concrete surface, clutching his lower leg, and as he did so, another kick landed on the same spot.

I stood by pathetically as Max Miller then turned and marched purposefully towards Chaney, who threw Jorge free and backed away, raising his palms in submission. Jorge ran towards the lion and grabbed it, then started stuffing his belongings back into his schoolbag.

At that point, Mad Dog emerged from the direction of the car park, clutching his tattered leather briefcase and juggling a large pile of jotters. He ambled past the group, eyeing us up and down.

'What's going on here, then?' he asked.

'Nothing, sir,' Max Miller said.

We all shuffled nervously. Chaney looked edgy and panicked. Lugton was writhing on the ground, trying to hold back tears.

'What's the matter with you, Chaney?' Mad Dog demanded.

'Nothing, sir,' Chaney said, his voice strained with pain.

Mad Dog stood silently surveying the scene for a few moments and a thin smile appeared on his face.

'All right, as you were,' he said before striding off towards the school building.

8

Ever since my phone call with Connie I'd been preparing myself for the inevitable, and I knew before I opened the front door that Cheryl was gone. It was late afternoon and still light outside, but the hallway was unusually gloomy. The house felt cavernous and overwhelming, bringing to mind Cheryl's frequent complaints, when we were thinking about buying it that it was much too big for our needs. Even for London it was an impressively proportioned space – a detached Arts and Crafts conversion, with access to a shared garden. Its value would rocket, I'd assured her, and I was right, it was worth well over a million now. But Cheryl had a point. It *was* much too big – the three of us had been rattling around in it for several years, growing more and more distant from each other.

It felt odd standing there alone, like a stranger in my own home. Nothing was out of place, yet it seemed alien, as though someone had taken my mental image of the space and moved everything slightly to the left. Perhaps it was an unconscious realisation that this was the first day of my new life without Cheryl, a mental readjustment to the home that would no longer have her walking around in it.

I dropped my holdall on the floor and wandered across the hallway to the sound of my own footsteps. The kitchen was cold and tidy, with not an unwashed saucepan or mug in sight. Cheryl had obviously cleaned the house before leaving as a parting shot – it was my place now, to do with it as I wished – she was no longer answerable to my serial grievances about order and cleanliness.

I wandered through to the living-roonm, which had the same unlived-in feel, and I looked around for a note, but there was nothing. I climbed the stairs with a growing feeling of loneliness and entered our bedroom – it too was immaculate, and I could tell that she hadn't slept there for several nights.

I opened the door of the large walk-in wardrobe that we shared. Some of her clothes remained, but the ones she wore regularly were gone. I looked up to the overhead shelves where we stored the suitcases. Two were missing. I wandered through to the bathroom – she'd taken away all her toiletries.

I walked back into the bedroom and my legs buckled. I don't know how long I lay on the bed, staring into space, the distant hum of the city and the rush of traffic on the street outside dancing around my ears. I had no idea what to do. The evening stretched out before me. Ben would be back, but I didn't know when. Suddenly I panicked: what if Ben didn't return? Perhaps he'd left as well. Perhaps that's why it was so tidy.

I forced myself to stand up and made my way along the hallway to his bedroom. My legs were heavy and slow, as if I was wearing rain-drenched trousers, and a light-headed nausea crept over me. I pushed open the door and switched on the light. It was its usual wasteland: randomly discarded clothes, surfaces cluttered with empty bottles and beer cans, empty food tins relieved of their cold contents with teaspoons, and coffee cups lined with green mould. Several large ashtrays, emblazoned with the logos of lager brands, were piled high with fag-ends and roaches spilling volcanically on to the floor. The carpet was shrouded in a thin blanket of dust and crumbs and other, unidentifiable detritus. Eerie wisps of cobwebs hung from lampshades and down the sides of the curtains that hadn't been opened for God knows how long.

I knew from this fetid abyss that I hadn't been abandoned. Ben would be back – his mother would never have allowed him to leave me with this much ammunition. As I stared into the apocalyptic scene of post-pubescent filth I tried to laugh, but ended up choking on my tears.

I needed a distraction, so I returned to the coldness of the lounge, turned my laptop on, and Googled Alguaire. Despite other preoccupations, I'd been unable to stop thinking about the village and what Papa had told me about his family. It was mentioned only in the context of a cycling trail and a new regional airport being proposed nearby to serve Lerida. If, as Papa told me, it had for a short time represented a tiny strategic lifeline to those fighting for the Republic – a lifeline for which my grandparents paid with their lives – why should it fail to merit even a mention?

I typed in 'Lerida and Spanish Civil War', which produced more hits, but they were virtually all tourism websites mentioning in passing that the town had fallen to insurgent forces in 1938 after Franco had ordered a push from Saragossa towards the Mediterranean. A photojournalism website included a collection of black-and-white stills of desperate street fighting following the Nationalist bombardment. Buildings were pockmarked and ruined after being shelled and shot up, and men lay in the streets surrounded by fallen masonry. One of the pictures featured a soldier falling backwards after being wounded, with La Seu Vella, the town's elevated medieval cathedral, in the background. I recognised the street in which they were fighting – it was only a few yards from the bar where Papa and I had eaten a few nights before.

Another website included an account of the aerial bombardment of the town by the German Condor Legion. Despite a public profession of neutrality, it said, Hitler had put the flagship unit of the Luftwaffe at Franco's disposal. As well as supporting a common cause, this allowed the Nazi air force to hone the military strategies it would use to bomb Allied cities during the Second World War. The depleted and under-resourced Republican defences could hold out for only so long. Their troops were holed up in a series of defensive, flat-topped ridges that ran along the western edge of the town. At the start of April, a squadron of German dive-bombers, nicknamed *angelitos* by the Spaniards, closed in on the town. At first the Republican machine-gunners held their positions, restricting the aircraft to a height of around a thousand metres, but soon the order came for the pilots to dive, and in a series of strafing runs they picked off the gunners one by one. Among them, according to my father's account, was my Uncle Pepe.

I must have drifted off, because I woke to the sound of the front door slamming shut. I looked at the carriage clock on the mantel-piece – it was shortly after midnight. I'd been sleeping with my mouth open, and my throat was dry and sore. My body ached. I sucked my tongue hard to build up some moisture in my mouth and sat upright too quickly, feeling a sharp, piercing pain above my eyes.

Ben walked into the room, dressed in the same black leather ensemble he'd been wearing the last time I'd seen him. He now appeared to be wearing black eye make-up as well.

'Where have you been?' he asked.

'I was in Spain with your grandparents.'

'Blimey. Spain. I thought Abuelo was allergic to Spain.'

'Where have you been so late?' I asked, remembering my parental responsibilities.

'I was at Natalie's.'

'Who's Natalie?'

'She's my girlfriend.'

'I didn't know you had a girlfriend.'

'You don't know much about me.'

'How long has all of this been going on, then?'

'Six months – and don't make it sound like I've been deal-ing drugs. Why does a conversation with you always end in confrontation?'

'Don't talk rubbish,' I said.

'It's true. You do it effortlessly with Mum and now you're doing it with me. Why can't we just have a normal chat without you blaming me for something? '

I didn't want to have an argument with Ben. I was sick of argu-ments. I wanted to calm things down. 'There's something I've

89

been meaning to tell you about Abuelo, but I didn't know when the right time was,' I said.

'Oh yeah?'

'I'm afraid he's not very well.'

'What do you mean?'

'I mean he's dying. Of cancer.'

He frowned and his face reddened. Even with all that aggressive leather clothing, he still looked touchingly young.

'Shit.'

'Yes, it is shit.'

'I'll go and see him.'

'Okay, but you'd better not leave it too long.'

'How long has he got?' he asked, his voice husky.

'I don't know, not long.'

He leaned over and grabbed my wrist, over my sleeve, and held it for a couple of seconds.

'I'm sorry. I'll go and see him.'

I felt like crying for the second time that day. My head was pounding and I needed to be in bed, alone and in the dark. I stood up slowly and balanced my weight on the back of the chair until I was confident that my legs weren't going to buckle.

'Have you spoken to your mother?' I asked.

He sighed. 'Let's talk about it in the morning.'

I knew we wouldn't.

'I'm not going to go chasing after her. I only want to know where she is.'

He looked up and smiled. 'We'll talk about it another time, Dad.'

I was too weary to argue.

9

I was woken by the piercing ring of my mobile phone. The display said it was half past six. It was Kevin was calling to say that The Editor wanted to see me in his office later in the morning. He imparted the news, as he did most information, without comment or favour, simply with an expectation of compliance.

'Is this about my trip to Spain?' I asked Kevin, a little too anxiously.

'Don't know.'

'Because it was a family emergency, not a holiday. I explained that to you.'

'I know.'

'Did you not tell that to Prowse?'

'Yes.'

'So why does he want to see me?'

He hung up.

I'd worked with Kevin for ten years, and I doubted there was a single item of personal information about him I could relate. Like many news editors, he didn't have any ambition beyond a caffeine-fuelled, dead-eyed, single-minded commitment to filling pages with print. His appearance was shabby-corporate, as though he'd been dressed in the dark by a party of drunken middle-managers. He seemed to take no interest in his image because, I suspected, his head was crammed to bursting point with other priorities – page leads, drop intros, secondary sources, direct quotes, balancing quotes, standfirsts, affidavits, WOB headlines, cuttings searches, hidden mikes, snatch photos, vox pops, timelines, cold type, column inches, wire copy, banner ads, baseline shifts, butting heads, column rules, hammer heads, hanging indents, standalone pictures, summary decks, white space, widows and orphans.

Perhaps it was the industry's relentless demand for more that made him the way he was. There was no room for reflection, congratulation or remorse in his world, because whatever went before was in the past, and he was already on to the next thing. There wasn't a conversation I could remember having with him that wasn't conducted in the tight, primary-colour parameters of tabloid certainty. Reality for him was a series of rigid opposites – good or bad, success or failure, boom or bust, smart or stupid, tart or virgin, saint or sinner.

He had an unambiguous disregard for the conventions of human interaction. He didn't speak much, but he listened to everything, assimilating its implications, calculating its possibilities. Despite his lack of social graces, he was fearsomely good at his job, and that made him, within his narrow professional ambit, untouchable.

I didn't even know if Kevin was married. I wondered if he had some kin – an elderly mother, perhaps, with whom he still lived, who brushed stray items of breakfast from his clothing before he left for work. I thought he might be gay, non-practising and sexually repressed of course, telling anyone prurient enough to inquire that he was still playing the field, or that he just hadn't met the right girl.

He was one of the few members of staff who referred to Clive Prowse by his first name, a practice that carried an implicit entitlement, like they were friends who just happened to work together. In reality Prowse had no friends, or none prosaic enough to work for him. Most people in the building called him by his surname, spitting it through pursed lips, or they referred to him simply as The Editor. The very mention of his name was enough to instil fear, more so in recent weeks when any brush with senior management carried with it the threat of redundancy.

Prowse's office was large and, by comparison with the rest of the utilitarian concrete-and-glass building, absurdly plush, with its dark wood furniture and deep bordello-red decor. He ushered me in and introduced me to Uli, who shook my hand from a seated position. I'd met him once before, during his guided tour of the newsroom shortly after his company, Bayerische Zeitungsherausgeber, had bought out the Mercury Group titles, but I had no expectation of him remembering me. He'd tried to ingratiate himself with the staff then by demonstrating his encyclopaedic knowledge of vintage British comedy – according to his Wikipedia entry, he had the world's largest collection of Norman Wisdom memorabilia – but it had fallen embarrassingly flat, as few people could make out what he was talking about through his thick German accent.

'What is your opinion of your new leader?' he demanded curtly, our hands barely having parted.

I was unsure whom he was referring to. Was there some tier of new management in the building that had passed me by? Or was he, perhaps, fishing for compliments?

He sensed my hesitation. 'You are the political chief of your paper, no?'

'Oh, you mean our new prime minister,' I said, the penny dropping.

'Uli wants to pick your brains,' Prowse explained, nervously motioning for me to sit down.

I eased myself into a leather armchair while Prowse took his place behind his desk.

'Well, he's the only millionaire I know who buys his clothes from Asda,' I said, smiling. 'Still, I suppose he has a little pile of Boden cashmeres that he keeps at the back of his wardrobe like a guilty secret.'

Uli's expression didn't alter. 'What taxes will he reduce?' he demanded.

'I believe he's against any tax cuts at the moment until the economy recovers.'

'I am talking to your treasury minister, who is telling me of foreign leveraged investment programmes and offshore portfolio investment possibilities.'

'Well, you would seem to have better contacts in the government than I have,' I said, smiling. 'They don't talk to us because we didn't support them in the election.'

Prowse rested his chin on his cupped hand and stared intently at the Anglepoise lamp on his desk.

'And he had some very interesting ideas concerning tax mitigation,' said Uli.

'Sorry, tax what?'

'Mitigation. For large corporate entities.'

'You mean tax avoidance?' I said.

'Mitigation,' he corrected.

'Well, whatever you call it, I wouldn't say it's much of a priority for our readers, most of whom are on the minimum wage.'

Prowse's chin slipped clumsily from his palm, and his face reddened as he attempted to regain his composure. 'Antonio's preparing for the start of the party conference season,' he said, obviously flustered.

Uli eyed me with scepticism. 'Where is this accent from? You are English, no?'

'Scottish,' I said emphatically.

His eyes widened. 'You are knowing Ronnie Corbett?'

'Umm, not personally, no.'

'I am finding the sketches of the Two Ronnies in the women's clothes very funny,' he said with an unsmiling glare.

I nodded uncertainly. The oppressive silence unnerved me, and I felt coerced to fill it. 'I once saw Benny Hill at an airport,' I ventured.

His eyes appeared to moisten and a rare smile creased the fleshy folds of his face. 'Ah yes, Benny Hill – a great, great, great man,' he said wistfully.

I couldn't face going home to an empty house, so I phoned Max Miller. He picked up on the second ring and sounded flustered and hesitant when I suggested dropping by for a chat, claiming he had too much work to do. I felt angry.

'Oh, come on Max, surely you can give me an hour,' I pleaded. He always seemed to be at the disposal of any dysfunctional misfit who needed re-housing or had to be kept out of jail. And now, when I wanted a friend to talk to, he wasn't available.

He prevaricated, but I wore him down and told him I'd be round in an hour. 'Make it two,' he said. 'I've got things I need to do first.'

Max Miller had rented the same two-bedroom flat in Wandsworth for years, sharing it with a succession of lodgers, but now he was living alone. I pressed the buzzer of the modern yellow-brick block and waited, but there was no response. After a minute or so I pressed it again and it crackled into life.

'Hold on, I'll be down shortly,' he said.

He arrived at the front entrance a few moments later wearing an old parka.

'The flat's a bit of a mess. Let's go somewhere for a coffee,' he said, striding off down the road.

'I don't care what your flat looks like,' I said, struggling to catch up with him.

'No, there's a small place round the corner, come on.'

He led me up a short, narrow sidestreet which barely started before it ended, abruptly and apologetically, at a graffiti-covered railway arch. The pavement was black with oil leaking out of the workshop of a second-hand-car garage. On the far side of the garage was a shopfront with whitewashed windows and a hand-painted sign above the door that said 'Nav's Caff'.

Max Miller led me inside. A kettle and a glass display with a few wan-looking sandwiches appeared to be the establishment's only concessions to its stated purpose. A man I assumed to be the eponymous Nav stood resolutely behind the sandwiches.

We ordered two coffees and sat down at one of the plastic tables.

'So, what's going on with you and Cheryl?' Max Miller asked.

'She's left me.'

He didn't seem surprised. 'Just like that?' he asked dryly.

'Just like that.'

'What led up to it?'

That was a difficult question, and I felt tired just thinking about it.

'I don't really know – that's what's so troubling. She's been in a mood over the past few weeks and we haven't been talking, but there was no big bust-up or anything. Then, when I arrived home from Spain, she wasn't there. I wasn't that surprised, so I guess I must have seen it coming.'

'What was Cheryl working on?'

It was a question I wasn't expecting, and it threw me. 'Sorry, what do you mean?'

'What was she doing at work?'

'I don't know.'

'What did you give her for her last birthday?'

It clicked. 'Oh, right, I see where you're coming from. That's typical of you to take her side.'

'I'm not taking her side – and why does it have to be about sides anyway?'

I felt betrayed. 'Because it does, that's all. And you're taking hers.'

'Go on – tell me, what did you give her for her last birthday?' he demanded.

I remembered her last birthday, I'd been late home after doorstepping the leader of a paedophile ring in Cumbria. Or was it Northumberland? Anyway, I'd bought her something in a boutique in Carlisle or Penrith or somewhere like that. Only what was it? 'I can't remember, but it was bloody expensive, I'll tell you that.'

Max Miller smiled wryly.

We chatted some more, but we had to leave because I was desperate for a piss and Nav didn't have a toilet. Max Miller suggested I pop into a pub on Wandsworth Road.

'What's the matter, don't you want me in your home or something?'

'Don't be ridiculous,' he said, blushing.

His flat was compact, colonised by flat-pack furniture and reminiscent of one of the tiny showcase areas in Ikea that demonstrate how comfortably people with no imagination can live. It was late afternoon and the dull sky cast a gloom inside his living-room. He struck a match and lit a handful of tea-lights floating in a water-filled glass bowl. Using candles rather than electric bulbs was one of Max Miller's most irritating affectations. I excused myself and made a dash for the bathroom.

Another habit, which annoyed me, was the way he left small piles of paperback novels placed strategically throughout his flat. Standing upright on the cistern were well-thumbed copies of *The Go-Between*, *If This Is a Man* and *Leviathan*. The effect, I guessed, was to convince visitors that he was both romantic and humane.

I returned to the living-room and sat down on a small, cramped sofa, rubbing my hands to generate some heat. On a coffee table sat copies of books by Umberto Eco and Richard Dawkins, along with some New Age tract that looked like something Cheryl would read.

'Look, I don't want to rush you, but I've got a lot of work to do,' he said.

I did feel rushed, and slightly self-pitying. He was supposed to be my friend, and I didn't impose on him often. In fact, I couldn't remember an occasion when I'd done so before.

'What about a quick coffee?' I pleaded. 'I couldn't drink that stuff in the café, it was rancid.'

He sighed.

'Okay, but you'll have to make it yourself. I've got three family conferences to prepare for.'

The kitchen, like the rest of the flat, was prim and immaculate. I often wondered how Max Miller managed to keep his place so spotless when it had such a procession of chaotic individuals traipsing through it. I filled the kettle and searched the cabinets for a jar of coffee. In one of the cupboards I came across a bottle of organic wheatgrass cocktail, exactly the same brand Cheryl used – she claimed it helped to purify her blood. I stood in the doorway to the living-room and held the bottle up.

'You don't know where Cheryl is, do you?' I asked.

Max Miller's pale features reddened. 'Me, how would I know where she was?'

He never could lie convincingly.

10

It was the weekend of my thirteenth birthday and, for the first time, I was allowed to go fishing with Papa and Pablito. Papa was against taking me on the trip – he said I was too young to spend a night in the outdoors, but Mama insisted he bring me along, if only to stop my endless begging. Joining this grown-up, exclusively male pursuit felt to me like a step towards adulthood.

Fishing was one of the few activities Papa still took part in after Mama forced him to stop playing cards for money with his fellow baggage-handlers. When there was a card game on he often stayed out through the night until breakfast time, arriving home looking dirty and unshaved, with his shirttail hanging out over his trousers and his eyes red and pinched. On those occasions he'd either be deliriously happy, kissing us all in turn and laying out banknotes like a cover across the kitchen table, or he'd be foul-tempered, not speaking other than to demand coffee and cigarettes. Then we knew we'd be in for a difficult week. Mama had eventually put her foot down.

Fishing, on the other hand, was permissible. Papa went on these overnight trips two or three times a year, initially with his workmates and latterly with Pablito. I envied those times they had together, when they set off in high spirits and returned ruddy-faced with contented smiles, their spirits replenished.

More often than not they came back empty-handed, but, as Papa pointed out, catching fish was not the main thing, it was the taking part that counted. He and Pablito seldom volunteered details of their expeditions other than brief references to the weather, and Mama and I rarely asked. It was as if we knew this was a space they shared, that was exclusive to them.

For me, that only added to the mystique, and I was excited to finally be part of it, to learn more, to occupy the same space, close to Papa. I pored over the items in his fishing-tackle box that sat under the stairs, marvelling at those obscure objects – the plastic, weightless floats, the shiny metal spinners and coloured fly lines, the lethally sharp hooks of varying size, the lead weights – running my fingers over their irregular shapes and pondering their purpose. I marvelled at the geometry and engineering that went into the construction of a fishing reel, a perfect tool that appeared to serve its purpose so smoothly and completely. Instinctively I knew I'd be at home by the riverside or on the banks of a loch.

The night before our trip I barely slept, willing the hands of my alarm clock to move closer to morning. I'd never been away from home, or Mama, before, and I felt sure this was where my relationship with Papa would begin proper, father and son, something at last to bind us, something we could plan for, discuss and look forward to. I could barely contain my excitement.

The day before we left I accompanied Papa and Pablito on a trip to buy a small Primus stove, which we'd need to heat soup and boil water. The one they had used on previous trips had given up the ghost. We went into a shop on Victoria Road that sold camping equipment, and near the doorway we saw one that was ideal in the middle of a display that included a tent, a picnic table and various other camping accessories.

Papa approached the sales assistant to inquire about the price. It was ten pounds – too expensive, Papa said. As we left, I watched with a sense of exhilarating horror as he lifted the stove from its display, bundled it inside his jacket, and carried on walking out of the store.

My heart pounded as we paced speedily along the crowded street. I was convinced that the eyes of hundreds of shoppers were trained on us and that at any moment I would feel the firm, apprehending arm of the law on my shoulder. When we reached the car, Papa and Pablito laughed uproariously and warned me not to tell Mama. Back at home I felt complicit in their crime, expecting the police to appear on our doorstep and the three of us to be led away to cold, darkened cells.

The following morning we were up early, dressed in old clothes suitable for the countryside, preparing to leave. Pablito went into the garden with a shovel to dig for worms, and Papa gathered the items we'd need to subsist – the stolen Primus, a saucepan, old ginger bottles for water, tea bags, a loaf of bread and a tin of John West salmon. He packed everything into the back of a battered old van he'd borrowed from the airport, along with an overnight bag and three moth-eaten sleeping bags.

We set off, buoyed by a sense of release, loudly singing 'Porompompero' by Manolo Escobar. I mouthed the occasional word I remembered in the verses and then joined in with the chorus, which was easy.

Porompom pón, poropo, porompom pero, peró, poropo, porom pompero, peró, poropo, porompom pon.

I'd no idea what it meant, and it sounded daft. If any of my friends had heard me, I'd have been mortified, but it was a happy song, and that was all that mattered. When we stopped singing, Papa teased Pablito about how few fish he was going to catch. I'd never seen my father so cheerful and liberated.

The van stuttered noisily through the Highlands, its rasping exhaust pumping oily black fumes into the vast, tranquil expanse of Loch Lomond, and then the Cairngorms. We passed through Fort William and pressed on until we reached the hamlet of Bridge of Orchy, where we turned off down a remote single-track road. It ran alongside the banks of Loch Tula and was punctuated by signs warning of boulders falling and deer crossing. Papa and Pablito pointed out remembered landmarks, arguing between them about the location of the best fishing spot.

We settled on a stretch easily accessible from the road, sheltered by a circle of overhanging trees. It was a hot and still summer's day, and clusters of midges congregated in shafts of sunlight. Swathes of rough purple heather covered the hills, which rose grandly from the glacially smooth loch. There was a smell of peaty freshness, and the silence was broken only by the occasional whoosh of a car passing in the distance. I'd never witnessed anything so achingly beautiful – it was as though the scene had been conjured up especially for me, for my first fishing trip.

While Papa lit a cigarette and admired the view, Pablito set about preparing the rods, attaching reels and tackle. Then he grabbed a handful of worms from the jar and selected the fattest; he pinched it between his fingers to stop it wriggling and clumsily skewered it on to the fishing hook. The tip pricked the worm's skin and a small squirt of green slime trickled over Papa's nails. He repeated the procedure another two or three times until the worm was wound around the hook, then he did the same with the other fishing rod.

Papa explained that there were only two rods, so we'd have to share. He ordered me to stand back while he cast. He turned so he was facing away from the loch with his rod held outstretched, then he spun a hundred and eighty degrees, releasing the line from the reel and sending the weighted, baited hook far out on to the water. I heard the soft plink of the worm hitting the surface of the loch. Then he gently laid the rod down behind a large rock, its tip pointing in the air. Pablito cast his line, not gaining quite the distance that Papa had managed.

And that, it appeared, was that. They seemed content to stare blankly at the rods, Papa drinking coffee and smoking cigarettes. I'd been expecting more. I wasn't quite sure what, but I thought there must be greater excitement to fishing than this, something that would hold my imagination. After twenty minutes I was bored, so I suggested we move to another spot where there might be more action, but my proposal was met with frowns of disapproval. After an hour of fruitless contemplation, I decided to go and explore.

I wandered through the nearby woodland and over a couple of hillocks, among the acres of fern and the droppings of a multitude of rabbits. Suddenly I heard an eruption of noise from the bank of the loch. I rushed back in time to see Pablito grappling with his rod, while Papa gave him rapid instructions. At last, some excitement. The rod was bent, with the line held tightly in place as Pablito fought to steady himself. He was struggling to hold firm and was slowly dragged into the loch.

'*Despacio, despacio*,' Papa called. 'Slowly, slowly.'

There was a flurry of splashes at the point where the line disappeared below the surface of the loch. Pablito steadied himself and took a proper grip on the rod, and, as he transferred his weight on to his right leg and hauled the rod back over his shoulder, weakening the tight resistance on the line, he began to wind the reel clockwise until the line went tight again. The flapping became more intense, catching Pablito off-balance, and he slipped, landing on his backside. He let go of the rod.

'*Rapidamente, rapidamente!*' Papa shouted. 'Quickly, quickly!'

I was breathless, and I willed Pablito to rescue the situation. He got to his feet, drenched, and waded deeper, catching hold of the cork handle of the rod before it was dragged out of his reach. As he hauled it back, I heard the reel whirring freely as the fish pulled on the line.

'Wind, wind!' Papa shouted.

Pablito steadied himself and grabbed hold of the handle of the reel, winding it so quickly his hand became a blur. When the line was tight again, he heaved the rod over his shoulder and wound up the slack. I could see he was getting tired, but with Papa shouting encouragement he kept going.

Suddenly the splashing stopped and the rod straightened. Pablito stood upright and continued to wind the reel, but the resistance had dropped and he became more relaxed. After a few moments I saw the fish emerging, breaking the tension of the water surface, flopping and splashing in the shallows, heading towards us. Judging by the fight it had put up, I was expecting a shark. It wasn't quite that, but it was still pretty big.

Papa waded into the loch and lifted the end of the line. The fish emerged with the hook caught through its bloody lip, flapping wildly. I felt a pang of pity. Papa pulled on the hook, breaking through the gristle of its jaw. Spurts of blood splashed on to the rocks. The fish was wriggling so much it slipped from Papa's grasp. He reached down and grabbed it firmly between his hands and battered its head against a rock.

'What are you doing?' I shouted.

Papa looked at me.

'I kill it,' he said neutrally.

'No, don't do that,' I pleaded. 'Throw it back.'

Papa and Pablito looked at one another and laughed. The fish was still struggling, so Papa whacked its head on the rock again, and it went limp.

The other two stood admiring their catch, debating its size and weight. Papa reckoned it was at least three pounds, and Pablito agreed. It was around two feet long, silvery grey, with flecks of blue and red – a magnificent rainbow trout. Papa dropped it into a polythene carrier bag, which he left at the bank of the loch with a couple of rocks placed on top to stop it drifting away. Pablito re-baited his rod and cast again, and we all settled back, bursting with self-satisfaction.

There was a mood of togetherness – Pablito might have caught the fish, but now he willed us to do the same. I asked Papa if I could wind his reel in if he got a bite, and he said I could. We discussed Pablito's catch in the smallest detail, going over every stage, from the first twitch of the line to the successful landing of the fish on the shoreline.

I'd never talked so freely with Papa, making comments and offering opinions that he took seriously. After a while we drifted on to other subjects – football, boxing, fruit machines, street games. Papa took a long draw on his cigarette and reclined on a patch of lush moss, with his head resting on a rolled-up sleeping bag. I was sitting in front of him on a large rock, whittling a twig with a gutting knife that I'd found in the fishing-tackle box.

'This is how I imagine Scotland,' he said, sighing wistfully.

'What do you mean, Papa?' I asked.

'When I live in Tangier and I offer job here, I think this is how it will be – big mountains, calm water, green fields, beautiful peace.'

He wasn't normally so openly thoughtful, and I was taken aback. It was at times like these, I'd learned, that Papa could sometimes be encouraged to talk about his younger days. 'And what was Tangier like?' I ventured.

He peered at me for a moment, and I was worried he'd stop talking, but then his head dropped and he breathed deeply. 'There is a lot of Spanish in Tangier at this time. It is then a very exciting place . . . very, how you say, cosmopolitan. All Spanish in Tangier, they work in hotels. I have good job then – restaurant manager in the Hotel Continental, the best hotel in city.'

'What was it like?'

'It is big hotel, floor tae ceiling it's, how you say, mosaics with small tiles, all piece together like painting. In Moorish style. Rich guests, they come from all over, from Spain and France and America. We have famous writers and movie actors, all the time they come there.'

He was quiet for a moment and then he sat upright and laughed out loud, prompted by something dredged from the back of his mind. 'You know who I serve dinner?'

'No, who?'

'Wha's the name a this guy, this big Hollywood hot-shot guy, who act in film . . . wha's it call?' He slapped his forehead, frustrated at his poor memory.

'Humphrey Bogart,' Pablito prompted, as he returned from the lochside where he'd been checking his rod.

'*Si*, Humphrey Bogart. Humphrey Bogart. Wha's the name they call him . . . Bog . . . Boga . . . Bogus?'

'Bogie,' Pablito corrected.

'*Si*, Bogie, I serve Bogie.'

I could tell Pablito had heard all of this before. Papa lay back down on the moss, chuckling to himself, before sitting upright again. 'You know wha he eat for dinner?' he asked me.

'No, what?'

'Roast beef,' he announced triumphantly. 'I serve Humphrey Bogart roast beef. Nae other place in Morocco you get roast beef at this time, only in the Hotel Continental in Tangier.'

He stared at me, and I smiled enthusiastically.

'Wow, that's magic, Papa.'

'There is photograph of him in this hotel, I bet, still to this day. You nae believe me?'

'Yes, I do,' I insisted.

'You go see, in Hotel Continental, in Tangier, a photograph of Bogie in bar. After he eat roast beef, served by me, by your Papa.'

He sprawled back again, staring at the sky. It was early evening and the sun was setting over the top of Beinn an Dothaidh, casting a long, dark shadow over the blue, still loch. The heat of the afternoon had dissipated, and the midges were starting to emerge now in force. We hadn't brought anything to repel them, and I felt them burrowing into my scalp and the back of my neck, forcing me to slap my head and face every few seconds. I could see they were irritating Pablito too, but they didn't seem to bother Papa, who lay still on the ground.

'Tangier is rich at this time,' he said after a few moments. 'Everybody, they want come and spend money – businessmen, actors, writers, royals, these boys . . . how you say?'

'Playboys,' Pablito chimed in.

'*Si* playboys. It was international city, run by many governments, so no one make rule. Anything you wanna dae in Tangier, you dae, anything you wanna buy, you buy.'

'So why did you leave?' I asked.

'The Moroccans, they get independence, and is nae same any more. Now people they are told "you nae do this, you nae do that". The rich they no come and there is nae money, nae job.'

Papa announced that he was hungry. Pablito opened the tin of salmon and, using the gutting knife, smeared lumps of it on to roughly torn chunks of crusty bread. He filled a saucepan with water from the loch and heated it over the stolen Primus stove to make tea. Papa made a comment about what good value it had been, and I cringed. The tea tasted bitter.

Dusk was closing in, and there had been no activity on the fishing lines since Pablito's catch. Papa had run out of cigarettes, so he suggested that we go to the bar in the nearby hotel.

'What about Antonio?' my brother asked. 'They won't let a thirteen-year-old boy in the bar.'

'Ach, he sit in van,' Papa said dismissively. 'We nae be long. Is nae problem, eh son?'

We'd passed a small, whitewashed hotel at the turn-off from the main road, and I guessed from the familiarity with which Papa and Pablito discussed it that they had visited it before. They stripped and washed in the loch, and from the overnight bag recovered from the van Papa produced a pair of slacks, a neatly pressed shirt and smart, polished shoes, which he changed into.

He filled the saucepan with water from the loch and heated it over the Primus so that he could have a shave. He'd even packed a bottle of aftershave. He splashed some on to his cleanly shaven face and clapped his hands together loudly. I suspected this was part of a well-worn fishing-trip ritual.

'Okay, we go,' he said enthusiastically.

During the short drive to the hotel I tried to resume our earlier conversation.

'So what made you come here, to Scotland, from Tangier?'

Pablito sighed.

'I work in Hotel Continental, and this customer, a rich businessman, he say, "You come work for me. I give you good job, you run my hotel in Scotland."'

'What, just like that?'

'*Si*, just like this. He say, "I have hotel, how you say, *a la costa*."'

'At the seaside,' Pablito said with bored resignation.

'*Si*, at seaside. He say, "I pay for you come". I say, "I nae even speak English". He say, "I pay you learn". I say, "Wha about my family?" because I married tae your Mama and we have Pablito, and he say, "You bring them. I give you house tae live. You earn plenty money."'

He shook his head and laughed. 'You know wha I think?'

'What?' I replied.

'I think I come tae Scottish village like on bottle of Glenmorangie, you know, Glenmorangie whisky with cottage and sheep and beautiful water on label?'

I had no idea what he was talking about, but I nodded anyway.

'This is all I know of Scotland, from bottle of Glenmorangie in bar of Hotel Continental, nothing else. I come tae Scotland and you know where I arrive?'

I knew the answer, but I also recognised it was not the time to provide a response. This was a punchline he wanted to deliver himself with as much drama as he could muster.

'Saltcoats, stinking bloody Saltcoats,' he spat. 'This shithole full a stinking bloody chip shops and *borrachos* from Glasgow.'

We arrived at the hotel and pulled up at the car park. It was on the edge of a small village – just a post office and a few cottages – but I could tell from the noise emanating from the bar and the multitude of motorbikes parked outside that it was an attraction. Pablito said it was one of the most popular stops on the route of the West Highland Way. That explained the pile of rucksacks near the entrance.

'Wait here,' Papa told me. 'We nae be long.'

He strolled across the car park with the dry gravel crunching beneath the smooth leather soles of his Italian shoes. Pablito hesitated, as though he wasn't comfortable with the arrangement, but then he turned and followed Papa. They opened the door to the bar, releasing a loud blast of traditional fiddle music, and disappeared inside.

A few minutes later, Pablito emerged with a bottle of Coca-Cola and a packet of crisps that he handed to me with a sheepish look before returning to the bar. The Coke was warm, and the crisps were soft and stale. I had no appetite for either.

There was no radio in the van to listen to, so I moved into the driver's seat and fiddled with the gearstick, the handbrake and the various buttons and knobs for a while, and then I got out of the van and wandered to the far side of the car park, peering over the bridge on to the gushing river below. I looked across the open moors to the red, craggy hills in the distance, then climbed down the riverbank and collected a handful of stones, which I lobbed into the water.

After a while, when I could no longer stand the midges, I made my way back to the van. As I crossed the car park I heard the sound of clapping and whooping along to the music. It just didn't seem fair that I should be stuck outside, missing out on all the fun.

I opened the door to the bar and peered inside. The room had a warm, comfortable atmosphere, with a thick, deep-red carpet and dark, sturdy furniture padded with tartan fabric. The white, roughly Artexed walls were hung with paintings of Highland scenes and a mounted stag's head. Behind the bar, dozens of malt whisky bottles formed an impressive display. A sea of half-empty glasses and mixer bottles blanketed the dimpled copper-clad tables.

The customers were dressed in hiking gear or bikers' leathers and most were drunk. Two heavily-built men dressed in kilts were playing a traditional reel on a fiddle and a squeezebox. Papa and Pablito sat immediately beside them, talking to two women. I only managed to get a proper look at the one seated next to Papa. She was quite pretty, with blonde hair in a feather cut like Suzi Quatro, and she had large, sticky-out tits that were clamped tight inside a pink t-shirt. She held a cigarette in one hand and a pint of beer in the other. She was staring intently at Papa, who was talking at some length, as if he was telling her a story. She inclined her head towards him, draped her hand around the back of his head and pulled his face closer towards her ear. The gesture was so intimate it made me feel as though I was intruding.

I returned to the van and sat inside until it was dark. I hoped the customers might begin to drift off, but if anything the bar was getting busier as more cars and motorbikes arrived. At one stage I was sure I heard the familiar strains of 'Porompompero' emerging.

I curled up on the passenger seat and tried to sleep, but there was nothing to cover me – we'd left the sleeping bags in the tent back at the fishing spot, and the night's coldness was closing in. Eventually I could bear it no longer and I returned to the bar. I opened the door and peered inside. Through the crowds and clouds of smoke, I made out Papa, in the same seat as before – only now Suzi Quatro was sitting on his lap. Pablito had a stupid look on his face. He was talking to another woman, who had dark hair and was wearing a denim bomber jacket. Pablito tried to pull her on to his knee, but she resisted and slapped him on the chest playfully. I fought my way through the bodies and grabbed Papa by the arm.

'Can we go now? It's freezing outside,' I pleaded.

His face reddened and he manoeuvred the girl off his knee. 'You wait in van. We only be one minute.'

I returned to the van and waited for another twenty minutes. In the end I got out and walked around briskly to keep warm. Eventually, after another hour or so, the door of the bar opened and people started to drift out, into cars and on to motorbikes. Papa and Pablito were among the last to leave, and behind them Suzi Quatro and her friend teetered across the car park, clutching a bottle of beer in each hand, singing 'Viva Espana' at the top of their voices.

'We drop girls at their tent,' Papa said casually.

Papa drove, with Suzi Quatro in the passenger seat, and her friend, Pablito and I sitting on the bare metal floor in the back. The smell of stale alcohol and cigarette smoke made me feel nauseous.

'How dae ye say dildo in Spanish?' the friend asked.

They both erupted in braying laughter.

'Aye, and blow job. How dae ye say blow job?' Suzi Quatro added.

'Hey, I have young son, you watch language,' Papa said angrily.

We stopped at a field located off the main road about two miles from the hotel, where a small canvas tent was pitched alongside two motorbikes. Everyone got out of the van and Suzi Quatro disappeared into the tent, emerging seconds later with a bottle-opener. She uncapped two bottles of beer and handed one each to her friend and Pablito. She uncapped a third and handed it to Papa, but he refused and she drank it herself.

'Papa, can we go now? I'm freezing and tired,' I implored.

Suzi Quatro disappeared back into the tent and emerged with a sleeping bag, which she handed to me.

'Here you are, wee man, wrap this round yersel,' she said.

As she stood in the glow of the van's headlights, I caught sight of her face properly. It was lined and baggy and coated in a heavy layer of make-up. It was clear she wasn't as young as her dress implied.

'You sleep in van, we nae be long, only two minute,' Papa said.

Reluctantly I took the sleeping bag and climbed into the vehicle. There was a strong smell musky of bodies and cheap perfume from the quilted nylon, but at least it was warm. I huddled down into it and tried to sleep.

The sound of chatter and laughter stopped and everything was silent. I climbed into the front passenger seat and tried to look out of the windscreen, but it had steamed over with my breath. I rubbed a small circle in the bottom corner with the sleeve of my jumper to act as a spyhole. Papa had switched the headlights off, so it was difficult to make out what was going on. I squinted through the darkness, just managing to make out Pablito and Suzi Quatro's friend kissing.

After a few moments Papa and Suzi Quatro emerged from the tent. Papa's shirt was hanging out of his trousers, and she was wearing a long t-shirt that stretched over her thighs. As he walked away she slapped him on the back of the head, and he stopped and faced her. I thought he was going to hit her, but he turned away.

'*Mi cago en su padre,*' he shouted. It was a phrase Mama had banned him from using in the house. 'I shit on your father.'

Papa grabbed hold of Pablito, still in a clinch with the friend, and pulled him away.

'Oi, whit d'ye think yer daen?' the friend shouted.

I scampered over the seats into the back of the van and lay on top of the sleeping bag, pretending to be asleep.

'Who the fuck d'ye think ye are, ya dago bastard?' Suzi Quatro yelled.

The doors opened and Papa and Pablito hurriedly climbed in. Pablito was clearly irritated at the turn of events.

'What happened, Papa, what did you do to her?' he asked.

Papa turned the ignition and slammed the gearstick into reverse. The wheels skidded on the damp grass as the vehicle spun around.

'I tell her she is drunk, and she stink like bitch that is fuck by all dogs in street.'

Suzi Quatro came running towards the van as it pulled away and hammered her fists on the driver's side window.

'Gie's ma sleepin bag, ya fuckin greasy cunt,' she demanded.

The van halted abruptly.

'Give her this bag,' Papa shouted angrily.

Pablo leaned over and grabbed the bag from under me. He opened the door and threw it out on to the ground then Papa slammed his foot on the accelerator and the van tore off at speed, back to the fishing spot.

I woke first the next morning. I didn't know what time it was, but it was light and the birds were singing. I spent some time playing at the lochside, whittling sticks and throwing stones into the water before Papa and Pablito emerged from the tent looking groggy and sheepish. Papa boiled some hot water over the

Primus to make tea, and then he announced that we were going home. There was to be no more fishing.

The journey was almost entirely silent, except when we stopped at a public toilet in Tarbert. As the three of us stood at the urinals, I saw Papa catch Pablito's eye and motion his head towards me. Papa then said he was going to buy cigarettes and left. As I was drying my hands, Pablito took me by the arm.

'You know that what happens on fishing trips stays on fishing trips,' he said, staring me in the eye.

'What do you mean?'

'I mean we don't talk about it, like to Mama for instance.'

'Of course not.'

I knew it was wrong but I couldn't help feeling a surge of pride. I'd been taken into Papa and Pablito's confidence.

11

I hadn't heard from Cheryl for weeks and I was desperate to see her, to stand in front of her, to find out who she was with and what she was doing. It was like an itch I needed to scratch, that consumed me day and night, dragging me down, making me unable to function properly. At work I found I couldn't concentrate on anything for longer than a few minutes. In bed I lay tortured, conceiving alternative pasts for myself – if only I'd acted differently at particular junctures – and different possible futures too, speculating what lay ahead depending on the choices I could make. I couldn't eat or sleep, and I had no energy. Even the most mundane task that took me out of my routine – such as collecting shirts from the laundry or finding somewhere to buy a tube of toothpaste – seemed like a monumental effort.

Cheryl filled my every thought. I called her at work repeatedly and left messages on her voicemail, all of which went unanswered. I texted and emailed her without response. I called her friends and colleagues, but none had seen or head from her. Ben and Corrie claimed not to have had any contact with her, which I doubted, but I didn't press them, especially Ben, who was only a few weeks away from his mock A-levels.

Max Miller insisted he too hadn't heard from her. I tried to gauge from the tone of his voice whether he was being truthful. He sounded sympathetic enough, but was it the tenor of deceit? I felt sure he'd never forgiven me for stealing Cheryl from him at university, and perhaps now, after all these years, he was exacting revenge. But no matter how hard I tried to convince myself of that possibility, I couldn't make it ring true. Max Miller wasn't like that: he was principled and honourable. Surely he wouldn't steal my wife? It just wasn't possible. Was it?

I was about to embark on a crucial period at work; I was facing what I anticipated would be a captious and emotionally demanding divorce; and my father was dying. What I needed least at this time was the distraction of a wild goose chase going back seven decades into a corner of a country whose language and customs I barely knew. And yet, as though waking suddenly from a dream, I found myself back in Alguaire.

Despite having spent only a few hours there when rescuing Papa from the police station, I sensed that it held clues about what made my father who he was. Somehow, I felt, by returning there I would have a clearer understanding of him. There was no point trying to explain something like that to Kevin, so I told him I had flu and wouldn't be at work for a couple of days. He sighed with resigned disapproval. In the decade I'd worked with him I couldn't remember him being off sick for a single day. A broken leg, pneumonia and rampant gastroenteritis – which involved clearing a runway from his desk to facilitate his routine shuttle sprints to the bog – had all failed to dent his untiring work ethic.

I took a budget-airline flight to Barcelona and drove to Alguaire in a hire car. I parked on the edge of the village. The streets were cool and eerily quiet with a hint of morning mist. I wandered into the main square and sat outside at the pavement café. The only other customer was an old man, I guessed in his eighties or early nineties, wire-thin with tough, leathery skin and gun-dog eyes. He sat nursing a small glass of black coffee, smoking strong, toasted cigarettes, and greeted anyone who passed with a friendly '¿Qué tal?' He reserved his most cheerful smiles for the pretty young mothers, dressed in colourful skirts, who meandered across the square with their children in pushchairs. A few migrant workers were congregated outside the telegraph office opposite. Occasionally one or two of them crossed the road and teased the old man about this or that, and he accepted their attentions with good humour.

I wondered about his past, how long he'd lived in Alguaire and how he'd survived the war. Perhaps he'd known my grandparents; perhaps he was one of the villagers who'd betrayed them to the Falangists; perhaps he'd pointed to my grandmother and said, 'She deserves to die.' Perhaps he was one of the villagers who'd written to the Ajuntamente, objecting to Papa's request to recover his parents' remains from the field where they'd lain buried for the past seventy years.

I left the café and wandered through the streets to the outer edge of the village, where I found a steep set of narrow steps leading on to a promontory on which a stone statue of Christ was perched, his extended arms seeming to embrace the village and the countryside beyond. On the side of the hill was a series of loudspeakers from which municipal messages were being relayed to villagers – times and dates of meetings and community events, I guessed.

I climbed to the top and looked across the landscape, beyond the chaotic cluster of terracotta roofs below me, the olive and nectarine groves, and over the undulating plains. The green valleys, bordered by headlands of lime and red, marly sandstone, were interrupted occasionally by islets of yellow, parched scrub. In the distance, the craggy mountain range stood like a bold artistic statement. This was what had been fought over.

Below, I saw the building with the bell tower that had caught my attention on my previous visit. From this distance it was even more unsightly than up close. No one, it seemed, was prepared to do anything about its ruin. No one wanted to talk about the war: the building remained scarred and the dead lay where they were buried, untouched.

The thought made me suddenly and fiercely angry, and I wanted to do something about it. On my way back to the car I noticed the Ajuntamente office was open, so I went inside. It was attended by a pair of female clerks, attractive and smartly dressed, neither of whom had been there when I'd visited with Mama and Pablito. They both greeted me with a smile. I asked in faltering Spanish if there was someone around who might be able to answer some questions about the building opposite. They looked at me, puzzled.

'*Momento,*' said one, and she disappeared through a door that looked as though it led on to other offices.

She soon returned with a tall, grey-haired man dressed in a white short-sleeved shirt and camel cavalry-twill slacks that were pinched around a neat waist. He smoked a cigarette with urbane authority.

'Yes sir, how may I help you?' he said in English with just a trace of a Spanish accent.

I told him of my interest in the damaged building.

'Ah yes, *el almacén de granos.*'

'I'm sorry.'

'In English it is the grain store. Or, at least, it was historically. Today it is a municipal building for concerts and meetings and so on.'

'I wondered what had happened to it. Was it damaged during the Civil War?'

He paused. 'Umm, yes, that is correct.'

'And why has it never been properly restored?'

There was another, longer silence. 'I don't really know the answer to that Mr . . .'

'Antonio,' I said.

'Well, Señor Antonio, it all happened a long time ago.'

'How was it damaged exactly?' I asked.

'There is a lot of literature available in the public library in Lerida that will provide you with that kind of information,' he said in a polite tone.

'Don't you have any information here?' I pressed. 'It seems odd that the local municipal office doesn't hold any information on such a central building.'

He breathed heavily, as though he'd been confronted with a matter of particular inconvenience. 'I'm sure if you visit the library there will be a local historian who will be able to answer your inquiries.'

His response provoked a sudden and disproportionate change in my mood. 'Why is it that no one wants to talk about the war?' I demanded.

He didn't respond.

'All I'm asking for is some information about a public building. I can't believe you've sat in your office opposite that monstrosity and never wondered what happened to it.'

'Are you by any chance related to Señor Noguera from Scotland?' he asked.

'Yes, he's my father,' I sighed.

There was another long silence, and I thought he might try to usher me out of the door.

'I am sorry I was not in the office the day your father called, because I could have given a proper explanation about why his request was denied.'

'Yes, he was pretty angry about that.'

'It was not, as he suggested, that we thought it unreasonable or that anyone in the village had objected.'

'Oh really?'

'No, on the contrary, we would have been pleased to facilitate his wish, but to do such a thing we must have evidence that these remains to which he referred exist, and unfortunately he was unable to provide us with that.'

'What do you mean? My father says he knows where his parents are buried – is that not evidence enough?'

'I am afraid not, Señor Noguera. The war ended seventy years ago, and, for the first forty of those years, no records were kept of those killed by the Nationalist side. The only evidence that exists is the recollections of the survivors, but those are, as I'm sure you can imagine, notoriously unreliable.'

'So what are you saying, that my grandparents' remains must stay dumped in a shallow grave forever because my father's recollections are not reliable enough?'

'No, that is not the case, but we do need supporting evidence.'

'And where would he get that?'

'I'm afraid that is a matter for you and your father, but I suggest you start by going to the library in Lerida.'

His tone was equable, generous even, and I felt embarrassed and wrong-footed. It was typical of Papa to pile into such an issue half-cocked and accuse others when he didn't get what he wanted. I should have been more cautious – I'd been stung too many times before to accept what he told me without question.

Driving back to my hotel in Lerida I tried to phone Cheryl's mobile again, but as usual it diverted to voicemail. After the tone I hesitated, unsure whether to leave another message. I didn't want to give her the satisfaction of knowing I was wondering where she was and what she was doing all the time.

I decided to go for it. It shouldn't be important what she thought about me, I told myself – I should be above all that. She might have been prepared to end our marriage without explanation, but I was not going to allow her to think she was unaccountable.

'Hi, it's me. I've been home, and I know you're gone. I'm not interested in why or where. I just thought we should talk and make arrangements about where we go from here.'

Apart from a hint of dryness in my mouth, my delivery was controlled and impassive. I should have been pleased, but the moment I hung up I had doubts. Did I really want to give up our marriage without a fight? Even if she was determined to go, why should I make it easy for her? I thought about phoning her again and leaving another message, but I didn't want to seem too desperate either.

Back at my hotel I asked the receptionist for directions to the local library and was told it was within walking distance on the Rambla de Aragon. It was called the Biblioteca Pública de la Maternitat, she explained, because it was housed in a former orphanage. When I arrived I immediately felt like one of its former charges. It was a cloistered, imposing structure whose nineteenth-century shell had been recast as a cathedral of high-Modern open-plan design. My sense of awe was intensified by the fact that all the signs were in Catalan. Shards of sunlight streamed through a glass roof, and my footsteps echoed across the granite flagstones as I approached a librarian seated in a central atrium behind a large semi-circular walnut table. I could tell by the way she squinted at me as I approached that she had sensed I was going to be problematic.

'*Si señor,*' she said tartly.

I tried to explain what I was after, and, though she spoke a little English, she didn't understand. After several failed attempts she directed me to a section of the library that dealt with Spanish history. I made my way to a collection of shelves, more to avoid the embarrassment of having to retreat sheepishly from the building than because I thought I'd find anything of use there.

There were several multi-volume histories of Spain, each with a section, of varying size, on the Civil War. But these were general, academic treatises with none of the localised human dimension I was after. The only books dedicated entirely to the war seemed to be in a section chronicling the Catalan experience, with titles such as *L'Intent Franquista de Genocidi Cultural Contra Catalunya* and *Traidors a Catalunya: La Cinquena Columna (1936–39)*.

I took a few of the books to a reading table and thumbed through the pages, stopping at those which bore the now familiar wartime scenes – grainy stills of tired, middle-aged men in Homburg hats and old suits standing in bombed-out streets, looking hunted and angry; wagons of achingly naïve volunteers clutching ancient rifles with worn wooden stocks and rusting bolts; strutting, absurdly camp Fascist generals glad-handing cassocked clergy; dirty-faced feral youths scouring the rubbled ruins for signs of life or food or anything with a resale value.

I heard the sound of sharp footsteps and looked up to see the librarian I'd spoken to approaching me along with a short man who appeared to have been summoned from some backroom function.

'Hello sir,' he said. 'My name is Fermin. My colleague tells me you have a question about the Civil War.'

As his colleague stood by I explained to him what I was after. Requesting decades-old information about an anonymous building in a middle-of-nowhere hamlet made me realise how nebulous my quest appeared to be. Had I really come all this way to find out about a grain store, I wondered to myself. I flushed with embarrassment and found myself recounting the detail of my grandparents' death, as a way, I supposed, of legitimising my inquiry. Fermin listened politely.

'I do not have any knowledge of the building in question, but I could make some inquiries,' he said matter-of-factly.

He had a brief conversation with the other librarian in Catalan and she strode purposefully off.

'I should also say that, as well as being an historian, I am a local member of La Asociación para la Recuperación de la Memoria Histórica. Have you heard of this organisation?' he asked.

I shook my head. The librarian returned and handed me a glossy brochure. On its cover was a black-and-white picture of a soldier crouched in a doorway, his rifle pointing towards a crowd huddled at the end of a narrow street.

'It was set up a few years ago by a group of volunteers dedicated to recovering the remains of victims of Franco's regime. To date it has exhumed the corpses of several thousand war dead. If your grandparents died in the circumstances you described, then this organisation may be able to help you. I could make some inquiries on your behalf if you will permit me. It would involve reviewing existing records and speaking to any surviving villagers in Alguaire who might recall the incident.'

I noticed he was wearing a pair of rubber-soled house slippers. There were circular patches of damp under the arms of his short-sleeved shirt, and from the plumpness of his frame I guessed he would have some difficulty remembering the last time he had broken into a trot. He looked an unlikely hero, and yet I wanted to pull him towards me and kiss him. He was the first person who had given me, or Papa, anything like positive news regarding the search for my grandparents' remains.

'That would be fantastic,' I said, grinning.

Back in my hotel room I turned on my laptop and Googled the organisation Fermin had mentioned. In English it was the Association for the Recovery of Historical Memory. Its website described it as a collection of volunteer archaeologists, anthropologists and forensic scientists who had come together to redress the historical anomaly that, until the turn of the millennium, the remains of victims of Republican atrocities only had been disinterred for reburial. Association members collected oral and written testimonies from friends, neighbours and relatives of Franco's victims and exhumed and identified recovered remains, it said. Less than a decade after its formation, it had exhumed the bodies of four thousand supporters of the Republic who had been murdered and dumped in roadside ditches and mass graves. The website included a forum for families of war victims whose relatives were still missing, and for people who'd lost touch with family members and were now trying to trace them.

I was struck by its remote sadness, the random desperation of the people who continued to mourn and who still held out hope of information about those they'd lost. Plaintive messages filled its pages, from mothers whose babies were taken at birth as retribution because their husbands were *rojos*; children whose birth records were destroyed and who were raised by strangers in loveless institutions; sisters who had lost brothers; wives who had lost husbands; grandchildren who'd grown up knowing only that their grandparents had 'disappeared'. One of the entries was headed '*Setenta años sin Miguel*' – 'Seventy years without Miguel'; another sought information about a father who'd disappeared while fighting at the Battle of the Ebro; another who'd lost track of his brother, whose last known whereabouts was a hospital in El Escorial where he was being treated for a leg wound.

I stared at the screen with the possibilities racing through my mind. Did this have any relevance to me? Should it have any relevance? Papa had lost his parents and siblings in the war, but I had lost nothing. I had never known these people, so why should it be my responsibility, a generation removed, to get involved in seeking some kind of ill-defined justice on their behalf? Anyway, quite apart from the fact that I had other things on my mind, like saving my marriage, I didn't know if I could trust Papa's account of what had happened. It wasn't just that the alleged events had taken place so long ago and that he had a child's memory of them. More troubling was the question of his honesty, as much with himself as with others. He had a worrying ability to convince himself of the significance of partial truths. Moreover, if I did want to take this further, I would need his approval and co-operation, and I knew that would be my biggest challenge.

12

'Bobby never told me you were Spanish.'

Cheryl's height-of-summer smile lit up her gemstone eyes. It was the first time I could recall anyone referring to my nationality without it sounding like an accusation. If Max Miller hadn't told her that I was Spanish, then who had? Had she been asking about me?

'Eh, yes, that's right, I am,' I replied, resisting the urge to qualify my response.

'Are you interested in the Civil War at all?'

I hesitated – I couldn't tell her that all I knew about the Spanish Civil War was that there had been one. 'Eh, yes, I am, in a way,' I said.

In a way. What the hell did that mean?

I had first spotted Cheryl at the Freshers' Week Fair, and I'd been admiring her from a consistently retreating distance ever since. She'd been over at the Socialist Workers' Society stand, her head thrown back, laughing loudly, clothed simply in a pair of tight jeans and a baggy white t-shirt. Her skin was smooth, like polished new wood, and her long, cornfield-blonde hair was held in place at the back with a simple red ribbon. I had approached to talk to Max Miller, who was chatting to the people running the stand, and fleetingly my eyes had met hers. Then she'd returned to the conversation she'd been having with some friends. It was the briefest of glances, and yet it was enough to convince me I was in love.

I was now into my second term at university, and I continued to slope in the shadows, looking as though I didn't belong. Mama's constant refrain, that I'd be the first Noguera to have a university degree, only added to the pressure. Between lectures I wandered alone, trying to look purposeful and hide the fact that I felt friendless and out of place. Max Miller, in contrast, had adapted readily to student life, making friends effortlessly. By the third week he was on first-name terms with all of his tutors, he'd started playing football for the first eleven and had been elected treasurer of the Socialist Workers' Society. He knew Cheryl, but he called her Dolores. It was some kind of SWS nickname, an in-joke that only the members shared, and I wasn't going to reveal my ignorance of all things political by asking him about it. Recently I'd seen them together a lot, handing out fliers, drumming up support for society meetings and sitting together in the union bar. That had made me even less confident about ever speaking to her. But now here she was, sitting down right next to me in the lecture theatre, looking earnestly into my eyes.

'Did any members of your family fight in the war?' She pressed.

I had no idea if any of my family had fought in the war or not, and, what was more, it was the first time in eighteen years that it had even occurred to me that I didn't know. I was barely aware of the names of my extended family, far less anything they had done. 'Eh, I don't know, it's not something my parents speak about much,' I mumbled.

'Ah, *el pacto de olvido*,' she said.

I looked at her blankly.

'The pact of forgetting?'

'Ah yes, that's the one, the old pact of forgetting,' I said, nodding as though I knew what she was talking about.

'What side did they support?'

I felt the heat rising from my face as I sought frantically for the names of the opposing sides in the conflict. I was sitting next to the most beautiful girl I'd ever met, she was taking an active interest in my background and my family, and I was displaying all the erudition of a monkey.

I'd already let slip that I didn't speak Spanish, and now I risked revealing that I didn't know who had participated in the single most important event in my native country's recent history. I racked my brains, remembering from the time of Franco's death that he'd led one of the sides in the war, but what was it called? The Francoists sounded familiar, but was that too obvious? In any event, Papa hated Franco, so even knowing the name of the side he led was not much use.

Cheryl smiled with gentle curiosity as I continued to dither. I willed myself to speak, to say something – anything – to break the mounting silence. Then, suddenly, from a weed-strewn corner of my brain, I managed to dredge the contents of a long-forgotten argument between my parents.

'My dad was an anarchist,' I said hesitantly.

Her face broadened into a joyful, accepting smile. She edged back a few inches and scanned the length of my body as though she were reassessing me in light of this new information.

'God, an anarchist,' she said with unconcealed admiration. 'He'll have fought with the FAI militia, then?'

I grinned weakly.

'La Federación Anarquista Ibérica?' she said expectantly.

'Yes, probably,' I replied. 'Like I say, he doesn't really discuss it.'

Much to my surprise, Cheryl asked me to join her for the screening of a documentary film about the Spanish Civil War at the Glasgow Film Theatre the following week. I threw budgetary caution to the wind and bought some new clothes from Millets with the last of that term's grant money – a pair of stonewashed drainpipe jeans and a red plaid lumberjack shirt, which I wore with a blue velvet jacket I'd picked up at Paddy's Market for three quid.

I arrived at the union bar early and bought myself a pint of snakebite and blackcurrant, then sat in a booth and opened a copy of *Socialist Worker* I'd bought to impress Cheryl. By quarter past five, with no sign of her, I started to panic, convinced she'd stood me up. I waited another twenty minutes, then just as I was about to leave she walked in. My heart swam. She was laughing, chatting away with Max Miller, who followed close behind her. My heart sank.

'You don't mind if Max comes along, do you?' she asked.

'Course not,' I replied, forcing a smile.

The bombing of Guernica, said the crackling, blunt-needle voice of the film's narrator, was a landmark event, because it was the first air attack on a civilian population and a rehearsal by the Luftwaffe for subsequent bombing raids on London and Coventry. The market town in the north-east corner of Spain, he explained, was symbolically important as a centre of Basque ethnic nationalism and Republican resistance against Franco's rebels. On the afternoon of Monday, April the 26th, 1937, a market day, it was attacked by fighter planes of the Luftwaffe Condor Legion and the Italian Fascist Aviazione Legionaria. It had no aerial defences, and until then it had been untouched by the war. With no warning, the population was subjected to almost three hours of sustained bombing, during which time 1,654 people were killed and 889 injured.

Until then I had known little about Guernica, other than that it was the name of a Picasso painting, and I'd never felt compelled to find out any more about it or the bombing. It was part of a war anchored in a history that meant little to me and evoked no particularly strong emotional response. The Second World War, in contrast, had a central place in my world, and its primal, us-against-them, good-versus-evil dichotomy was embedded in my imagination and my culture. I learned about it at school, read about it in books and comics, devoured countless films about it, discussed it with my friends and played games with it as the backdrop. Its outcome defined my very existence.

I expected the film to be arcane and dryly academic, but instead it was gripping. A war correspondent who had covered the bombing described approaching the town as the German bombers flew low overhead, almost touching the tops of the trees, buzzing those on the ground, driving into them the fear of God. Women wandered unsuspecting and defenceless among the market stalls in the spring sunshine buying their weekly provisions. As the bombs dropped, they ran for cover. Machine-gun bullets whizzed past them, ricocheting off walls.

Some people stood transfixed as they were strafed by aircraft fire; others screamed, terrified, and soiled themselves. Amid the screaming and bloodshed, buildings crumbled and cars combusted, and soon flames lit up the sky for miles. Children lay in the streets dead, broken and charred, emitting a nauseating smell of scorched flesh. Survivors wandered from street to street or huddled together, crying and praying. At the end of four hours, all that remained standing was a church and a sacred tree, the symbol of the Basque people.

I stared at the floor and held back tears of pity for these long-dead people. Why, I wondered, had the Spanish war assumed such a low profile in my consciousness? The themes were similar to those played out in the wider European conflict that began just a few months after its conclusion. On the face of it, Franco was no different from Hitler – a Fascist dictator. Where were the British, the French and the Americans when this was happening? I wondered. Why, if Franco was Hitler's friend, hadn't he been our enemy?

After the film we went to the bar for a drink, and Cheryl bumped into a man she introduced as 'Mike from Modern History', who had the well-groomed, coiffed look of a newsreader. He stood over us, pronouncing on the merits of the film while Cheryl and Max hung on his every word. He was evidently an expert on the war, and he was enjoying the attention.

'Although Guernica's still a symbol of the one-sidedness of the power relations,' he said, 'other atrocities were just as horrific. Lots of people were shot by firing squad and dumped into pits or shallow graves. Some people were killed by neighbours and workmates who became their enemies after the coup.'

Old scores that had rankled in towns and villages for years were settled by people who acquired power suddenly, an accident of the side they had chosen, he told us. Their enemies were shot, clubbed, butchered or thrown to their deaths from buildings and cliffs. Others were worked to death in forced labour camps, for no other reason than that they had an association with people or organisations who supported the Republic.

'Why didn't Britain and France do something to prevent a Fascist uprising on their doorstep?' Max asked.

'I suppose it was because the elected government of the Republic included Communists and Anarchists, and Britain and France feared a Bolshevik-type uprising in Spain more than a Fascist government,' Mike said. 'Of course, there were atrocities on both sides. In fact, some of the worst violence was perpetrated by the Communists on other supporters of the Republic.'

He left to rejoin his friends, and Cheryl and I sat down at a table while Max got some drinks from the bar.

'Listen, I'd really like to talk to your dad about the Civil War,' she said. 'I'm thinking of writing my honours thesis about it.'

I stifled a laugh, not because Cheryl was already thinking about the subject of her honours thesis three months into the start of her first year, but because it was the first time anyone I knew had wanted to meet my father, far less try to elicit from him anything remotely detailed about his or his country's past.

'Oh, I don't know,' I said warily. 'He's not very forthcoming about that sort of thing.'

But as I considered the idea, it didn't strike me as so preposterous after all. Why shouldn't he be prepared to be questioned about the war? He didn't need to be an intellectual – all he had to do was to talk about his life and how the war had affected him. It occurred to me that he might even be an interesting person, given where and when he grew up.

What was more, ever since Franco's death, he'd taken far more interest in Spain. He'd watched with cautious optimism as political developments unfolded – the new king determinedly sweeping away the old guard, people voting in democratic elections, power being taken away from the previously unassailable

Catholic church and the Guardia Civil, the politically-controlled police force under Franco.

He'd commented on how the pages of the glossy magazines Abuela sent us had changed. I could see what he meant. No longer were they the state-censored organs of Franco's rule. Gone were the unquestioning line-ups of senior political and military figures; in their place stood the new Establishment of celebrities, entrepreneurs and minor royalty. They were younger, better-looking, more relaxed, and they smiled.

'Oh, I'm sure I could get him talking. I'm very persuasive, you know,' Cheryl said, holding my gaze.

My stomach fluttered. 'I'll give it a try,' I said.

'When could you take me to see him?'

'Soon, maybe next week,' I said.

'Okay, let me know. And thanks for coming tonight. I hope you enjoyed it.'

She finished her drink quickly and announced that she would have to leave as she had a lecture first thing. She put her coat on, leaned down and kissed me on the cheek. I breathed in her sweet smell, and as she raised her head her soft hair brushed gently against my forehead. She beamed a smile that I knew would sustain me until our next meeting. I felt light-headed.

'Are you coming, Bobby?' she asked Max Miller.

And I was suddenly thrust back into reality.

'Yeah,' he said as he drained the remnants of his glass. He slapped me on the back. 'See you later, Antonio.'

They drifted out of the bar together, hand in hand.

13

I flew back from Spain to Scotland, feeling more positive than usual about returning to my parents' home. I was certain that the information I had would bring Papa and me closer together. But when I saw him, I felt a painful sadness. He looked different even since the last time I'd seen him, only a few weeks before. He was characteristically well dressed, in a tailored shirt, slacks and a pastel-blue cashmere pullover, but they draped loosely over his depleted frame. He was stooped and shaky, and what I might otherwise have dismissed as the inevitable blemishes of age now appeared unmistakably to be signs of terminal illness.

Mama had gone to evening Mass, leaving him to make his own dinner. He negotiated the kitchen at an infuriatingly slow pace, plucking the components of a rudimentary meal of bread, olives and Ibérico ham from worktops and cupboards, placing them carefully and deliberately on the table. I stood over him as he ate at the kitchen table.

When I told him about my conversation with the man from the Association for the Recovery of Historical Memory and his offer, he stopped chewing and slammed his glass down, spilling water across the table. 'Why you dae this?' he demanded. His voice was harsh, almost tearful.

'I thought you'd be pleased.'

'You have nae right, I nae want these people tae dae nothing.'

'That's my grandparents were talking about, and I didn't know anything about them until a few days ago,' I protested.

'You nae speak tae me like this,' he said, waving his finger.

His response surprised me, and I thought he might not have understood properly what I'd told him. 'There's nothing to worry about, Papa, these people are on your side,' I said.

'Wha people? I nae even know these people.'

'The association. They're volunteers, archaeologists, anthropologists, historians. They want to help people like you who had relatives who were killed by the Falangists.'

He looked at me sceptically and resumed eating his sandwich.

'If we give them details of your mother and father, they will trace them through official papers. There may even be a record of their death that you don't know about.'

His face grew redder and he shook his head disapprovingly.

'They would also speak to people in Alguaire.'

'Who they speak?' he demanded.

'Survivors, people who have lived in the village for a long time. People who may remember what happened and who would be able to corroborate your story.'

He exploded with anger. 'I nae want this, you nae dae this. You tell this people nae, I nae want.'

A small bit of food caught in his throat and he began to cough. I had to pat him on the back to help him recover. He was red and breathless, and I felt guilty at having unsettled him.

'Look, I was only trying to help. I thought that was what you wanted.'

'I nae want. You leave alone. If I want, I dae myself.'

I was confused and disappointed. When I thought about the lengths to which he had gone in Alguaire, I found his refusal of help perplexing.

I told him I wanted to know about his brother, Paco, who had survived the bombing of Lerida but who, Papa believed, had later died. I wanted to know the circumstances. Was he killed during the war. If so, how? Or had he survived the war and died subsequently? And if he was still alive, what did he do? Did he have any family that I didn't know about? I knew that if I didn't push Papa now, I might never know. 'If you don't start to open up to me about this sort of thing, I'll be left with no option but to find out for myself,' I said.

He looked at me disdainfully, as though I had committed an unpardonable act of disloyalty, but then he began to talk, slowly and quietly.

'We go to Barcelona, me and Paco, and everywhere is ruin,' he said. 'The shops they are empty and people they are starving. Everywhere is how you say *sacos de arena . . .*'

I looked at him blankly.

'You know, this bags tae stop the bullets.'

'Oh, sandbags.'

'*Si*, sandbags. Like big walls at the end of every street.' He sighed. 'We try find unit tae fight but we nae find nothing. Everywhere is *communistas,* Russians who nae like *anarchistas.*'

I nodded appreciatively.

'We are in café, and soldier he say "Who you fight for?" We tell him *anarchistas* in Lerida, and he pull us close.' Papa leaned closer to me. His voice dropped and his eyes widened. 'He say "You nae say this tae anyone or you shot." He say "Where your paper?" We say "In our bag." He say, "You destroy paper. If *communistas* find them, they say you are *Franquistas.*" He say, "You leave Barcelona, there is only trouble for you here," but we have naewhere tae go. We have nae food or transport and we spend months here, nae know what tae do.'

'Where did you live? Where did you sleep?' I asked.

'We sleep in shops where owner they go away and in factories that nae make nothing. In buildings that are bombed. We look for food in rubbish and in bins of restaurants. We eat what we can – the skins of onion, fishes' head, seaweed, seagulls, and we smoke shells of nuts and leaves from trees. The worst is when we sleep on ground that is frozen, because when we wake our bones is so sore we cannae move.'

I'd seen recently, on websites and in books, pictures of deserted streets, their buildings pockmarked with bulletholes and shell damage, festooned with faded posters of muscular, square-jawed workers manning barricades and bearing standards of the peoples' struggle. I'd read about the foreign volunteers from Poland, Britain, America and Canada who'd come to fight the Fascists.

'We stand in La Rambla and the Plaça de Catalunya and we meet militia. We know them because they are dressed in blue *monos*, how you say, this uniform with name of party sewed on. They tell us wha happen in war and they give us cigarettes and sometimes coffee or chocolate.

'We talk with this people and they tell us news of the *Franquistas* and when they attack but we have tae be careful because we nae know are these people, how you say . . . *informantes?*'

'Informers.'

'Si, informer who go tae the Guardia Civil or the Guardia de Asalto.'

'So when did the Francoists attack Barcelona?' I asked.

He waved his hand at me in annoyance. 'I nae know dates, you nae ask me dates,' he said angrily. 'I live this. You listen to me and I tell you wha happen. You nae ask me dates.'

'Okay, I'm sorry. Just tell me about it the way you want to.'

He sighed. 'In the buildings where we sleep there is Gypsies. They are scared because they know when the *Franquistas* come they will be shot. They start tae leave, hiding on the ships at Barcelonetta, or they try walk across Pyrenees intae France, tae Marseille where there is ships that go Mexico where *republicanos* they are welcome.'

'So what did *you* do?'

'We hear German plane overhead, same sound as in Lerida. At this time we are sleeping in cave in Parc Güell and we say, "We must go, we cannae stay any longer." Paco, he say, "I go in city and look for food tae eat on journey." He leave in evening and I wait for him in park.' His face took on a troubled, resigned expression. 'I wait for him in cave for three hours, four hours, and he nae come. I sit and sit, nae able tae sleep. When is light, still he nae come, and I say, "I must look for Paco." I leave park and go tae the Carrer de Padilla, where I see Gypsy girl who sleep in our cave. She say, "Pablo, I see your brother, he is arrest by Guardia. They ask him where he live, and he say, 'I nae tell you,' so they hit him on head with rifle, and they say, 'You tell us *hijo bastardo de puta anarquista,*' but still he say nothing and they push him in truck and drive away."'

'What happened then?'

'I say to Gypsy girl, "I go look for my brother," but she stop me, she say, "You nae go, Pablo, or you are kill." She hold me back with all strength in her small body. She say, "You come with me tae Tangier where I have cousin. He say every Spaniard in Morocco is stranger and is easy tae hide." I never see Paco again.'

'But how do you know he's dead?' I asked.

'I know.'

'But he may have survived, Papa. You can't know for sure that he was killed.'

'He is dead, this I know,' he said emphatically.

The next morning I rose early to fly back to London. Mama had already left the house to attend morning Mass. I said I'd take a taxi to the airport, but Papa insisted he would drive me. He finished his breakfast, put on his sheepskin coat and led the way out into the cold morning, where the frozen wind stung my ears.

He opened the passenger door first and I climbed in. Then he reached past me and fished about in the glove compartment, retrieving the same small block of wood, planed to an acute angle and lacquered, that he'd used as a windscreen scraper since I was a child. It was one of a dozen relics, everyday items practical from which Papa continued to wring every last penny's-worth of value. On the driver's side of the window he proceeded to scrape a small patch of visibility in the layer of frost that covered the windscreen.

When he was finished, he lowered himself into the driver's seat alongside me. There was the sound of cracking bones and laboured wheezing. His breath clouded what little visibility he'd managed to create. He rubbed the inside of the windscreen with the back of his hand, but as soon as he'd cleared it it misted over again.

He put the key in the ignition and turned it. The engine jolted and coughed like a consumptive patient, but failed to spark into life. He tried again and again, but the engine wouldn't start. Stubbornly, Papa continued to turn the key until the battery was drained of power. Each cycle of the starter motor turned slower and with less conviction until it stuttered to a faltering halt. It reminded me of being a child, when the dark, freezing winter months were made longer and less hospitable by the grinding unreliability of Papa's car – I had grown up thinking that all cars failed to start nine times out of ten.

I took out my mobile phone and rang directory inquiries to ask for the number of a local mini-cab firm. He reached over and grabbed the phone from my hand.

'You nae take taxi, I have spare battery.'

'Look, this is ridiculous, Papa,' I said, but he was already out of the car and hobbling down the garden path.

To Papa, taxis were an outlandish indulgence beyond the means of people like us. We had no business pampering ourselves with such needless extravagance, hiring the labour of others to provide goods and services we could provide for ourselves. With the conspicuous exception of his clothes, he was of the belief that spending money on anything that could be home-made, self-provided or improvised was a waste. He never employed a professional if there was the remotest chance he could do the job himself. He never bought a stick of furniture, an appliance or a replacement fitting if he could mend the old one. Throughout my childhood we lived with a cracked toilet bowl, periodically patched up with duct tape and grout. Every room was painted with a covering of lime undercoat – large, standard-issue tins of which he'd liberated from the facilities room at the airport. When Mama ran out of cupboard space in the kitchen and requested a wall rack to hang her saucepans, he improvised with an uneven row of six-inch nails. At varying times, dining chairs doubled as deckchairs and deckchairs doubled as easy chairs; and redundant bed linen doubled as towels. When the element of our antediluvian boiler finally gave up the ghost, Papa refused to accept the problem was electrical, and we went without a bath for six weeks while he indulged an irrational conviction that our hot water was being stolen by the neighbours.

When I was younger, Papa's prudence had been a habit dictated by necessity, a fact I understood and tolerated. Circumstances were different now, but his attitude towards money had become so entrenched it was impossible to break. And still, I couldn't help thinking there was more to his attitude than frugality borne out of poverty. There was obstinacy in his refusal to accept that I'd grown up, that our relative circumstances had changed, that his role in our relationship had become equal and sometimes subordinate. He never asked me how much money I earned, but he knew it was enough to afford a taxi. He knew how much more comfortable his life and Mama's could be if he were to accept, even occasionally, my offers of financial help, but he never did.

He disappeared into the house and emerged a few moments later, bent double and gripping an oil-stained car battery. He edged his way along the garden path an inch at a time, the battery hanging tentatively between the tips of his brittle, twig-like fingers. I jumped out of the car to help him.

'Let me carry that, Papa,' I said, hastening towards him.

He brushed past me, his face scarlet and puffed. 'I dae, I dae,' he panted.

When he reached the car he let go of the battery, which dropped to the pavement with a dull thud, and he opened the driver's door to pull the seat forward. I'd forgotten that the battery was housed under the rear passenger seat, rather than next to the engine. He took a screwdriver and a single, tarnished spanner from the pocket of his coat and slowly bent forward to manoeuvre himself into the rear of the car, groaning with the effort. I stepped forward to help but he pushed me away. Despite his slight build and lack of power, his gentle shove was enough to wrong-foot me on the slippery surface, and I had to grab on to the roof of the car to stop myself falling over.

'Wha you dae?' he snapped when he saw me stumble.

'Let me do it,' I said. 'You're not fit enough to clamber about in the back of the car on a day like this.'

'Who isnae fit?' he demanded angrily.

He crouched in the gap between the driver's door and the back seat, breathing heavily as he attempted to fit the head of the spanner around one of the terminal bolts. As he crawled further inside, the tail of his sheepskin coat rode up his back, and, in this awkward, undignified position his frail, skinny frame was plainly visible. His entire weight was resting on his fragile, angular knees, which rocked uncertainly on the running-board, and he squirmed in discomfort. His thighs and buttocks were emaciated, the sharp points of his pelvis jutting beneath the folds of his expensive trousers.

After several minutes of shuffling and snorting, he managed to loosen the connecting wire around one of the terminals. He allowed himself a moment's rest to mark this minor triumph and then moved on to the next terminal. This proved more stubborn, as acid had leaked on to the surface of the battery, creating a white crust around the terminal head, and he didn't have the strength or purchase to loosen it. Whenever he applied any pressure, the spanner snapped loose. The more it happened, the more frustrated he became, and my offers of help only made him more irritated.

After several more failed attempts he relented partially, agreeing only to allow me to attempt to loosen the nut. I crawled into the tight space and manoeuvred myself over the battery. I was expecting a struggle, but after no more than a reasonably stiff turn of the spanner, the bolt loosened. He insisted on finishing the job himself, and we swapped places again so that he could prise the battery from its casing. Reversing out of the tight space, he manoeuvred an inch at a time, dragging the heavy block with him along the floor of the car until it was resting, precariously, on the running-board. I stepped forward and offered to take over, but as before he brushed me aside.

With the smooth soles of his shoes now resting on the uncertainty of the icy pavement, he stood up slowly and relaxed his weight against the side of the car. His body trembled as clouds of white, frosty breath escaped from his mouth and nostrils, hanging above his head. Small beads of sweat gathered along his hairline and trembled, threatening to launch themselves down his forehead.

After a few moments he took a deep breath and bent over to lift the battery, his red fingers clutching the oily, plastic surface uncertainly. As he tried to straighten up, the weight of the battery visibly pulled down on the base of his spine, and there was a dull snap, like a bar of chocolate being broken. Papa let out a deep groan and the battery slipped from his grasp. Instinctively I launched myself forward to catch it, but I was too far away.

There was an anguished yell as the battery landed square across the toes of Papa's right foot. His eyes creased and filled with tears as his face contorted into an ugly grimace. He hobbled on the frozen pavement and reached down to clutch his foot, and as he did so his back snapped again.

Everything happened in surreal slow-motion. I tried to grab him, but even as I was edging towards him I knew I'd be too late. The smooth leather soles of his handmade Italian shoes glided across the icy surface beneath him, propelling his body into mid-air. For a moment he seemed to be suspended, motionless, before he collapsed with thudding brutality.

His head smashed on the concrete surface and bounced, then landed again almost as hard. A small pool of blood appeared around the circumference of his head like a halo. For a couple of seconds serene silence descended, and I thought he was dead, I really did, but then he groaned and sat bolt upright, trying to wrest himself from the cold surface. I caught him before he was able to put any weight on his legs and held him down.

'Don't get up, Papa, you've had a shock.'

He ignored me and tried to force himself up, but I pulled him back and placed my hand at the back of his head.

'Papa, stay down for a moment!' I shouted. 'You've hit your

head, it's bleeding. If you try to stand up too quickly you'll fall over again.'

He looked at me, dazed and angry, and tried to speak, but he was too disorientated. Tears trickled down his rough cheeks and mixed with his blood. He turned away from me and buried his head in his hands. Then his resistance weakened, and his body went limp.

I carried him into the house and placed him on the sofa, where he sat hunched and small. The cut was not as deep as I'd feared. The bleeding had stemmed itself, but his scalp was grazed and his face was already starting to swell around his eyes. I was afraid he might have damaged his skull, and I gently tried to suggest taking him to hospital.

'I nae see doctor. I okay,' he said huffily, like a child refusing to eat.

I found some disinfectant and cotton wool in the bathroom and tried to dab his head, but he brushed me aside. Part of me couldn't help thinking he wanted to leave the wound open and bloody, in full view, as a *coup de théâtre* for Mama's arrival. Instead, he demanded that I hand him the telephone so he could call my brother.

'If you don't think you're injured badly enough to see a doctor, why do you need to bother Pablito?' I asked.

His eyes flitted evasively. 'You give me phone,' he demanded.

He grabbed the receiver and held it in his shaking hand, then he dialled uncertainly. After a couple of rings Pablito answered, and they proceeded to hold an animated conversation in Spanish, Papa breathlessly recounting what had happened. I knew it would be no objective depiction; rather he was building a case, putting forward his partisan interpretation of developments, with blame being unambiguously assigned.

'Let me speak to him,' I demanded, but Papa ignored me. After a few minutes' more talking to Pablito, he hung up.

I looked at my watch. My flight was due to leave in thirty minutes. It would have to go without me. There was another flight at midday which would still get me into City Airport at lunchtime. I rang Kevin and told him I'd be in the office by the early afternoon.

I made Papa a cup of sweet tea and he began to calm down a little. His hands stopped shaking quite so violently, and his voice lost its tremor. I put my hand on his shoulder and gave it a gentle squeeze. He looked up at me and managed a brief, flickering smile.

When he heard the sound of Mama's key in the door he appeared to suffer a sudden relapse. He placed his cup on the floor, to allow himself to tremble without the inconvenience of drenching himself with tea, and began to wail with melodramatic élan. Mama stood before him and threw her hand over her mouth.

'¿Díos mío, que pasa?' she demanded. 'Oh my God, what's happened?'

I tried to explain, but before I could utter a syllable Papa had leapt in to offer his take on events. It was the same diatribe he had proffered to Pablito, I suspected, but its tone was more intense, its delivery more compelling. Mama remained silent and attentive, save for the occasional glance of rebuke in my direction.

'He's fine,' I said several times, to no response.

Eventually, after another few rounds of Papa's breathless testimony, she broke in. 'Could you not at least have done something about his injury?' she asked.

'I tried, he wouldn't let me near him.'

Mama spun on her heel and marched from the room, removing her coat and throwing it on to the sofa. 'iMadre mía, yo no puedo salir la casa por diez minutos!' she exclaimed angrily. 'Mother of God, I can't leave the house for ten minutes!'

I heard her march up the stairs and rummage about in the medicine cabinet in the bathroom. '¿Dónde está el desinfectante?' she asked herself loudly.

I stood at the foot of the stairway, holding the items I knew she was looking for.

'The disinfectant is down here, Mama, along with the cotton wool.'

She came marching back down the stairs and grabbed them from me.

'What the hell did you think you were doing?' she asked in an angry stage whisper.

'That's what I was trying to tell you. I was trying to clean his head, but he wouldn't let me.'

'I don't mean after the fall – I mean before. You know how ill he is. What are you doing letting him change a car battery in this weather?'

'I didn't have a choice,' I protested. 'He insisted on doing it himself.'

'Why didn't you stop him? Why didn't you take hold of the battery and do it yourself?'

I stood facing her, my mind a blank. It was a reasonable question to which I didn't have an answer, or at least an answer that didn't make me sound as though I was an errant five-year-old.

'Or better still, why didn't you get a taxi?'

'He wouldn't let me.'

Her shoulders dropped and she looked at me in disbelief.

'He's eighty-three years old, Antonio.'

'I know, but he's my father.'

14

It was five years since Franco had died, and Papa was suffi-
ciently confident of the flourishing of democracy in Spain
– or at least of its failure to revert to dictatorship – that he and
Mama were talking openly about the possibility of returning
there. Every public utterance by King Juan Carlos, every magazine article charting the modernity of the new Spain, every trib-
ute from returning holidaymakers contributed to his growing
belief that things had changed, genuinely and irrevocably, for
the better.

Mama saw this as an opportunity to complete the circle of
their lives. Circumstance had forced them to move from Spain
to Morocco to Scotland, and now they had the chance to return,
to live out the remainder of their days close to her family and in
familiar surroundings.

Things came to a head shortly into my second term at university, when we received news from Tia Teresa, Mama's sister in
Malaga, that Abuela's health was failing. Now in her late eighties, she had suffered a stroke, and the prognosis was poor. Mama
wanted to be with her mother for the last months of her life. She
discussed the matter with Papa, and it was decided. One evening
they told us that they were leaving to start a new life in the old
country.

Papa asked me if I wanted to go with them, though there
was little conviction in his request, and he agreed it was sensi-
ble for me to stay in Scotland to complete my degree. I had
no inclination to follow them, and there was the dividend
of being able to move out of the family home and into university halls of residence, where I felt I'd have the freedom to grow

and to become myself. It was Papa who'd insisted I continue to live at home after I left school because that's how they did it in Spain, but I was in the minority among my friends, most of whom lived in the halls of residence or in digs.

Pablito had just started a new job, and he was planning to get married to Linda, his fiancée, whom he'd met at a late-night bus stop and whom he'd subsequently got pregnant – on the top deck of the bus, he'd confided to me. So he too would be staying in Scotland, though he went through the motions of suggesting he might join Mama and Papa in Spain at a later date.

Although Mama and Papa had talked in abstract terms about the possibility of returning to Spain for so long, now that it was actually happening it seemed unreal. Although I didn't want to move with them, I certainly didn't want them to go – not yet, at least. I was afraid I'd miss them, that I'd feel insecure without the anchor of my family. But there was something more elemental: I didn't speak Spanish, I knew little about the country, its culture or its history – all I really had was my Spanish parents and my name. And now, surprisingly and against all my expectations, I found that I wanted to feel Spanish. For the first time in my life my Spanishness had become an asset, a source of fascination to an attractive and desirable woman. Mama and Papa's intended departure could not have been less timely.

I had yet to raise with Papa Cheryl's request to meet him so that she could question him about the war. Introducing him to a friend, particularly a female friend, was fraught with danger. There was of course the very real prospect of him mortally embarrassing me with his imperfect English, his eccentricities, his chauvinism or his short temper. But there was something more potent, which, I'd come to suspect, was among the issues at the centre of my troubled relationship with my father: a conviction that, with his uncompromising maleness, his confident masculine deportment, any girl I brought home would find him more attractive than me. I'd seen it often enough with Pablito's girlfriends, who would enter the house smiling coyly, gripping Pablito's hand tightly, seeking reassurance. Yet within the flutter of an eyelash after meeting Papa, they'd move further from Pablito and edge ever closer to Papa, seduced by his charm.

I'd have to put my reservations aside, though. Now, with their intention to return to Spain confirmed, time was against me. Because of Abuela's illness there could be no delay, no long-term planning, and they planned to leave within a few weeks. I had been prepared to be patient in winning Cheryl over. I had known it would take time, planning, discretion, changing perceptions and orthodoxies and not a little deviousness, but it was a campaign I was willing to embark upon and to see through to the end. However, my plan hinged on Cheryl meeting Papa. I had to act quickly. And though I was still unsure of the wisdom of exposing one of my friends to Papa, especially one whom I held in such high regard, I felt as though I had little choice. My love life depended on it.

I planned in meticulous detail when to make the breezy, impromptu suggestion to Cheryl that she come round for dinner. I'd decided that it would be best to catch her before the start of our lecture on Monday morning, yet when the moment came I began jabbering.

'You know how we were talking about the Spanish Civil War and all that and how you were dead interested in it and all that?' I began.

'What?' asked Cheryl distractedly as she leaned against a wall, engrossed in a copy of *Marxism Today*.

'I was just saying that you know how you're into the Civil War and all that and how my old man fought in it . . . well I'm pretty sure he fought in it, although he's never said as much . . . but you know how you were talking about it and you were saying that . . .'

She looked up from her magazine and stared at me.

'Well, you know how you were saying you'd be interested in talking to my old man? Christ, why anyone would want to talk to him I don't know, but anyway, you know how you were saying . . .'

She sighed deeply and failed to stop her eyes rolling backwards.

'Anyway, just say if you think it's a non-starter, 'cause Christ, sitting in a room for any length of time with my old man is enough to make anyone lose the will to live, but I'll say one thing about my ma, she's a good cook, if you like that sort of thing that is, and it's not everyone's cup of tea but . . .'

'Antonio.'

'But she makes lots of typical Spanish dishes, and to be honest I'm not a huge fan of Spanish food, but I'll say one thing . . .'

'*Antonio*,' she said, loud enough to turn the heads of several of the students standing around us. 'I'd love to come.'

That night I told Mama and Papa about the visit. I'd thought carefully about whether I should tell them that Cheryl was fascinated by the Civil War and that she wanted to interrogate Papa about his anarchist past, but I decided against it, reasoning that if he were to object now, he might veto the whole enterprise. If it were sprung on him as a surprise, he'd be forced to co-operate. It was a risky strategy, but better than having to cancel on Cheryl.

He beamed with delight at the news that I was bringing a girl back to the house for the first time. 'This is good,' he said slapping me heartily on the back. 'You should dae this more. You ashame a your family or something?'

'No, of course not.'

Mama was excited too, and she promised to cook a special Spanish meal to impress her, oxtail with prunes – a speciality from her native Andalusia. She also agreed to banish Pablito from the house for the evening. Things were coming together nicely, and I was confident I might actually be able to carry this off without any disasters.

During the bus journey to my parents' house I tried to warn Cheryl about Papa, but I found it difficult to put what I felt into words – that was the problem with him: meeting him a hundred times would still fail to provide a full picture of what he was really like. You had to live with him to learn that.

'Don't be so anxious. I'm sure he'll be enchanting,' she said, squeezing my hand.

As I opened the front door to the house, there was an unnerving quietness and none of the warm, inviting cooking smells I'd expected. We took off our coats in the darkened hallway, and I led Cheryl into the living-room. Papa was in his usual seat, still dressed in his airport overalls, rocking gently on his seat, sucking determinedly on a cigarette. He didn't look up. Mama and Pablito were on the sofa, both white, and Mama appeared close to tears.

'What's wrong?' I asked.

No one answered.

'What's happened? Has Abuela died?'

Papa looked at his wrist, but his watch, which he never wore to work in case it was damaged by a suitcase, was missing. '*¿Qué hora?*' he demanded anxiously. 'What is the time?'

No one responded.

'*¿A qué hora son las noticias en la televisión?*' 'When is the news on television?'

'*En otros quince minutos,*' Mama said quietly. 'In another fifteen minutes.'

We continued to stand uncertainly in the doorway.

'What's happened?' I repeated.

Mama stood up and ushered us into the room.

'Come in and sit down. You must be Cheryl,' she said, forcing a smile. 'I'm sorry, we're not organised, you must forgive us. Something has happened in Spain that we are worried about.'

'Maybe I should go – I don't want to intrude,' Cheryl whispered in my ear.

'What's happened, Mama?'

'We don't know yet for sure. We're waiting to hear the news, it's something political.'

We sat in silence for a few minutes, then Mama asked Cheryl if she would like a cup of tea. Cheryl said she would make it and asked me to show her where all the things were kept. I followed her into the kitchen and watched her fill the teapot and put some biscuits on a plate, warmed by the sense of intimacy such a prosaic function created between us.

We returned to the living-room just as the six o'clock news was starting. The programme opened with some unannounced footage, the way they do when there's a big, important item, pictures telling the story because they have more impact than words.

The film was grainy and unfocused. A speaker was address-ing a meeting inside a grand, formal building that looked like a conference hall or a political chamber. Then suddenly he was interrupted by a group of soldiers carrying machine-guns who entered from a side door. One of the soldiers strutted purpose-fully into the centre of the hall and began to shout excitedly in Spanish.

It was a moment of compelling theatre. The man was short and absurd, a touch effeminate and grossly self-important. He had a large moustache, and he wore a stiff black hat that resembled the shape of an upturned boat. He was like a parody of a baddie from a children's film. Suddenly and without warning he raised a pistol above his head and fired several shots. Papa twitched violently and Mama threw her hands in front of her mouth.

'¡Dios mío!,' she gasped.

Inside the chamber there was a series of loud thuds as bodies hit the floor and chunks of masonary fell from the ceiling on to the wooden pews below, and there were screams of anguish and panicked instructions. The camera jerked violently and its focus was trained suddenly away from the action towards the ceiling, then down to the floor, before it fizzed and went blank.

The sudden, contrasting image of a composed, smartly suited BBC newsreader sitting in a London studio was unnerv-ing. He announced in measured, neutral tones that a group of civil guards, led by a lieutenant-colonel in the Spanish army, had attempted a coup d'état earlier in the day. They had entered the Cortes, the Spanish parliament in Madrid, and fired several shots, before ordering King Juan Carlos, the head of state, to make a statement.

The coup appeared to have been originated by former supporters of Franco in Valencia, where tanks had been ordered on to the streets and a state of emergency had been declared. The joint chiefs of staff had issued a communiqué declaring that all measures had been taken to put down the rebellion and to restore order.

'*Supe que esto sucedería. No es seguro. Nunca será seguro en España, a pesar de que los políticos digan,*' Papa said angrily. 'I knew this would happen. It's not safe. Spain will never be safe, despite what the politicians say.'

'Be quiet, Pablo,' Mama ordered. 'I want to hear what is happening.'

Before I'd met Cheryl, the symbolism of what was happening might have been lost on me, but I knew enough about Spain's past now to realise the events were shockingly similar to those that had foreshadowed the outbreak of the Civil War. At that time Franco, then an army general based in the Canary Islands, had flown to Spanish-occupied Morocco, from where he led a military uprising that was the prelude to three years of fighting and bloodshed, culminating in four decades of unbroken fascist rule. I began to appreciate why Papa should be agitated.

'*Llame a su hermana,*' he ordered Mama. 'Phone your sister.'

This confirmed the gravity of the situation. Papa never encouraged Mama to make expensive international calls. Mama pointed at the television set, indicating that she was still watching.

'*Llame a su hermana,*' he repeated.

She dialled, and Teresa answered immediately, launching unsolicited into an account of the day's events. From the other side of the room we could hear her tinny, animated voice through the receiver. Mama remained calm, repeatedly saying '*Claro.*' After a few minutes, Papa demanded to speak to Teresa.

He held the handset tight against his ear, constantly interrupting Teresa, who in turn shouted louder to be heard over him. Eventually he remembered the cost of the call, bade her goodbye and hung up.

The room descended into a melee of claim and counter-claim, point and rebuttal, all conducted in high-decibel Spanish. Not since the day Franco had died had I felt such an outsider in my home. Even Cheryl, though by no means fluent, had more of a command of the language than I had, and I was forced to suffer the ignominy of relying on her to keep me abreast of what was being said.

According to Teresa, the streets of the capital had been mobbed with people panic-buying food, and already the shelves of several shops had been emptied. The rebels had taken over local radio and television stations, and while there was no sign of any military presence on the streets where she lived, that wasn't necessarily the case in the rest of the country.

The BBC newsreader said the next twenty-four hours would be crucial in determining whether the coup had genuine support or if it was a stunt by a handful of extremists. The king was due to speak on Spanish television soon, and all we could do was to wait for the next main news bulletin at nine o'clock to hear what he had to say.

I apologised to Cheryl and asked her if she'd rather postpone her visit until another night, but she said she would like to stay. She was clearly intrigued by what was going on, and seemed to appreciate that she was witnessing such an event in the presence of authentic emotion.

Mama prepared a tortilla, which she laid out on the table with some lettuce leaves, sardines and bread spread with tomato paste and olive oil. We all tucked in – I'd eaten nothing all day in nervous anticipation of this evening, and I was ravenous – but Papa remained in his seat, chain-smoking, staring intently ahead. The room descended into silence, broken only by the sound of chewing and forks clinking on plates.

'Tha's it, we nae go back tae Spain now,' Papa said.

Mama sighed. 'Let's wait to see what happens, Pablo, we don't need to make any immediate judgements.'

'I nae wait, I know wha happen.'

'That general looked like a nutcase to me, Papa,' Pablito said. 'I don't think anyone's going to take him seriously.'

'This is wha they say about Franco.'

Hush descended again, but it was broken by Cheryl. 'If there was a civil war, I'd volunteer to go and fight,' she said confidently.

I cringed. Despite what I guessed were her best intentions, the statement sounded naïve and inappropriate. Papa turned and stared at me, but I avoided his gaze and continued to eat, hoping that her comment would go unacknowledged.

'Lots of people from this country joined the International Brigades that fought in the last civil war,' she continued. 'It was the last conflict where it was a straight fight between idealism and tyranny. My generation hasn't had that opportunity. If this develops into a conflict, I would have no hesitation in fighting against fascism.'

Papa eyed her incredulously. He had a familiar glint in his eye that signalled he was ready for a fight. 'Wha you talk about?' he demanded aggressively.

She tried to respond but he cut her dead.

'You nae know wha you talk, woman.'

Cheryl bristled. 'I don't see what me being a woman has got to do with anything,' she said defensively.

Papa's eyes widened, and his body seemed to contract as though he were a cat sizing up its prey. I tried to intervene. 'The point she's making, Papa, is . . .'

'You know nothing about war. You nae talk about wha you nae understand.'

I felt events slipping out of control. I couldn't trust Papa to bring the exchange to an end without causing further offence. 'All she's saying, Papa, is that . . .'

'I know wha she say, and she talk rubbish. What she know about fight?'

'I just think it's important to fight for what you believe in and not run away from it,' Cheryl said, probably more pompously than she'd intended.

There was silence, like the moment of absolute serenity before a bomb explodes.

'Who run away?' Papa asked menacingly.

Cheryl's face turned scarlet and her voice faltered. 'I'm not saying anyone's . . .'

'You say I run away? Who tell you I run away?'

'I'm not saying anyone has run away, Mr Noguera, I was just making the point . . .'

'You nae make point. You nae come in my house and talk about what you know nothing. You grow up in country with money in nice house with food and plenty of clothes. You nae know wha I do.'

'Look, I'm sorry, I didn't mean to . . .'

'You know wha age I leave school?'

Cheryl breathed deeply as though to compose herself, but her hands were shaking. She shook her head.

'Twelve. I leave school when I twelve and by thirteen I fight in war. So you nae tell me I run away. You shut your stupid mouth.'

'Pablo, that's enough!' Mama shouted.

'I'm sorry. Again,' I said as we stood at the bus stop.

'It's all right, honestly. I shouldn't have said what I did,' she mouthed, almost in a whisper, tears running down her cheek.

'But he had no right to speak to you like that.'

'I didn't mean to offend him. It just came out wrong. I wasn't passing judgement on him. He took it the wrong way.'

I wondered if she was right. She was eighteen years old, and even then I recognised it was her prerogative to be direct and guileless. Papa had suffered in his youth, but I didn't see why those closest to him had to suffer too as a result. He'd misrepresented what Cheryl had said – wilfully, I strongly suspected – and I was too mortified to admit that such episodes were common.

'He still had no right. He may have endured terrible times, but it was seventy years ago. I don't see why he still acts like his life's in danger.'

'Francoist killings and revenge attacks went on long after the war ended. It was Franco's intention to eliminate all opposition. So I understand your father's fear and anger, I really do.'

I braced myself against the driving wind and rain, and Cheryl stood close to me with her chin tucked into her chest, squeezing my hand tightly. The lights of the bus appeared on the crest of the hill in the distance.

'Why don't you come back to my flat? I don't want to be alone tonight.'

She raised her head slightly, and despite the darkness I could see her blushing.

'What about Max Miller?' I asked.

'Don't worry about Bobby,' she said, smiling.

I was woken the following morning by shards of winter sunlight streaming through the curtains. Cheryl's golden hair was fanned across my chest. I felt rested and more confident, clever and attractive than I could remember. I leaned over her and switched on the radio on the bedside table. The morning news was all about Spain, where the rebellion appeared to be petering out. The king had made a television address, offering his reassurance that all necessary measures would be taken to defeat the rebels.

It was half-past eight and my first lecture was due to start in thirty minutes. 'Cheryl,' I whispered, gently shaking her awake.

She opened her eyes and smiled.

'There's something I've been wondering,' I said.

She nodded her permission for me to ask.

'Why do they call you Dolores? Max and all those guys in the SWS.'

'It's a nickname, after Dolores Ibárruri, La Pasionaria.'

153

'Who?'

'She was the leader of the Spanish Communist party. She coined the phrase *"¡No pasarán!"*, they shall not pass – meaning the Fascist rebels.'

'And is that what you believe?'

'Well, I didn't let you pass by, did I?' she said, and kissed me on the lips.

15

'How are you, Kevin?' I asked, breaking the silence of the early-morning newsroom.

I beamed what I thought was an authentic, endearing smile. Several of those dotted around the office raised their heads slightly above their computer screens and lowered them just as quickly. Kevin, who was speedily going through the daily newspapers, looked up and frowned.

'Sorry?' he asked as though it was an accusation.

'How are you?'

He thought for a moment. 'I'm fine,' he replied before returning to the papers.

There was a photo on his desk that I hadn't seen before. The picture featured three people – a woman and two children – sitting astride expensive mountain bikes in a sunny Alpine location. I looked closer. The figures were surprisingly attractive, beautiful even – all flashing, white teeth, healthy golden complexions and freshly-laundered primary colours.

'That's never your wife?' I blurted out. 'I mean, is that your wife?'

'Yes, that is my wife. And my two daughters, aged ten and twelve.'

'She's gorgeous,' I said. 'I mean, she's very nice.'

The others in the room shuffled uncomfortably and returned to their screens.

'Thank you very much,' Kevin said uncertainly.

I looked at the picture again. His wife really was very attractive, sexy in fact – ludicrously so, considering whom she was married to. She had blonde hair that kinked over her forehead, framing a face dominated by pouting lips and demure film-star eyes. She was wearing a yellow cotton dress with a bodice that only just managed to cup a pair of stunningly fulsome breasts. She looked like a model, a trophy wife, if that was possible with Kevin. I consoled myself with the thought that she must be lacking in personality and intellect. He'd been lucky enough to bag a beautiful wife. A beautiful, intelligent wife was beyond him. The odds against it were too high.

'What does she do for a living?' I asked, smiling.

'She's a psychiatrist,' Kevin replied.

After work I wandered distractedly along the rough-hewn back streets, past the pawn shops, ethnic cafes and cheap rents, in the direction of the tube station. London to me was increasingly a city of the past rather than the future, of cracked paving slabs and pot-holes, streets unplanned and unfinished, buildings plotted randomly like gap-toothed smiles, with poorly maintained exteriors defaced by unintelligible graffiti and the long, iron-streaked scars of leaking pipes.

It was late afternoon and the sun was setting but still bright, its rays fleeting and unreliable respite from the biting chill. I'd left home without a coat, and all I had to keep out the cold was my suit jacket. I pulled up the collar tightly around my neck and dug my hands deep into my trouser pockets. A thin, crisp layer of silver ice coated the pavements, giving them a veneer of respectability they didn't deserve.

I arrived home to find the house in disarray. I'd been away for less than a week, and in that time Ben had turned the house into a slum. Magazines, food wrappers and empty cigarette packets littered the surfaces and various items of clothing lay discarded where they'd been shed. The kitchen had a warm stench of decay, and the worktops were strewn with discarded carrier bags and polystyrene containers. On the floor lay fragments of discarded toast and a chunk of orange Cheddar, shrunk and cracked like a dry river bed.

'Oh Christ,' I thought. 'Is this my future?'

Ben appeared, yawning, in the doorway. He was wearing a pair of crumpled boxer shorts and a t-shirt that said 'PISS OFF' in bold lettering.

'What the hell's going on?' I demanded.

He sauntered lazily into the kitchen. 'What do you mean?'

'I mean why are you living like this? You told me you were old and responsible enough to look after yourself. So why is the place falling apart?'

He plucked a bowl from the cluttered sink and rinsed it under the cold tap before emptying the remnants of a box of breakfast cereal into it. A few flakes dropped out, along with a mound of what looked like sawdust. He retrieved a milk bottle from the fridge and sniffed its contents before splashing some on to the cereal and sat down at the kitchen table, clearing a space for the bowl.

'It's not falling apart, I just haven't got round to cleaning the place, that's all.'

'Ben, it's six o'clock in the evening and you're eating breakfast.'

'Give me a break, Dad,' he said defensively. 'I haven't got my shit together yet.'

'Why weren't you at school?'

'I've left school, I'm at college.'

'Don't be a smartarse. Why weren't you at college?'

'I'm studying for my mocks. Natalie and me were up until four this morning revising.'

The events of recent weeks crystallised suddenly into a coherent, elegant thesis – Ben and Cheryl were in this together, and I was the victim.

'Take a look at yourself, Ben, you're a mess. You've got no drive or self-discipline. You're living in a shithole and you don't seem to be bothered. What kind of way is this to live?'

He snorted derisively. 'What do you care?'

'That's not fair, Ben, I work hard to keep this family –'

'I haven't seen you for weeks. Where have you been?' he said loudly.

'I've been in Spain. I had important things to sort out . . .' I began, immediately recognising the ludicrousness of what I was saying.

'Spain? Important? What's more important than being here with your family?'

I didn't have the strength to argue. I shook my head and left, walking slowly upstairs before collapsing on to the bed. I closed my eyes and tried to recall the last time Cheryl and I had had sex. It could have been six months ago, or it could have been a year – or more. I found myself envying Kevin, actually desiring that I could swap places with him, however fleetingly, to occupy his holiday snaps, with his shiny children and his busty, luscious wife.

My mobile phone rang and Cheryl's number flashed up. 'Hi, it's me, how are you?' she asked.

My heart raced and my mouth dried up instantly. I hadn't imagined that hearing from her would make me feel so anxious. 'Fine. And you?'

'Ben told me about Papa. I'm sorry.'

'Yeah, well, what can you do?'

'How is he? I mean, how's he coping?'

Why should it be that she could walk out on me and devastate my life, and then decide to be magnanimous when it suited her? She wasn't expressing concern about my feelings or even those of my father – this was about servicing her conscience.

'I'm busy, Cheryl, what do you want?'

She paused. 'Umm . . . I want to know how your father is.'

'He's ill. He's dying. Now, is there anything else?'

'I'm concerned about your dad, Antonio. There's no need to be hostile.'

She was right, and I felt embarrassed. 'I know you are. Sorry, I'm tired. So where are you staying?'

'I'm staying with a friend, just until I get myself sorted out,' she replied, a little too fluently for my liking.

'Anyone I know?'

She paused. 'No, no one you know, just a friend.'

I wondered whether to say what I was sure she already knew, that I'd been to Max Miller's flat. 'Is it someone from work, perhaps?' I asked.

She paused again, this time a little longer. 'Look, I don't want you to come looking for me, Antonio. I just need some time to think things through, to sort myself out, and then we can meet to discuss where we take things.'

'I know all that. I just wondered who you were staying with.' I was quite pleased with the reasonableness of my tone.

'I told you, I'm staying with a friend and it's no one you know.'

'Is it a male friend or a female friend?'

'What are you getting at, Antonio? There's no one else, if that's what you're suggesting.'

'Are you sure about that?'

'Of course I'm sure,' she said emphatically. 'Look, I'm not going to continue this conservation because I don't think it's getting us anywhere. I'll give you a call when I'm ready to talk.'

She hung up. I hated being cut off like that, but I was glad I'd asked the question because it had stopped my mind whirring. Now I was convinced she was lying.

16

'Y ou are terrible, but I like you.'

'I'm sorry?'

'You are terrible, but I like you,' Uli repeated in a monotone.

A cold silence ensued, the soundproofed windows sealing us from the bustling Berlin traffic eighteen storeys below.

'Hello, honky tonks, how are you?' he said in the same unsmiling tone.

'Ah,' I said, the penny finally dropping. 'Dick Emery. No, it's awful.'

'You think so?' he asked, looking slightly hurt.

'No, I mean it's "You are *awful*, but I like you", not "You are terrible".'

'Ah yes, you are awful but I like you. I am also finding great humour in the mother-in-law jokes of your Jimmy Tarbuck,' he said enthusiastically. 'A man, he walks into his house and says to his wife, "Pack your bags, I won the football pools" . . .'

By a stroke of luck my mobile phone rang at that point, and I pulled it quickly from my pocket. I told Uli I was expecting an update on my father, who was ill, and hurriedly left his office.

The call was from Fermin at the library in Lerida, who told me he was sorry to say he had bad news. He said he'd looked into my grandparents' alleged murder but could find no evidence to support my father's story. There was, he said, a Nationalist advance on Alguaire early in 1938, but there was no record of villagers being shot or of their bodies being dumped in a field.

'The problem is that there are very few people still alive who might remember such an event,' he said.

I felt more demoralised than I could have imagined just a few weeks before. Papa had been so certain of his facts that he'd been able to identify the general area of the grave in the olive field.

'We could commission a thermal imaging test, but it is an expensive business for an organisation such as ours, and we would not do so unless there was convincing supporting evidence.'

'I see.'

Fermin could hear the disappointment in my voice and he tried to remain positive, insisting this was not necessarily the end of the matter.

'Could you ask your father if there is any other information he could provide us about the event? Even small details that do not appear relevant to him may still be useful in helping to build a picture we can attempt to corroborate further.'

'I'll try,' I said.

'Are you sure there are no other existing members of your family who might be able to provide additional information? Often it helps to have an alternative perspective, because people's memories are not always reliable, no matter how sure they think they are.'

'No, my father is the only surviving member of his family,' I insisted.

'That's very unusual. He has no siblings, no aunts or uncles or cousins?'

'Not that I am aware of.'

'You should ask him if it is possible that some members of his family, no matter how distant, may have survived. If he thinks it is possible, we could use our website to post an appeal for them to get in touch. A lot of families have been reunited in this way.'

I'd hoped to be able to give Papa news of a positive development. I felt sure that, despite his protestations, he'd welcome my involvement if it led to some kind of resolution. This was a setback, and it made me realise it wasn't going to be as straightforward as I'd hoped.

I hung up and steeled myself to return to Uli's office. I still found it slightly surreal that I was here at all. I'd been on a train travelling to Blackpool for the start of the third party conference of the season, having missed the first two, when Prowse called me, ordering me to Berlin first thing the following morning. Improbably, it seemed Uli had been impressed with me during our previous meeting, and he wanted to talk with me again. He volunteered no further information and I knew better than to ask. I pointed out that Kevin was expecting me to attend the party conference, but he said he would 'take care of Kevin', which had made me smile.

I knocked gently on Uli's office door and entered. He was tapping sporadically on his computer keyboard, staring intently at the screen. Without looking up, he waved a hand imperiously to usher me in, and I made my way gingerly across the thick-pile carpet to the seat I had previously occupied. His screen was positioned at a slight angle, visible enough for me to see that he appeared to be surfing a film website.

'Look at this video, Antonio. You like *Carry On*, yes?

I sat down, rubbed my forehead and sighed. 'My father's dying, I'm getting a divorce and I need to be back at work, Uli. Can we get to the point about why I'm here, please?'

I was astonished at my bluntness, but I felt somehow fearless. It had occurred to me on the flight to Germany that I could no longer think of a single redeeming feature of my job or the people I worked with. With this realisation, Uli's power over me had seemed suddenly to diminish. He gazed at me with an expression of vicious incomprehension, and for a moment I thought he might summon a posse of security guards to usher me from the building. Instead, he smiled. 'We are having some plans for your newspaper,' he said slowly and deliberately.

'Oh really.'

His attention returned momentarily to his computer screen. He tapped several keys before looking up and swinging his chair around, confronting me with another ingratiating smile. 'We are moving your newspaper to China.'

I choked. 'Sorry?'

'Yes, this is what we are doing.'

'But it's a British newspaper. How can you produce a British newspaper in China?'

'We transfer production to Guangdong.'

'But the journalists will remain in Britain, surely?'

He shot me a look of irritation. 'No, journalists will be in Guangdong, with the exception of perhaps one or two in London.'

I wondered whether this was some kind of old comedy routine he was rehearsing. 'But it's a British newspaper.' I knew I was repeating myself, but I couldn't think of a more profound way of registering my confusion.

Uli smiled provocatively.

'With British news,' I added.

His smile broadened.

'Why would you want journalists writing British news for a British paper to be based in China?'

He looked at me as though he found it ridiculous that I should find anything remotely odd about his plan.

'China has a highly educated labour force that earns a fraction of the salaries expected in Britain. No union-negotiated employment rights. We save money.'

I tried again. 'But what do people in China know about producing a British newspaper?'

He laughed heartily. 'No, Herr Noguero. You are missing the point. They will be producing a global newspaper.'

'I don't follow.'

He sighed. 'We publish tabloid newspapers all over the world – in Britain, in Germany, in Australia, in America, in South Africa. And what do our readers in all of these countries want? They want to read about Brad Pitt and Angelina Jolie, about Jay-Z, Beyoncé and Tiger Woods. So why do we need staff in all these countries writing the same stories about the same people?'

'But they also want to know about what's happening in their own countries, with their own politicians and public services and celebrities and sports teams.'

He yawned and shook his head as though I was detaining him with trifles. 'We will have maybe one or two freelance journalists in the UK to take care of that. Soon all of our titles will be online, and all of our advertisers global brands. We did not buy your newspaper because we are interested in Britain. We are interested in the world.'

'That's not a very patriotic message to send out to our readers. How are you going to sell it to them?'

'I'm not, Herr Noguero,' he said smiling. 'You are.'

17

There was no way I was getting a 2:1. With the amount of
work I'd put in, I'd be lucky to get a third. I didn't really want
a 2:1 anyway. I didn't know how they expected anyone to get a 2:1
with the questions they'd set. None of the subjects I'd expected
came up. I mean, how did they expect anyone to anticipate
obscure Italian legal philosopher Del Vecchio? *No one* had revised
for Del Vecchio. Having said that, I could have got a 2:1 if I'd
tried, but I couldn't be bothered. I didn't understand why it was
so important to get a 2:1 anyway. It was a nebulous distinction
given to academics by other academics to keep them in work. It's
not like you wouldn't get a job with a 2:1. Most people got 2:2s.
The only people who got a 2:1 were spotty nerks with no mates,
no life and nothing better to do with their time other than worry
about whether they were going to get a 2 fucking 1.

'Antonio, why don't you shut up and drink your coffee?' Cheryl
said. 'Talking about it all the time isn't going to make the results
appear any quicker.'

Those twenty-seven-and-a-half days waiting for results after
my final exam were the longest, most tense period of my life.
Of course I wanted a 2:1. Everyone wanted a 2:1. Well, everyone wanted a first, but that idea wasn't even worth entertaining.
Getting a 2:1 was all I'd thought about. I was convinced that if I
came up short the rest of my life would be a desperate, downward trajectory into a black pit of abject, humiliating failure and
death.

I got a 2:1. It would have been a pitiless bruising injustice had
I got anything less after all the hard work I'd put in. Cheryl
got a first. Standing in front of the results boards we hugged

each other tightly. We were now officially both high achievers, and that meant that our relationship was more than a student romance: we had the same life goals and we could achieve them together.

After the high of learning my grade, I faced the low of the graduation ceremony with my father. Until then I hadn't given it a thought because I'd been so focused on my exams. Now it was a reality – my first formal outing, as an adult, with Papa.

He was determined to be a sartorial standout, arriving resplendent in a pure-wool, double-breasted navy suit, a camel cape and spats. The ensemble was rounded off with a brass-headed cane that he'd picked up at a junk shop, and which he carried, ostentatiously, in full view of all the other graduands and their parents. This was his interpretation of how a British gentleman presented himself in society. He looked more like a Mafia don.

'Papa, will you put that cane away? It's embarrassing,' I pleaded as we gathered in the medieval quadrangle among a sea of black gowns and wedding hats.

'Wha you say embarrass? This is good cane,' he said loudly. 'This good quality. You know how much it cost?'

I ignored the question, hoping he would drop it.

'You know how much this cost? I get you one.'

'Leave it, Pablo, he doesn't want a cane,' Mama said.

She had bought a new outfit for the occasion, though typically for her it was cheap and off-the-peg and did little to draw attention to her. She sloped and withdrew into herself, fearful of exposing her social inexperience in front of the other well-groomed mothers. Fortunately, students were limited to two guests – it was a good excuse not to invite Pablito. Not that he'd have come anyway; he was still at home in bed, sleeping off a hangover.

As I strolled across the stage to accept my degree I picked out the faces of my parents in the crowd – red, joyful and proud. There were tears in Mama's eyes. After the ceremony we'd planned to return home, where she had prepared a special lunch of rabbit in an almond sauce – one of Papa's favourites – but Cheryl invited us to join her and her parents, who were going to The Ubiquitous Chip, a posh restaurant on Ashton Lane. I really didn't want to go, and I could tell from the expressions of pained prevarication on the faces of my parents that they weren't keen either. We'd been going out together since first year, but our respective parents had never met before this day. They had little in common. Her father was a director of a large drinks company and her mother was a GP. They lived in a large detached house with a walled garden on the outskirts of Edinburgh. But Cheryl seemed to think that us sitting down together was the most natural thing in the world and insisted that we come.

The Ubiquitous Chip specialised in Scottish fine dining in a rustic, informal setting, which seemed to confuse Papa no end. He was edgy and suspicious, not least because of his inability to read the menu properly. Although my experience of eating out was confined entirely to cheap curry-houses, he and Mama clung to me as though I was a lifeline, and they were appalled when Cheryl suggested they sit apart at the table. Ordinarily Mama would act as Papa's interpreter and adviser, but with her at the opposite end of the table from him it was left to me to talk him through the options, which I did as best I could. Given my own inexperience, I wasn't much help with some of the culinary terminology, and Cheryl ended up ordering for us. Mama knew enough to know what she liked and seemed to warm to the experience. Cheryl's dad, Mr Bruce, who insisted that I call him Greg, announced that we should all have champagne.

'So are you going to break the habit of a lifetime, Pablo, and join us in a glass of bubbly to toast Antonio's success?' Cheryl asked him with pushy good humour.

There was a brusqueness about their relationship. Though Papa denied any uneasiness, there was little of the familiar, forced sincerity that characterised his exchanges with the girls Pablito brought home. With them he was flirtatious, encouraging them to giggle with him over some perceived misunderstanding or saucy faux pas. With Cheryl he was distant and polite – I think he was afraid of being bettered. Of course, there was also the possibility he didn't fancy her, though from the way I often caught him looking at her, I doubted that was the case.

He shot Mama a panicked glance at Cheryl's suggestion.

'Cheryl's asking if you'll have a glass of champagne,' I said quietly in his ear.

He offered a watery smile and shook his head.

The conversation had moved on – to the weather, the grandness of the ceremony, the difficulty in finding a parking space in the West End – before he spoke again.

'Wha ya try, tae get me drunk?' he demanded loudly.

The sound of chatter stalled as Cheryl's parents looked on bemused. They turned to Cheryl.

'I say, wha ya try, tae make me drunk?' he repeated.

I cringed, praying for Cheryl to temper what I feared would be a full-blooded response.

'Don't flatter yourself, Pablo, you're cheeky enough when you're sober,' she responded.

Her parents smiled indulgently.

More graduates and their families arrived, and soon the restaurant was rocking with the sound of braying laughter and the self-satisfied clink of champagne flutes. Mama soon warmed to the jovial atmosphere of the place and sat contented, sipping champagne and exchanging easy chat with Cheryl's mother.

Papa remained silent. When the food arrived, he seemed to relax a little – it was unfussy and delicious – but he still didn't join in the conversation. Several times I caught Cheryl's father looking at him, and midway through the main course he addressed him directly for the first time.

'So, Mr Noguera, what do you think of these two skiving off to Africa instead of getting proper jobs?' he asked cheerily.

Papa would have caught barely a quarter of the question, and

I was hoping against hope that the reference to Africa had passed him by.

'Wha you say, Africa?'

I squirmed. I'd deliberately avoided raising the subject of Africa with Mama and Papa, principally because I hadn't made up my mind if I was going yet. It had been Cheryl's idea, to take a year out and work on a charity project before launching our careers. She'd had her future mapped out by the end of her second year – a year in Ethiopia teaching English before returning to the UK to sit her diploma in legal practice, after which she'd get a job as a human rights lawyer.

I wasn't close to deciding what to do with my life. All I knew was that I wanted a job that I enjoyed and one that, if possible, was reasonably well paid. Working for an African charity seemed like a good idea at the time – I'd be able to help people, consider my career options and be with Cheryl – but I hadn't come to a firm decision about it, largely because I knew how unpopular it would be with Papa.

'I'm saying to this pair, rather than going to Africa to help the poor, they should be knuckling down to the world of work,' Mr Bruce said, chuckling. 'I mean, charity begins at home and all that, don't you think?'

He took a large swig from a glass of expensive claret that he'd ordered to accompany his rump of Perthshire lamb.

'Dad, don't be so crass,' Cheryl scolded. 'There are people starving in Africa.'

Papa leaned towards me with his forehead furrowed.

'Wha they talk Africa?'

'It's nothing, Papa, I'll tell you about it when we get home.'

His face tightened and he returned to his food.

After that Mr Bruce turned his attention exclusively to Cheryl, and they became involved in an intense discussion about something or other which I couldn't hear over the din of the other guests. Papa and I sat silently through dessert, and by the time the coffee and the petits-fours had arrived he'd abandoned any pretence of conviviality. He glanced at his watch and shuffled on his seat.

Abruptly and without excusing himself, he rose to his feet and made his way to the Gents. En route he stopped and chatted briefly to one of the waiters. We all watched him leave and the conversation faltered. A few moments later he came and took his seat again. Then the waiter arrived, handing him the bill.

'Now, don't be silly, old man, we'll get this,' Mr Bruce said expansively and a little pompously.

'Nae, I pay,' Papa said huffily.

'No, really, that's not fair, it was our invitation, after all.'

'I pay,' Papa insisted.

'Well, at least let's go dutch.'

This was an idiom too far for Papa, who hugged the bill protectively to his chest. 'I pay, I pay, you nae invite me, this is my son, you nae tell me who pay.'

'That's enough, Pablo,' Mama ordered.

I felt tears forming at the corners of my eyes. I knew Papa had been looking forward to this day for a long time. He would never, in normal circumstances, have volunteered to pay for anything so extravagant, but this was his way of reclaiming his place. Such a gesture, however misguided, was as close as he got to a declaration of love.

'No, he's absolutely right,' Mr Bruce declared magnanimously. 'It is his son, and he has every right to treat him to lunch on the biggest day of his life.'

Papa unfolded the bill and looked at it. He placed it face down and then retrieved it and looked at it again. He held it closer, as though he didn't trust what his eyes were telling him, and the colour drained from his face.

'Are you all right, Pablo?' Cheryl asked.

He sat back in his chair and held the table with both hands. I tried to catch his eye, but he was staring intently at the table. Mr and Mrs Bruce exchanged furtive glances as the waiter hovered uncertainly in the background. After a few moments he stepped forward.

'Would anyone like anything else? More coffee perhaps?' he asked.

'I no feel well,' Papa said quietly to me.

Mr Bruce waved the waiter away.

'Why don't you step outside for a bit of air?' he suggested. 'It is blasted hot in here.'

I took Papa by the arm and led him gently from the table into the street outside. He stood hunched and trembling, gazing coldly into the distance.

'Why don't you go and wait for Mama and me in the car?' I suggested.

He nodded in agreement and shuffled slowly along the cobbled lane towards the car park. I returned to the restaurant, where Cheryl's dad was paying the bill.

I drove the car home in silence. I could tell from the smile on Mama's face that she was tipsy from the champagne, though she knew better than to make it obvious to Papa, who sat slumped next to her in the back seat. When we arrived home we changed out of our formal clothes – Mama and Papa had bought me a suit from Burton's, and I wanted to keep it clean for job interviews – and Mama made a pot of coffee.

Pablito was sitting on the sofa in his dressing-gown, watching afternoon television, with an empty cereal bowl at his feet. He was unshaven, and his eyes were red and moist. He'd packed in his most recent job, as a fitted-kitchen salesman – his third in a year – a fortnight before, and he hadn't been out of bed before midday since then.

'Are you not going to ask how it went?' Mama asked.

Slowly he looked away from the television and cast an uninterested glance in my direction. 'Oh aye, how did it go?' he asked unenthusiastically.

'It went fine,' I said.

'Great.'

Papa sat brooding, smoking a succession of cigarettes, staring out of the window while Mama and I talked about the ceremony and the restaurant. Intermittently I caught her glancing at Pablito, and I saw in her face a growing sense of impatience. 'Should you not be dressed by now? It's past three o'clock.'

He ignored her.

'Pablito, go and get dressed,' she said firmly.

He continued to stare at the television screen. 'I'll do it after this programme has finished,' he said distractedly.

We continued to talk about the meal, but I could sense her attention wasn't properly on the conversation. 'Pablito, should you not be out looking for a job? That's another wasted day.'

I'd arranged to meet Cheryl in the evening, to join up with some friends for a celebratory drink. After I'd finished my cup of coffee I made to leave the room to get ready, but Papa stopped me. 'Hey, where you go?'

'I'm going out.'

'Why you nae spend time with your family? Why you always go with friends?'

'I don't,' I protested.

He waved me away and pretended to watch the television.

'I don't spend all my time with friends,' I insisted. 'I've been locked away in the library for the past three months studying. I deserve a bit of free time.'

'Oh, you deserve, always you deserve,' he said sarcastically.

Mama tensed, and Pablito got up from the sofa and left the room.

'What are you talking about, Papa?'

He bristled and shook his head despairingly – a gesture that suggested that if he had to explain, then his point was already made.

'Is this about Africa?' I asked. 'I was going to tell you. I just hadn't got round to it. Besides, I haven't made up my mind that I'm definitely going.'

It was enough for him that I was even considering such a thing. 'Why you wanna go away? Who force you? Is anyone force you?'

'No, no one is forcing me. If I do decide to go, it will be because I want to.'

'Why you dae this? I have tae leave my country. I have nae choice. You nae have to leave.'

'But Papa, this is completely different. I'd only go for a year and I could return when I wanted to.'

'Wha about your family? Your family here. Here is your responsibility.'

'Responsibility? For what?'

I felt a surge of resentment and a strong desire to hold my ground, but he stared me down and my self-assurance dissolved.

'You stupid. You know this. All time you read books and you stupid.'

'I'm not stupid.'

'Why you go Africa? Wha you think find in Africa? I live in Morocco. I know more than you. There is nothing. Nothing for you in Africa.'

'I'm not going for me, I'm going to help other people.'

'Other people?' he scoffed with mock laugher. 'There is other people here. Your mama, your papa, your brother, why you nae help us?'

'You're not starving.'

'What you talk, starve?'

'A million people have already died in Ethiopia because they don't have access to food. I think their need's greater than yours, don't you?'

His eyes narrowed and his body jerked with frustration. 'Why you nae get job? You know wha age I am when I get first job?'

'Thirteen,' I said.

'*Si*, thirteen, thirteen. Wha age you now?'

I ignored him.

'You wha, twenty-three, twenty-four . . . ?'

'I'm twenty-two.'

'Okay, twenty-two, and I pay you spend four years to sit and read books. Now is time tae get job and earn money, like your brother, and you go tae bloody Africa.'

'You want me to be like my brother?' I asked. 'Divorced by twenty-seven with a son he never sees, unable to hold down a job and still living off his parents?'

'Okay, you smartarse,' he said witheringly. 'You nae be smart little shit.'

'What do you *want* from me, Papa?' I screamed.

It was the first time I had ever raised my voice to him, and he recoiled. I waited for a reaction, not knowing what to expect. I thought he would be outraged, perhaps even violent, but instead he just stood, his eyes wide with incomprehension. I couldn't hold back any longer. 'What do you want? Tell me!'

'Hey, you nae shout, you show respect. *Poco de respeto.*'

'But it's the only way to get through to you! You never listen to anything I say.'

He eyed me suspiciously and retreated a step. 'You nae shout.'

I sat down and put my head in my hands. I could hear his laboured breathing, and I sensed Mama's tension from across the room. Eventually I raised my head and looked directly at him, but he refused to make eye contact.

'What are you saying, that you want me to stay at home to help out financially? That you want me to bring money into the house? Is that what this is really about?'

'Why you dae this to me?' he asked, pleadingly. 'I work tae give you good living, tae give you education, so why you make your papa small?'

I was late arriving at the pub. It was full of excited new graduates, celebrating their freedom. I joined Cheryl, who was sitting in a group of classmates, along with a few friends from other faculties. Most of them had been drinking all day and they were grinning and half-cut, trading slurred non-sequiturs. She squeezed my hand and asked me if I was all right.

A short time later Max Miller arrived, looking serious. He had been at a meeting of the Socialist Workers' Society general council, where, he explained, there had been an attempted putsch against a senior office-bearer who was guilty of some unpardonable ideological betrayal. He talked at length, and, though I wasn't really paying attention, I was glad to have the company of someone still capable of coherent speech.

My friendship with Max Miller appeared to have recovered after a difficult period. I'd been uneasy around him after cuckolding him with Cheryl, but he seemed to have gotten over it. He hadn't had a proper girlfriend since they'd split, despite the harem of attractive young women who perpetually surrounded him. Cheryl was unusually reticent about discussing their break-up, but she insisted that he wasn't heartbroken, just a loner.

Max Miller had graduated with a first in philosophy the week before, but he hadn't attended the ceremony, claiming he didn't need a bourgeois trinket to validate his self-worth, but he was gracious enough to buy all of us a drink.

'So you're really going to work in Ethiopia?' he asked.

Cheryl beamed. 'Yes, it's all systems go, we've been approved by the charity and we're going to book our flights tomorrow. Aren't we?' she said, squeezing my hand.

I smiled weakly.

'This time next month we'll be teaching in a village school in Eritrea.'

'That's great. I really wish I was coming with you, but there's so much going on in the Party at the moment. I'm worried that if I left now the whole branch would fall apart,' Max Miller said.

He put his hand around the back of my head and pulled it towards him. Our foreheads touched, and he squeezed closer.

'You're doing a great thing, mate, you know that, don't you?'

I tried to nod, but he had my head caught tightly against his.

'I'm really proud of what you're doing.'

18

I was going abroad for the first time and was determined to make the most of it. I had to admit the circumstances weren't ideal: I was travelling with Mama and I was going to attend my grandmother's funeral. Abuela had survived the stroke five years before, the stroke which had almost prompted my parents' repatriation to Spain, but eventually she had succumbed to the twin afflictions of a weak heart and a rampant appetite.

I felt strangely unmoved by the news of her death, and consequently guilty. I told myself I'd never had a proper relationship with her and that such emotional detachment was understandable. I'd met her only once, after all, as a child, and we'd never spoken more than a few words of Spanish to each other. The only lasting memory of her was my embarrassment at the size of her pants. I tried to put these misgivings aside and think of the visit as a horizon-expanding opportunity to sample a new land and culture, to bask in the Mediterranean sun and enjoy the chance to relax, with a bit of bereavement and solemn genuflecting thrown in.

It was actually a good thing that only Mama and I would be making the trip. Papa had already established that he wouldn't be going, and Pablito, as usual, had followed his lead. Papa justified his decision to stay at home by claiming he had no wish to "pray for dead *franquista* in room full a bloody *Franquistas*".

I had no more wish to sit in a room full of bloody *Franquistas* than he did, but I was prepared to do so to support Mama. I also needed a change of scene and routine. I was less than a year into my career as an assistant on the local evening paper, and already I felt as though I'd been doing it for a lifetime.

Every morning I arrived in the office at six o'clock and minis-
tered to the whims of a cadre of ill-tempered hacks until it was
time to go home, where Mama had prepared my dinner, which I
ate before settling down to watch television for the remainder of
the evening until it was time to go to bed, to sleep so I could wake
the following morning to go through the whole will-sapping
routine again.

Weekends were uneventful. Sometimes I went out with Pablito.
His favoured haunt was Cleopatra's nightclub, known locally as
Clatty Pat's, an unpretentious venue where your feet stuck to the
floor and a night wasn't a good night without a fistfight at the
bar. It was a peculiarly democratic environment, where wealth
and status stood for nothing in the darkened, late-night charge
of alcohol-fuelled confusion and carnal desperation. A limited
Egyptian theme amounted to the Ladies and Gents toilets being
renamed 'Pharaohesses' and 'Pharaohs' and a large stuffed camel
in a sandpit which was occasionally used by customers as a urinal.

I had never seen Pablito more at home than when he was
propped up at the bar of Clatty Pat's with a glass in one hand
and an inebriated female attendee hanging on his every double-
entendre. Inevitably I'd leave earlier than him, incoherent and
bloated with strong lager. Pablito would return home the following mid-morning and climb beneath his bedcovers, rough and
sated, smelling of stale cigarette smoke and cheap sex.

Mostly I stayed in and wrote to Cheryl. Although I'd decided
after all to stay at home and get a job, she had gone to Africa as
planned. And because telephone communication to Ethiopia was
unreliable and expensive, we'd only spoken twice in ten months.
There was a slight time delay too, which meant that both conversations had been disjointed and annoyingly faint. We'd had to
shout, so it had been difficult to gauge her tone. And of course
I couldn't be as intimate as I'd have liked with my parents in the
next room. Letter-writing was equally unsatisfactory. She sent
detailed, effusive stories about the great work she was doing
with the collection of dynamic, committed people she'd met, but

she wrote very little about us, about whether or not she missed me, whether she still felt the same about me. Her new friends sounded glamorous and infuriatingly middle-class – they all had names like Nadia, Brett and Corey, and they'd been brought up on game reserves in Tanzania and Zambia, or had attended American schools in Switzerland, or both. They all had 'really amazing plans for the future' – studying multimedia and Sanskrit at Columbia, joining the International Red Cross, or working in bonds on Wall Street. Whenever a male name appeared in one of her letters, I felt a painful stab of sexual jealousy. If the same name was mentioned more than once, I collapsed into a pit of self-hating despair and tortured myself imagining them all having vigorous, exotic sex in a great altruistic gap-year orgy.

In one letter Cheryl told me that Max Miller had recently joined the VSO programme and that he, too, was being posted to Ethiopia. I hadn't seen him since we'd left university. I wrote back, hinting that I was upset he hadn't told me about it in person, but she wrote that he'd only recently accepted the posting and she had found out about it after seeing his name on a list of new appointees. She went on to point out, unsolicited, how he'd be based in Addis Ababa, almost five hundred miles away from where she was, so it was unlikely they'd ever see one another.

My trip to Spain could not have been more timely. At last I felt as though I too was being adventurous and achieving something. From the moment I stepped off the aircraft, into the hot buffeting wind on the runway, I felt surprised and liberated, as if colour had suddenly been introduced into my monochrome world. The landscape was rough, with a dry, smoky smell from the parched earth. The airport workers were dark-skinned and attractive, and their manner was pleasantly informal. They smiled at me as we passed them, and I felt somehow they were familiar.

We moved through the terminal building at an agreeably relaxed pace and hailed a taxi whose engine clattered and clunked as we pulled on to a busy dual carriageway. The smiling driver, who chain-smoked and wore sandals, drove speedily and volubly, giving us what I assumed was a running commentary on the events of his day. We drove into the narrow steets of Malaga, past residential blocks with candy-striped canopies, boxy air-conditioning units and chaotically draped items of laundry. Mama's family had moved here from Tangier in the late 1950s after Morocco had gained independence, shortly after she and Papa had moved to Scotland.

It was mid-afternoon when we arrived at Tia Teresa's apartment, located in an unremarkable neighbourhood near the centre. The street was eerily quiet, its shops closed for the *siesta*. Next to her building a municipal basketball court lay empty, its concrete pitch baking in the afternoon sun. As we emerged from the taxi I felt the intense heat drain my limbs of strength. I began to sweat heavily, the moisture causing my shirt to stick hard to my back.

Mama rang the buzzer and the glass door clicked open. It was a relief to step into the coolness of the polished stone hallway. We struggled up to the first floor with our suitcases. Teresa greeted us warmly, ushering us into a dim apartment that smelled of garlic and perming lotion. We moved along a row of grinning strangers, like guests in a line-up at a wedding reception, who clutched us and kissed us vigorously, reminding me of Abuela's arrival in Scotland all those years ago.

Someone relieved us of our suitcases and we were guided into a cool parlour furnished with a mock-leather three-piece suite, a dining table and a matching display cabinet filled with cheap wine glasses and photographs of various children attending their First Communions.

Teresa emerged from a small kitchenette, carrying a tray with a bottle of red wine and bowls of nuts and olives. She retrieved some glasses from the display cabinet with a degree of reverence that suggested this was not a frequent occurrence. There wasn't enough room for everyone on the suite, so several people sat on upright chairs and on the floor.

We spent the afternoon chatting endlessly about this and that. Although I couldn't follow all of what was being said, I could recognise enough words to know roughly the theme of the discussion, and that none of it concerned anything of great importance.

I'd been expecting, with some trepidation, sober observance of Abuela's death and even, perhaps, an open display of her cold corpse, but neither of these things happened. There was passing reference to the sad event, but no one seemed keen to dwell on it.

'*Ella era una señora mayor,*' said one of those present. 'She was an old lady.'

'*Si, es por la major,*' said another. 'Yes, it was for the best.'

Much of the conversation revolved around me – how well I was doing, which side of the family I resembled most, when I was getting married, why I hadn't visited Spain before, why I didn't speak Spanish. It made me feel self-conscious, yet also flattered to be the centre of attention.

Gradually I was able to work out who was who. Teresa was smart and attractive, with a lively demeanour. She was dressed in a youthful, brightly coloured cotton dress that accentuated her curves, and she had obviously recently visited the hairdresser because her dark, curly hair was freshly set. She was several years older than Mama but looked younger.

Her husband, Salvador, was grey and overweight, dressed in cheap, ordinary clothes. He had warm, expressive eyes and an unremittingly jovial demeanour, laughing throughout the afternoon, making witty observations and cracking jokes that I instinctively found amusing, although I had no idea what he was saying. He seemed to be unlike Papa in every regard.

Their sons, José and Fabio, were about my age, one a little younger, I guessed, slim, swarthy and with jet-black hair. Facially they looked like me enough for it to be slightly unnerving, but as time passed it seemed less so. It was even quite gratifying as they were both good-looking. They sat dutifully, enthusiastically engaging in the conversation.

They had an elder sister, Sancha, who was bookishly pretty and around Pablito's age, and a brother, Cesaro, a year or two older than her, who had a beard and whose contributions were quietly authoritative. The others were an assortment of uncles, aunts and cousins whose names and provenance I had yet to establish.

What struck me was how affectionate they were to each other and to Mama and me. They weren't the collection of murderous fascists that Papa had made them out to be, and although I didn't know them, and couldn't understand everything they said, I felt a sure sense of belonging.

As the afternoon progressed more wine appeared, followed by bottles of cold beer, plates of cured meat and seafood and salads, then an assortment of stews and bread, then sweets, fruit and pastries, and finally coffee and brandy, until it was well into the night. Eventually, around midnight, the guests began to return to their homes. I was ready to turn in, but José and Fabio had plans to take me out into the town. I was tired and unsteady, but they were so excited by the prospect that it seemed rude to decline. I freshened up in the bathroom and changed my shirt. As we stepped out my cousins kissed their parents and embraced them tightly, and I felt obliged to do likewise.

Because the alcohol had relieved me of any inhibitions I might have had about trying to communicate through hand signals and the few words of Spanish that I knew, and we managed to keep a lively conversation going as we meandered along the warm streets. Though it was midweek and after midnight, the bars were crowded and the streets buzzed with chatter and laughter. I felt relaxed and utterly happy.

We flitted from bar to bar, where José and Fabio seemed to know everyone, and I was continually introduced to smiling, friendly people who kissed me on the cheeks and offered me drinks and cigarettes. Though none of them spoke much English, they went out of their way to engage me in conversation and ask me questions about where I came from and what I did.

After several drinks we went to a nightclub, accompanied by a coterie of friends gathered along the way. It was a high and cavernous building, like an aircraft hangar, with whitewashed brick walls and an uneven stone floor. In the hazy atmosphere I found myself standing with my arms around a girl who'd been with us since the second or third bar. She was trim and petite – even in her high, scarlet heels she only just reached my chest. She had long, straight black hair that reflected the light like a still pond, and large chestnut eyes. We'd had a brief conversation sometime before we arrived at the nightclub in which I'd told her I didn't speak Spanish, which she seemed to find intriguing. She'd told me her name but I'd forgotten it. It could have been Lucita. Or Paulita. Or perhaps something else entirely.

Next to us, rolling a joint, stood a tall, thin member of the entourage with long greasy hair and nicotine-coated fingertips the colour of burnt toffee. When the spliff was ready, he lit the end and took two drags in quick succession before inhaling long and deep and holding his breath. He passed it to me and I waved it away.

'*¿Por qué no?*' he asked on the exhale. 'Why not?' His voice was deep and gruff, like that of a voiceover actor in a low-budget melodrama.

'*Porque no quiero,*' I said. 'Because I don't want to.'

He looked at me sceptically, his mouth arched downwards. '*¿Querría algo mas?*' 'Would you like anything else?'

I didn't know what he meant, and I frowned.

'*Heroína, cocaína, anfetaminas?*'

I flushed with sudden conspicuousness, afraid that even by talking to him I was somehow doing something wrong.

I pulled away and went off to look for my cousins. José was standing on the other side of the bar, next to a plump black woman dressed unfussily in a cheesecloth shirt and a long patterned skirt and sandals. She was drinking beer from a bottle and looked somehow out of place. José introduced us and she extended her hand.

'Pleased ta meet yer, love,' she said in an east London accent.

Her name was Rachel. She'd come to Malaga the previous year, to work as an au pair with the children of a banker and his wife. She'd arrived without speaking the language, but had picked it up in a matter of months, she said, and now she planned to settle in Spain because she loved the country so much.

It was a relief to speak English, having spent the day struggling to be understood, taking an age to convey the simplest communication. It was also interesting to be able to question someone from back home about their perceptions of Spain. If only I could get my brain to function properly, I thought.

'You 'ad a few, darlin'?' she asked as I swayed from foot to foot.

I ordered a glass of iced water, and slowly I felt my senses return. We stood shouting above the pounding, deafening beat of Europop booming through the speakers, with me firing questions at her and at José through her. I was surprised to learn that both José and Fabio lived with their parents, despite having worked since they were seventeen and both having well-paid jobs.

'Don't you live with your parents?' José asked.

'Yes, but not through choice,' I replied.

'Why then?'

I couldn't think of a convincing answer. It certainly wasn't a financial issue, not now that I was working and earning a decent wage.

Lucita/Paulita wandered over and nestled into me. Her perfume was sweet and intense, and it made me feel suddenly sober and aroused. José smiled. '*Creo que le gustas, primo,*' he said. 'I think she likes you, cousin.'

I felt a rush of warm satisfaction. I couldn't remember the last time I'd had such an enjoyable day. I was also embarrassed at how modest my expectations had been, and I felt a desire to tell José how pleased I was to be here and how my father had misrepresented things.

'My papa warned me that you were all *Franquistas*,' I said.

It wasn't something I'd have said had I been sober, and immediately I feared I might have overstepped the mark. The remotest hint of a smile creased José's mouth. 'We are,' he said.

I couldn't tell from his expression whether he was joking or serious.

It was cool when we emerged from the club, and the early morning sun was starting to peek through the gaps between the high buildings. The area looked different from when I'd walked through it in the darkness. It was smart and opulent, with fine Renaissance buildings lining broad, leafy avenues. Lucita/Paulita was holding my hand, but she broke away and ran ahead to catch up with Rachel, and they walked arm in arm while I brought up the rear with José and Fabio. I grabbed hold of Fabio's wrist and looked at his watch. It was seven o'clock, which meant we'd have three hours sleep at the most before having to leave for Abuela's funeral.

Lucita/Paulita and Rachel stopped ahead of us at a crossroads and waited for us to catch up. Rachel was heading in the opposite direction. She took me to one side while Lucita/Paulita stood by, smiling expectantly.

'Angelita wants to know if you'd like to have sex with her,' she said.

Of course, Angelita, I thought, feeling a warm glow of pride. I took hold of her hand and kissed her gently on the cheek.

'Tell her I'd love to, but I've got an early appointment, and I need to get some sleep,' I said to Rachel.

Mama and I returned to Glasgow in the rain. Despite her grief at Abuela's death, she had enjoyed being in Spain with her family and she was in good spirits. The mood was tempered by Papa's surly attitude on our return. He didn't make any mention of the funeral and wasn't interested in anything else we'd done, even though I was keen to pass on my opinions and observations about his country.

There were two letters waiting for me. One was from a national newspaper to which I'd applied for a job as a trainee reporter.

They'd invited me to their head office in London for an interview the following week.

The other letter was from Cheryl. I took it to my bedroom so that I could go through my usual ritual of speed-reading it first to make sure I hadn't been chucked and then re-reading it several times slowly, scrutinising it line by line, looking for any hidden meanings. On this occasion, though, there was no need for the latter. It was a short message of about half a page, informing me that she was cutting short her stint in Ethiopia and returning to Europe. VSO had offered her a position as a fundraiser at its office in Amsterdam, and she'd be starting within a fortnight.

My life was running away from me. If she moved to Amsterdam she might never come back. I had to take some initiative, make a meaningful gesture. I had to ask her to marry me.

19

I was sitting in the airport departure lounge in Berlin returning from my meeting with Uli when my mobile phone rang. Before I had a chance to say anything, Mama burst into tears. Papa was refusing to go to the hospital, and she couldn't persuade him to change his mind.

'He's frightened, and I understand that, but if he doesn't go, what hope is there for him?'

I wondered if he'd given up, deciding the fight wasn't worth the pain. But I knew that wasn't what Mama wanted to hear. She was in a terrible state, and I felt helpless.

'What about Pablito, can't he persuade Papa to go?'

'Pah, I haven't seen Pablito since we returned from Spain,' she said.

I was shocked. I knew my brother hadn't taken the news of Papa's illness well, but he was never usually out of contact with my parents for more than a couple of days at a time.

'I just don't think he wants to face the truth. I really need you here, Antonio. Normally I wouldn't ask such a thing, but I can't cope on my own any longer.'

I told her it was a bad time for me, but even as I spoke I knew I sounded selfish. Her husband was dying and she needed help. What relevance did the business of newspapers and corporate relocations have to her life? I told her I could spend the rest of the weekend in Scotland but that I had to be back in London first thing on Monday morning – Uli had asked me to prepare a series of articles and leaders justifying the company's move to China.

I landed at Heathrow and walked slowly, head bowed, through the long airport corridors, feeling tired and agitated. I realised

I could make the next shuttle flight to Glasgow, but something held me back.

I'd continued replaying my last phone call with Cheryl in my mind, and the more I thought about it, the more I was convinced that she and Max Miller were carrying on behind my back, and the angrier I became. I needed to see them, to confront them if necessary, if only to save my sanity.

I made my way to the Heathrow Express platform. At Paddington I caught a tube to Clapham Common and walked briskly in the direction of his flat on Wandsworth Road. It was mid-morning and the roads were already noisy and gridlocked, the pavements bustling with shoppers and gangs of mini-cab drivers drinking coffee from polystyrene cups, with rolled-up tabloids under their arms.

I'd lived in London for fifteen years, but I'd never felt entirely certain, walking along roads like these, about what I would hear or see or smell, or the people I would encounter. Things changed constantly. At this time in the morning, the air was filled with the smell of spices and freshly baked flatbreads from the Punjabi and Bangladeshi snack bars, preparing lunch for the crowds who would emerge from the mosques at midday.

I hadn't yet worked out what to do – I didn't know Max Miller's movements on a Saturday morning, and I didn't fancy hanging around in the street in the hope that he – or they – might emerge. The alternative was to force my way into the flat and confront them. I'd been rehearsing an admittedly ridiculous scenario in my head for a month which involved breaking down the door and bursting into his bedroom, catching them naked, engaged in exotic and physically improbable acts, standing in the doorway, tall and imposing, delivering a series of poignant, morally superior facial expressions before . . .

The scenario got a bit vague after that. What would I do, exactly? Would I drag my naked former best friend from the scene of his treachery and beat him to a pulp? Would I turn my back on them and retreat, quietly vindicated, dignified and alone?

The sky was the colour of wet concrete and the air was shrouded with fine drizzle that clung to me, forming a cold, creeping layer on my face. I stood on the opposite side of the road trying to summon the motivation to act. Then the front door to the flat opened and Cheryl and Max Miller emerged, arm in arm.

Even though I'd been expecting it, I could barely believe that they really were together. I became breathless, my vision blurred, and I had to hold on to a railing for support. I tried to regain my composure, to force myself to be alert and purposeful for the moment I had the upper hand: I knew about them and their deceit, and they didn't know I knew. They were already fifty yards ahead and I crossed the road, hurrying to follow them and feeling a curious, masochistic sense of elation that, after weeks of helplessness, my suspicions had been proved correct. It was liberating and empowering, even though I knew it would be short-lived.

They strolled along Wandsworth Road, chatting casually, sharing jokes, and then they stopped to look in the window of a shop that sold New Age trinkets. I froze. There was no shop doorway or bus shelter for me to hide behind, and I knew that if they turned around I would be spotted. Max Miller whispered something into Cheryl's ear, and she removed her arm from around his waist and slapped him playfully on the shoulder. They joined hands and continued to walk. Cheryl was wearing tight jeans, flat shoes and a long, slim-fitting rainjacket. As ever, her clothing was simple but she still managed to look heartbreakingly desirable. Even after all these years I couldn't look at her without being consumed with admiration.

They came to a pedestrian junction and crossed the road, heading in the direction of a supermarket. As I followed them through the car park towards the entrance, I decided I'd have to confront them now – if I prevaricated any longer they'd be inside, and I didn't relish airing my marital problems in the middle of the freezer section.

'Hi, Cheryl,' I said casually.

Both she and Max Miller spun around with identical expressions of guilty shock, as though they'd been caught stealing. Cheryl ripped her hand from Max's.

'Antonio, what are you doing here?'

I did my best to sound emotionless. 'I'm on my way to Glasgow. Thought I'd look you up.'

We stood in a tense stand-off. A family with a shopping trolley appeared behind me and asked if they could squeeze past as I was blocking the entrance. I excused myself and moved aside. Max looked intently at his feet. Cheryl sighed nervously.

'Look, this isn't what you think,' she said falteringly.

I didn't trust myself to speak without my voice breaking, yet somehow I felt disconnected, as though I'd been cast in a drama, an actor playing the part of me. The most appropriate direction for the narrative would be for me to turn and walk away, ruined and humiliated, my heart and life shattered. But what if Cheryl just let me carry on walking without calling me back?

'We need to talk. Let's go inside for a coffee,' she said.

I almost collapsed with relief. She signalled to Max that he should leave us alone. He waved apologetically and sloped away while we walked briskly and silently towards the cafeteria.

Cheryl went to order while I looked for a couple of seats – even agreeing on doing that was awkward and painful. Already we seemed to have lost the easy intimacy I'd taken for granted during twenty years of marriage.

Cheryl arrived with two coffees and we sat, silent and awkward.

'So how have you been?' she asked at last.

'Not great.' I wanted to elaborate, but I didn't know where to start.

'That . . . eh . . . outside, it wasn't what you think,' she said.

'You told me.'

I wanted to ask her what exactly it was if it wasn't what I thought. How the hell did she know what I thought it was anyway, as if it wasn't blindingly obvious? What did she take me for, a moron?

'Look, I didn't tell you where I was staying because I knew you'd come looking for me, and I need some time on my own to think things through.'

'Not because you have something to hide?' I asked, fixing my gaze on an empty sugar sachet that lay at my feet. I couldn't look her in the eye, I felt pathetic and embarrassed even posing the question, and she sighed impatiently.

'No, I told you on the phone, there's no one else. That's not what this is about.'

'So what is it about?' I asked continuing to stare at the sugar sachet.

'You know what it's about. You can't have lived in the same house as me for the past few months and not know.'

'So you've only been unhappy for the past few months?' I asked, hurriedly and more desperately than I intended.

She didn't answer. I looked at her fleetingly and dropped my gaze again.

I'd wanted this discussion to take place for weeks, but now that it was happening I wanted it to end. It was going the wrong way, and I didn't know how to change direction. I'd tried to prepare myself for the worst, but now I realised I'd never properly allowed myself to consider what the worst amounted to – betrayal, estrangement and prolonged loneliness.

'So how long has it been?'

She didn't answer.

'A year? two years?'

Still no response.

'So what are you saying, Cheryl, that you've never been happy in our marriage?'

'I don't know, Antonio,' she replied reluctantly. 'I just don't think we have the same goals, I don't think we ever did.'

I felt angry, like a switch had been flicked in my head.

'Is this still about Africa? Christ, Cheryl, it was twenty years ago.'

'It's got nothing to do with Africa.'

'You know how much I wanted to come, but I didn't have the freedom to make the choices you did. I had a living to make. I didn't have wealthy parents to back me up. What was the alternative for me, to end up drifting and broke like my brother? Or worse, like my father?'

'You're more influenced by Papa than you care to admit,' she said.

'What are you talking about?'

'You are, you know.'

I couldn't believe what I was hearing.

'I'm nothing like my father. I'm settled, even-tempered, committed to providing for my family. I've never had an affair. What's the big problem with me? What makes me such a bad husband?'

'I never said you were a bad husband. And I never said you were like Papa. I said you were influenced by him.'

'So what's the difference?'

'You've spent your whole life trying not to be him rather than trying to be yourself. I don't know what you're really like, and I don't think you do either. You keep your emotions in check, you never say what you really feel, you travel the country doing a job you hate, that keeps you away from the people you say you love.'

'I just want financial security for myself and my family. What's wrong with that?'

'There's nothing wrong with that, but you don't have to dedicate your entire life to it. You're intelligent, educated and successful. There will always be opportunities for you. You don't have to live with the same fear of failure that your father has. You're not running away from a war.'

I didn't know whether all of this meant our marriage was over or not. It wasn't as though she was saying that, having assessed my character and personality, she didn't like them. Rather, she hadn't seen enough to be able to make a valid judgement because, in her view, I hadn't allowed my true character and personality to

192

reveal themselves. Surely that was a good thing? All I had to do was to be more like myself for us to make things work. That was easy – no one was better at being me than me.

'OK, so I'll change then.'

'It's not as simple as that.'

Christ, it never is, I thought.

'It *is* simple. You don't think I'm being me, and what I'm saying is I'll change to be more like me . . .'

'No, stop, Antonio. That's not what I said.'

'You did, you said . . .'

'No, I didn't. What I said was that you are too heavily influenced by your father. Our problems can't just be fixed by you promising to change.'

'Am I the man you fell in love with?' I asked.

'What?'

'Am I the man you fell in love with?'

'Look, I don't want . . .'

'Just answer the question, Cheryl. Am I the man you fell in love with?'

'Yes, but . . .'

'No – no buts. If that's the case, and I agree to be more like that man, rather than not being my father, then there's a chance for us, isn't there?'

'Look, I don't know why –'

'No, please, just say there's a chance for us.'

She stared at the floor and shook her head. 'I don't know, Antonio.'

'I don't believe you.'

'You don't believe what?'

'Any of it. It sounds like the kind of tortured logic that people use to justify their actions when they don't have the courage to admit the truth.'

'And what is the truth?'

I nodded in the direction of the entrance to the store to indicate that I was referring to what I'd witnessed outside.

'What?'

I nodded again.

'Bobby?'

'I know what I saw.'

She laughed. 'You don't know what you saw.'

'I followed you from the flat and you were all over one another like cheap suits – you could hardly keep your hands off him, whispering into his ear and playing with –'

'He's gay.'

I stared at her.

She shook her head in exasperation. 'That's so like you, not to know that your best friend is gay. You know that you're the only person he knows who isn't aware of that?'

'Fuck off.'

'It's true, and do you know why he hasn't told you?'

'Don't say it's because I'm homophobic – there's no way I'm homophobic.'

'No, it's because he doesn't think you'd be interested.'

'What?'

'You're not interested in anything, except what's going on in your own little world.'

'That's rubbish, is that what he said?'

'He didn't have to. He's a caring and considerate man, and he'd never think of being negative or critical if he could avoid it. No, I worked that out for myself because I'm used to you.'

The shock of being told Max Miller was gay was tempered by the relief of knowing Cheryl wasn't having an affair with him, but now I was being accused of having other deficiencies I was unaware of. Not only was I unduly influenced by Papa, but now, it seemed, I was uninterested in those around me.

'Until last year, I hadn't seen him since university, so how am I to blame for not knowing that he's bloody gay?'

'Well, why hadn't you seen him in twenty years? Did you ever wonder why that was?'

'Oh right, so that's my fault, is it? Now I'm being blamed for not keeping up with my friends. Well I'm sorry that I was otherwise occupied building a career so that I could provide a comfortable life for my family.'

'That's the problem, Antonio. Our lives would have been more comfortable if you were at home once in a while, rather than Ben and I sitting around in a big house waiting for you to return from your latest trip.'

I didn't have any response to that, and we sat in silence for a couple of minutes not drinking our coffee. Cheryl sighed and placed her hand over mine. I couldn't help feeling that, as far as she was concerned, I just didn't measure up. I wasn't like her, angry and resentful at injustice, driven by a burning desire to change the world. I was apolitical and consensual, a talker not a fighter. I wasn't the Spanish anarchist she'd hoped for, imbued with the spirit of La Pasionaria and the International Brigades. It occurred to me that what I needed to win her over was a conviction, a cause to fight for. I needed to find my grandparents' remains.

20

My flight touched down at Glasgow Airport late in the afternoon, and I was feeling guilty I'd have so little time to spend with Mama and Papa. I'd have to leave after lunch the following day to ensure I was back in the office first thing on Monday morning to write Uli's articles. I hadn't even told my parents Cheryl had left me yet, and I didn't have the energy for that conversation now, so I resolved to blame my late arrival on flight delays.

I took a taxi to their house. As I walked in I met Papa, clinging to the doorframe of the living-room for support and looking so much frailer than before. His face was drawn and anguished, and the skin on his face hung loosely from his cheekbones and chin. His pupils were grey and vague, anchored at the foot of his eyes as though they were being drawn downwards by gravity. What was left of his hair was thin and white, lying in sad strands across his flaking scalp. A pair of blue corduroy trousers, which only weeks before had appeared little more than slightly baggy, now draped loosely around his hips and buttocks. He looked as though he was literally clinging to life.

A look of recognition flitted briefly over his face as I closed the front door, but he didn't smile. Perhaps he didn't have the strength, or the inclination. He reached out his free hand in my direction.

'You help me go upstairs,' he said in a dry, throaty voice.

I moved towards him and he put his hand on my shoulder, transferring his entire weight on to me. He felt as light as a small child. I put my arm around his waist, resting my palm gently on the surface of his clothing. I didn't want to grab him any tighter, fearful that I might damage him.

'How are you, Papa?'

He didn't say anything, but shook his head as he walked slowly across the hallway, moving one foot ahead a few inches and then catching up with the other. When we reached the foot of the stairway, he paused for breath before beginning a painfully slow ascent, one step at a time.

We reached the upstairs landing and he stopped, holding on to the banister while he sought to regain his breath. I patted him gently on the shoulder and leaned my head towards his, kissing him on both cheeks. His skin was cold, and he didn't respond.

'Are you all right, Papa?'

He lifted his head and sighed.

'I go sleep now,' he said quietly, almost in a whisper, indicating his bedroom.

I wanted to tell him about my telephone conversation with Fermin, to quiz him more about his family, about the possibility that there might be some survivors, but I was shocked by his rapid deteriation. Somehow it no longer seemed urgent.

I made my way downstairs and found Mama in the living-room, dressed in her black nylon housecoat, cleaning the windows. The vacuum cleaner was parked in the middle of the floor, its flex attached to the wall socket. A strong smell of disinfectant and furniture polish permeated the air. The house was spotless.

'Sit down and I'll pour you a drink,' I said.

'I can't stop cleaning. I'm determined the house doesn't smell of death,' she said with a weak smile.

'How long has he been like this?'

She stared at me as though I'd asked her what shape the earth was.

'He is very ill.'

I made us both a cup of tea and sat down, staring out of the window as Mama fussed around me, dusting and polishing. Eventually she stopped cleaning and sat down to drink her tea. She was flushed and tired-looking. She smiled as she grabbed hold of my knee. I'd never worried about her health or her ability to cope as I had with Papa. She was strong, and she always seemed to know what she was doing. Whatever fate threw at her she handled before moving on to the next challenge quietly and uncomplainingly. I knew she'd come to terms with Papa's illness pretty quickly, and her priority, as with most setbacks, was to minimise its drama.

'I'm glad you came,' she said cheerfully. 'I suppose I could have coped if I really had to, but it's nice to get some support.'

'I knew you could.'

She smiled again.

'I'm sorry I can only stay until tomorrow, Mama.'

Her smile waned. 'Couldn't you change your plans and stay a little longer?' she pleaded. 'Your father is very ill.'

'I'm sorry, but I've got a lot on at work.'

She sank back into her seat and her shoulders dropped. Perhaps she wasn't coping as well as I'd imagined.

'You really need to get Pablito to pull his weight,' I said.

She sighed. 'It's not just you who's busy. He has a lot on at work as well, you know.'

I raised my eyebrows.

'And . . . he doesn't cope,' she said dejectedly.

From upstairs I heard the sound of Papa's voice. It was weak and gruff, like a strained whisper, but it sounded distressed, and I shot to my feet. Mama dragged herself from her seat and moved slowly towards the door as though it was all part of her normal routine.

'Don't panic, he'll be stuck on the toilet again,' she said wearily.

I followed her upstairs and into the bathroom. Papa was lying naked on his back in the bath, and he was crying.

'*¿Qué hace?*' Mama asked. 'What are you doing?'

'*Ayúdeme*,' he pleaded. 'Help me.'

Mama moved towards him and put her hands under his arms. I edged in beside her and tried to take hold of his legs, but he cried out and pushed me away.

'It's all right, I can manage,' Mama said.

I stepped back and watched helplessly as she lifted his emaciated frame until he was sitting upright.

'*¿Qué hacía?*' she pressed. 'What were you doing?'

'*Estaba tratando de bañarme y me caí al suelo.*' 'I was trying to bathe and I fell down.'

'Why are you trying to bathe yourself?' she asked in English.

'*Porque estoy sucio. Y huelo*,' he replied, tearfully. 'Because I'm dirty. And I smell.'

She leaned forward and he wrapped his arms around her neck. She strained, trying to raise herself upright until he was kneeling.

The bathroom hadn't changed since I was a child. It was cold and sparse, and the enamel coating on the cast-iron bath had become thin and abrasive to the touch. The chrome taps were dated and tarnished with limescale. A slight breeze rattled the sash windows.

Papa clasped Mama's hands tightly in his bony grip, and slowly he lifted himself into a standing position. The sight of his sickly, wasted body was painful. His skin was dry and jaundiced, like a piece of cured meat, and the frame of his skeleton was almost entirely visible. Inflamed, weeping sores were scattered along the pressure points on his backside and the underside of his thighs. He continued to cry hard, not, I suspected, because he was in particular pain, but because of his helpless indignity.

Mama dried his body and dressed him in a pair of thick winceyette pyjamas before putting him to bed, like a mother would a child. We returned downstairs and sat in silence. I didn't know what to say, and I couldn't trust myself to speak without my voice breaking.

'You need to think about your priorities, Antonio,' Mama said quietly. 'What are you going to remember in five or ten years' time? Whether you were at work to write on this bit of paper or that bit of paper, or whether you were there for your father when he died?'

I woke on Monday morning exhausted and with a sense of disorientated panic. I looked at my watch – it was seven o'clock, which meant Kevin would already be at his desk, and I hadn't yet informed him I wouldn't be in. I felt a sick, knotted sensation in my stomach – the same feeling of dread I experienced when I was late for school.

I showered and made my way downstairs, where Mama was in the kitchen frying doughnuts and making coffee for breakfast. I'd agreed to take Papa to the hospital. His appointment was at nine o'clock, but he was still in bed.

'He's refusing to get up. He says he doesn't want any treatment,' Mama said, her voice taut with anger.

'Would it help if I tried to talk him round?' I asked.

I was hoping that she'd say no.

'It's worth a try, I suppose.'

Papa's bedroom was dark, and it had the helpless humiliating smell of a geriatric ward. He lay hunched on a small portion of the mattress with the blankets pulled tightly over his head. He was facing away from me, towards the drawn curtains, but I sensed he knew I was standing behind him.

'Papa, you need to get up, you'll miss your hospital appointment.'

He ignored me.

'Papa, you have to go to hospital.'

'I nae have tae dae nothin,' he said groggily.

I sighed heavily, which prompted him to twitch. For a moment I thought he would turn around to face me, but he simply readjusted his pillow. I knew from experience that nothing I said would make him change his mind, but for Mama's sake I resolved to press on.

'Papa, you can't just give up.'

He continued to ignore me.

'You've got to keep fighting.'

He remained still and silent, and I steeled myself for one last push.

'Papa, you're being selfish. This isn't just about you, it's about the people trying to help you and the effect your stubbornness is having on us.'

He raised himself slowly and turned to face me, the pain of movement evident in his eyes.

'Wha you know about me?' he asked disdainfully.

I decided to go to the the hospital without him, to speak to his consultant about his prognosis. I waited for an hour in the oppressively hot corridor of a crumbling Victorian hospital before a harassed, unshaven medic approached me with an outstretched hand and a look of exhaustion. We went to a closet-sized room with a treatment table and a cracked sink. I insisted he sit down on the only chair, as he appeared to be on the point of collapse. His accent was indeterminate – I guessed it might have been Arabic, though he might just as easily have been from the Balkans.

I apologised for Papa's absence as he skimmed through a file containing his notes. I got the impression he wasn't listening to a word I was saying. Abruptly he closed the file, looked at me and smiled.

'To be perfectly honest with you, Mr Noguera, I see no benefit in your father attending this clinic,' he said matter-of-factly.

'But I thought he was booked in for chemotherapy treatment.'

'That would be one of the options, but my judgement is that, at this stage in the development of your father's carcinoma, the disadvantages, in terms of trauma, pain and side-effects, outweigh the possible benefits.'

'What are the possible benefits?' I asked.

'Extra longevity.'

'You mean he's better off just waiting to die?'

He smiled benignly. 'At this stage, quality of life is often more important than quantity.'

'You said that's your judgement?'

He nodded.

'What factors do you take into account in arriving at that judgement?'

He opened the file of notes and closed it again just as quickly. He sighed and glanced at the ceiling, as if he was seeking a very precise form of words.

'Well, I spoke to your mother and to your father's GP, and I made my own analysis of his psychology. Your father is not the sort of person who would deal very easily with the reality that he is about to die. Your mother asked that I didn't use the terms cancer or tumour when I dealt with him.'

'Surely he must know he has cancer?'

'I think that deep within himself he recognises it, but it's not something he's willing to admit. He has, as I understand it, had a troubled life, and it is often better to let the dying make the best of what they have left.'

'So how long does he have? Weeks? months?'

'I wouldn't go very far away from him if I was you.'

I sat in the Beetle in the car park and cried. I wasn't sure why. I wanted it to be about Papa, but it might also have been a delayed reaction to the break-up with Cheryl. I tried to be sad for Papa, but it seemed I'd forgotten how.

I drove to the petrol station on Paisley Road West, where I knew Pablito worked. I couldn't see him, so I filled up the tank and went to the checkout to pay. The cashier looked unnerved when I asked where my brother was.

'Eh, dunno, you'll huv tae ask the boss,' she said.

'I thought he was the boss.'

She smirked.

'Lewy husnae been in fur a couple a weeks.'

'Lewy?'

'Aye, ah call um that cos it gets oan his tits,' she said with a grin.

'Why's he been off?'

'Like ah said, you'll huv tae ask the boss.'

I couldn't imagine why Pablito would have taken more time off work. I drove down to his flat at Springfield Quay. It had been several years since I'd visited him, and so much new residential development had sprung up since then that it took a while for me to be certain I was in the right place. The new streets felt ghostly quiet and empty.

The first of the apartment blocks had been built on the site of the former shipyards a decade before, a brown-brick and brushed-oak monument to upwardly mobile, expense-account post-industrialism, each flat box-built and fully alarmed. Pablito had bought his tiny studio flat on the back of a messy divorce.

I found what I believed to be the front entrance to his apartment block. His name wasn't listed on the entry system, although there was an unlabelled buzzer for a second-floor flat. I pressed it and waited for a few moments. There was no response. I tried it again, unsuccessfully, and walked back along the path towards the pavement. I looked up towards a pair of French windows – the curtains were drawn, but I was sure I saw them twitch. I returned to try the buzzer for a third time, but again there was no response, so I decided to leave.

As I put the key in the car door, I heard my name being called out, and I looked up to see Pablito's face at the window. He beckoned me and buzzed me through into the vestibule. I walked up the stairs to find him waiting for me at the door to his apartment, dressed in a dishwater-grey bathrobe, blemished with what looked like old curry stains. Without greeting me, he turned his back on me and returned inside.

I closed the door behind me. His flat was dank and fuggy, with the moist texture of a teenager's duvet. There was a sofa bed, and a portable television set resting on the cardboard box in which it came; an open-plan kitchenette area overflowing with filthy crockery and discarded fast-food containers; and a small shower room. The walls were yellowed by nicotine, and around the edge of the French windows, which led on to a small balcony, the plaster wall was bubbled and flaked, evidence of water damage that had never been attended to. Below, the carpet was rotting and mottled, peppered with fag-ash, crumbs and other remnants of wasted living.

Pablito sat down on the sofa bed. He stubbed out a cigarette and switched off a video game he'd been playing on the television. 'I don't have any coffee.' He refused to look at me, preferring to stare out of the window as though preoccupied by something outside. 'I thought you were in Paris or some fucking place.'

'Berlin,' I corrected.

'Aye, wherever.'

'I came back to see Papa.'

'That was good of you.'

I didn't respond.

'And how is he?' he asked, glancing at me furtively before returning his gaze outside. He reached for his cigarettes and lit another.

'He's not great. In fact, I've just been to see his consultant, who said he's beyond help.'

Pablito took a hard drag on his cigarette and pinched the corners of his eyes at the top of his nose.

'Bloody smoke,' he complained.

I opened the French doors and a draught of air blew in, circulating the swirls of grey smoke that hung at head height.

'I dropped by the petrol station on my way over,' I said.

He looked at me, expecting me to elaborate, but I stayed quiet. I wasn't going to do all the running.

'And?'

'And what?'

'What did they say?'

'They didn't say anything. Just that you weren't there.'

'Uh-huh,' he said, nodding.

'So why aren't you there? Are you ill?'

He considered the question.

'Yeah, that's right, I'm ill.'

'You don't look ill.'

I removed an empty sherry bottle from the sofa and sat down beside him. He smelled of alcohol and stale sweat.

'Why don't we go out for a walk? It will do you good to get some fresh air.'

He ignored me.

'Well, get back to work then. You're not doing yourself any favours cooped up in this shithole.'

He collected the ashtray from the floor and stubbed out his cigarette end.

'I know why you're doing this,' he said.

'You know fuck all.'

I seemed to have spent my life being told by members of my family how little I knew. 'I know how hard you're taking Papa's illness, but you can't just give up, not now when he needs you most, I said.'

He sat forward and shuffled uncomfortably.

'You need to keep yourself together, for Mama's sake.'

He remained silent.

'What do you think Papa would say if he saw you like this?'

He put his head in his hands.

'What's the matter, Pablito? Talk to me.'

He looked up. 'It's my work,' he said plaintively.

'What about your work?'

He started to sob. This wasn't how it should be. He was my older brother, and for most of my life he'd exercised authority over me. He looked vulnerable, broken, and I didn't know what to do for him. 'I took some money,' he said through his tears.

'What do you mean you took some money? You mean you stole it?'

'I was going to pay it back.'

'Why did you need to steal money?'

'To pay for the holiday in Spain. I was going to return it, but my boss found out and now he's going to the police.'

I felt a sudden pain in my chest. No matter how hard I tried, I couldn't sustain any pity for him. 'Oh, Christ, how much?'

'Two grand.'

'Oh, Christ.'

I felt like a boy again, at the mercy of my family's foibles and weaknesses. It was the stolen camping stove. It was having to tell lies to Mama. It was opening the letter to Mr McKendry and discovering my father was illiterate. It seemed that no matter how much I tried to improve myself or to be truthful and honourable, there was always someone close to me to drag me down. For most of my life I'd been answerable for the failings of my father. Now he was dying, and still there was no respite. I couldn't bear to be in my brother's company any longer.

'You should go and see Papa. You owe it to him.'

'I owe him nothing,' he protested.

'How can you say that? Whatever shit you're in, at least you have a good relationship with him. Despite all of his faults, he always stood up for you.'

'I have no relationship with him,' he insisted.

I couldn't believe Pablito could say such a thing. 'But he loves you. He respects you.'

He laughed. 'No, he uses me – he always has done. But he has no respect for me. I allow him to behave badly because I do too. It's you he respects, because you stand up to him. In fact, he's jealous of you.'

'Jealous? Why should he be jealous of me?' I asked incredulously.

'Because you're a success, and he's a failure. You've done all the things he was never able to do. He resents the hell out of you for it, but deep down he thinks the world of you.'

21

I received an email reply from the Association for the Recovery of Historical Memory's messageboard in response to a posting I'd made. I'd decided to defy Papa and had asked if anyone had information about the fate of Paco Noguera from Alguaire, who hadn't been seen since September of 1938. My heart pounded as I logged on to my computer. By the time it booted up I was beginning to have doubts, troubled by the kind of guilty trepidation that accompanies challenging a parent, even in adulthood.

'Hi, my name is Montserrat, and I think I may be related to you. Please call me,' the message said.

There was a phone number with an overseas dialling code, which I Googled. It was for Mexico. I thought about dialling the number there and then, but I stopped myself. It would still be the middle of the night in Mexico, but that wasn't the only thing holding me back. I didn't know if I could go through with it without Papa's approval. I tried to reason that what I was doing was justified and that he'd be pleased at the discovery of one of his relatives, but I wasn't convinced. It also occurred to me that something in his story didn't ring true. If it had been this simple for me to track down a member of his family, why had he never done it himself?

I'd been in Glasgow for a fortnight, and I'd already slipped into an unbroken routine of sleeping, working and helping Mama to look after Papa. She continued to do the bulk of his caring – lifting, carrying, cleaning, feeding, changing and dressing him, laundering his clothes, administering his drugs, keeping him amused and stimulated, boosting his spirit and stopping him from dying.

The only respite she had was early in the morning when she left to visit Pablito's flat, where she did much of the same for him.

Pablito continued to languish in despair, despite having had the immediate threat of police charges lifted. I'd visited his boss at the petrol station, who agreed not to pursue the matter of the stolen two grand, provided that I repaid the money and that he never clapped eyes on my brother again.

In return for helping him, I demanded that Pablito get out of his flat and look for a job, which he did for a short time, but without much conviction or success. I also persuaded him to visit Papa, but he didn't stay for long and he left obviously traumatised, his eyes swollen and red.

I'd already decided I was leaving the paper, so I had no misgivings about leaving Uli or Kevin in the lurch. I hadn't yet told anyone of my decision to quit – that conversation could wait until later – only that I'd be taking an extended period of compassionate leave. The paper had a small regional office in Glasgow, and I'd agreed to work the odd day from there if there was an emergency.

Mama had taken to leaving the house to visit Pablito before Papa was awake, so I looked in on him every morning. It became a ritual for me, knocking gently on his bedroom door and edging my head around as he was waking up, helping him to sit upright and plumping up his pillows to give him support before serving his breakfast on a tray.

On the first morning I made him a boiled egg with soldiers and a cup of tea, rather than his customary fresh coffee and *churros*. He seemed to enjoy it. As he ate, I perched on the edge of the bed and we talked. I had never felt completely relaxed in his company, and the prospect of his death made things more tense. It hadn't occurred to me how difficult it would be to hold an ordinary conversation with him, knowing that he knew he was dying. Compared with the unspoken issue that hovered between us, any topic seemed trite and immaterial – the weather, the consistency of his egg yolk and the strength of his coffee, how well he'd slept, his plans for the day.

I made to leave, and he smiled, which made me nervous because I hadn't seen him smile for such a long time.

'You are good boy,' he said quietly.

I hovered at the end of the bed, half-standing, half-sitting, unsure of what to do, whether to interpret it as a off the cuff observation or as a belated attempt to instigate some closer connection between us.

'I wish you'd told me a bit more often,' I said.

He raised his skeletal hand and waved it downwards. 'You go now. I wanna sleep.'

Mama was looking forward to the family being together at Christmas for the first time in years. She told us to forget about Papa's illness and concentrate on having a good time. I spent several days ferrying her around the little continental food shops that she and Papa had unearthed and patronised over the years, so that she could buy all the esoteric ingredients she'd need to create an authentic Spanish Christmas.

We stocked up on several kilos of seafood and a bream – to be baked and eaten with potatoes – as well as a large leg of lamb that Mama planned to roast with tomatoes and paprika. We bought toasted almonds and marzipan, and I talked Mama into choosing a couple of bottles of cava to drink chilled, when Papa was out of sight.

Ben flew up from London to spend a couple of days with us the week before Christmas. When he was young, Ben had told me he was frightened of his *abuelo*. Now it was Papa who looked alarmed at the sight of his grandson, dressed in a long black leather coat and wearing studded cuffs and a large silver pentagram hanging around his neck.

Ben took time every day to sit on the end of Papa's bed and try to have a conversation with him, which wasn't easy given that he was now virtually comatose with morphine. Cheryl, he informed me, was spending Christmas with Connie and her husband. Ben had planned to stay at his girlfriend's family's house, but he offered to remain with us in Glasgow instead.

'That's okay, Ben, but thanks for offering,' I told him. It was obvious he was mightily relieved, but I appreciated the gesture nevertheless. I hugged him close and planted a kiss on the top of his head.

It was a peculiar feeling, preparing for a Christmas at home with my parents for the first time in almost thirty years. Choosing a Christmas present for Papa was upsetting. I wandered the city-centre shops, contemplating the purchase of clothes I knew he'd never wear, books he'd never read, music he'd never listen to. I opted for a multi-pack of pure silk socks from Marks and Spencer on the principle that, even if he didn't wear them, he'd appreciate their sartorial value. It also occurred to me fleetingly and, at a deeper, almost subliminal level, that I had the same size feet as him and was in need of new socks.

Mama was up before anyone on the morning of Christmas Eve, cleaning the house and preparing the meal. I was awake early but chose to lie in bed for a couple of hours longer, staring at the ceiling. My life promised to be significantly different in the coming year – Papa would die, and I'd have to decide how I'd feel about it; my marriage was over; Ben might or might not be at university; and I'd be out of a job. Of all the changes that were coming, what worried me most was not the certain grief, loneliness, or shortage of cash, but the loss of control over my life, which until now had been built of what I believed to be certainties. I was throwing a pack of cards in the air, unsure of where they would land.

I showered and dressed and helped Papa walk downstairs. I lowered him on to the settee in the living-room and swaddled him in a duvet. He sat expressionless, his eyes flickering as though he was doing his best to stay awake.

Pablito arrived shortly after midday, smelling of stale drink. It didn't take him long to discover the cava, and after a few glasses his mood became spirited and expansive. He sang a few verses of 'Viva el vino y las mujeres' by Manolo Escobar, and even managed to get Papa to smile.

We decided to eat mid-afternoon rather than waiting until the evening, as was customary, as we knew Papa would be too tired by then. Mama set all the courses out on a coffee table in the living room. I tried to assist her but she insisted on doing everything herself.

'You are a man, you sit down.'

'Mama, let me help,' I pleaded. 'Modern Spanish women don't think like that.'

'What do I know how modern Spanish women think?'

Papa picked at some of the seafood and a few pieces of lettuce while we tucked in to everything else. The one thing I appreciated more than anything about staying with my parents was the home-cooked food, and I set about the fish and meat with gusto. The highlight of Papa's day seemed to be the single cigarette he was permitted after his meal. The consultant had told Mama that, while he shouldn't be encouraged to smoke, he was beyond the stage where the occasional fag could do him harm.

After the meal, presents were unwrapped with as much ceremony as we could muster. Papa considered his socks uninterestedly and dropped them at his side without comment. Mama unwrapped a tube of cheap face cream she'd bought as a present to herself from Papa and feigned surprise and delight. I unwrapped the suit carrier she'd bought me and mentally stored it alongside the foldaway coathanger, the plug-in teacup element, the mini-alarm clock and the countless other travel-related products she'd bought for me every birthday and Christmas since I could remember.

It was mid-afternoon and still daylight when Papa said he was tired and wanted to return to bed. Pablito and I carried him upstairs. After Pablito returned to the living-room I hung back to make sure Papa was comfortable.

'Did you have a nice day?' I asked when he was settled.

He nodded slowly.

'You no bring egg tae me this morning,' he reprimanded me.

I laughed. 'Papa, it's Christmas.'

'I still like egg.'

I sat on the edge of his bed as he dozed, and I tried to guess how long he had and how much of a relief it would be when his time came. I hadn't mentioned the email from Mexico, but it continued to prey on my mind. Should I ask him about it or should I let it lie? Was it too late to mean anything to him? I couldn't understand why he appeared willing to see out his life with such an important part of his past unresolved.

'You remember the scientists in Spain that I told you about, Papa? The ones who recover the bodies?'

He turned his head slowly towards me.

'They can also help to find relatives who are still alive.'

He looked pained. 'And I was thinking, what if Paco didn't die after you left him in Barcelona? What if he survived?'

He smiled lazily. 'Paco is dead.'

'They have a website that has thousands of names of people who lost relatives during the Civil War, and it helps them to reunite if they are still alive.'

'Paco is dead.'

'But you don't know that. You just assume that because you lost touch.'

He tried to lift a hand to wave me away, but he didn't have the energy, and he closed his eyes. 'I know,' he said quietly.

I bent down to kiss the side of his face. A tear had rolled down his cheek.

'Have you had a happy life, Papa?' I asked him.

He sighed. 'You know when I am happiest?'

'No, when?'

'When I am in Tangier.'

'Why was that?'

'Because I can still see Spain across the water.'

I returned downstairs. Mama had made coffee that Pablito had laced with cheap brandy from the off-licence. The television was on, but both of them were asleep. I sat and sipped at my coffee, thinking about what Papa had said. I remembered what Cheryl had told me in the supermarket canteen – that, unlike mine, his actions could be excused because he was still affected by the war.

I considered myself, Pablito and Mama – a self-absorbed workaholic, a dysfunctional semi-inebriate and an exhausted old woman doing her best to keep the whole charade going – and it occurred to me that Cheryl was wrong. The reality was that all of us, in our own ways, continued to bear the scars of the war.

Kevin rang my mobile phone early on Christmas morning, ordering me to take part in a conference call with Uli, from the Glasgow office, within an hour. Uli was keen to start the new year by announcing the paper's move to China, hence the urgency of calling me on Christmas Day, he said. I suspected pissing me off was also an added bonus for him. I didn't have time to make Papa's boiled egg, and when I popped my head around his bedroom door he was fast asleep, so I decided to leave him.

I had a keen sense of the reception that awaited me, and, as expected, the conference call was terse. Uli was in a foul mood because I wouldn't commit to returning to London to handle the media storm that would inevitably be prompted by the announcement of the move. He threatened me with the sack. I told him I'd take him to the cleaners at a tribunal. I also told him I was taping the conversation, which I wasn't, but it was fun hearing him squirm. Knowing that I was leaving anyway gave me a warming sense of empowerment.

I came away from the call smiling. I hadn't felt so cheerful in ages, and I was looking forward to talking with Papa. His reaction to my suggestion of trying to track down his relatives had, I felt, actually been quite positive. He'd dismissed it, but not as vehemently as I'd feared, and I certainly thought it was worth pursuing. I resolved that I would tell him I'd been contacted by Montserrat from Mexico.

It was the middle of the afternoon and the city centre was

post-apocalyptically quiet, so I had no trouble hailing a taxi. The cab approached my parents house' just in time for me to see an ambulance disappear around the corner at the end of the street. I told the cab driver to wait and made my way into the house, which was eerily quiet. I hurried upstairs and opened the door into Papa's bedroom. The duvet and top sheet were stripped back, and the window was wide open. Biting cold air was blowing into the room.

22

I stood by the graveside, shivering in the chill of the after-noon. It had been pleasantly warm when I left the hotel in Barcelona earlier in the morning, and I was surprised at how much the temperature dropped the further I drove into the mountains.

I'd fallen in love with Collbató the moment I saw it – a fairy-tale hamlet nestling at the foot of the silver-grey range, halfway between Barcelona and Lerida, dotted with whitewashed stucco villas and polished pitch-pine chalets. The countryside around it was wooded and lush, and it was difficult to imagine this was the same country that housed the dustbowl of Andalusia.

My family had no connection with the village, but we'd stopped here on a coffee break following Papa's arrest in Alguaire, and I remembered the picturesque cemetery on its gentle slope, enclosed within a square of drystone and flanked by fir trees and tall black pines.

I stood alone, waiting for the priest to arrive. Fermin had asked whether I wanted a humanist celebrant – many of the people the Association dealt with were the relatives of atheists and didn't want a religious service. Mama didn't know if Papa's parents had been religious, so I opted for a Catholic priest to be on the safe side. Papa never went to church, but he had always been tolerant of Mama's faith.

The service was supposed to have started ten minutes earlier – typical Spanish efficiency, I thought – but there didn't appear to be another funeral party waiting to follow us. After another ten minutes or so a small red car drew up outside the gates and a priest got out. He was youthful – I didn't know why, but

I'd been expecting an older man – and he wore a black cassock and an expensive-looking pair of designer glasses. He walked briskly towards me, smiling, and shook me firmly by the hand.

'How do you do? I'm Father Carballo. I'm sorry I'm late. I was held up making arrangements for a wedding in the cathedral in Lerida,' he said in English.

The coffins containing my grandparents' remains were sitting on the ground next to their graves, draped with ornate purple sashes that would be used to lower them into the ground. The priest looked around expectantly.

'I'm the only mourner,' I explained.

I'd been disappointed that Mama and Pablito had decided not to attend. Mama had become more tired and frail since Papa's death, and I hadn't really expected her to make the journey, but my brother's refusal was a surprise. He'd sold his flat and moved in with Mama, and he'd held down a job in a call centre for the past year. I thought he, more than I, would have wanted to make this gesture, but he told me he was starting to get his life back on track and was worried that travelling to Spain would stir up memories of things he'd sooner forget.

Four men, who looked like labourers appeared at the gate and moved slowly towards us. They stopped a few yards away and stood with their backs to the stone wall, their heads bowed respectfully. One, who was wearing a baseball cap, removed it and clutched it tightly to his chest.

I'd provided the priest with as much personal detail about my grandparents as I had been able to collect, which wasn't much. He explained that he would say a few words about their lives. Since I'd refused the option of a funeral Mass, it would be a short ceremony, consisting of a scriptural verse and a committal prayer, at which point the coffins would be lowered into the ground. He would then recite an intercession – which, he explained, was a prayer to God on behalf of my grandparents – followed by the Lord's Prayer and a blessing.

'Would you like me to deliver the service in English?' he asked.

'No, in Spanish, please. This isn't for me – it's for my father,' I explained.

His manner was sympathetic, and he took nothing in my knowledge of the Catholic liturgy for granted. He asked if I wanted to conclude the service by taking part in a song, affirming hope in the resurrection, but I politely declined.

As he began the service I became aware of a woman entering through the gates, moving hurriedly across the cemetery. As she moved closer I recognised her from the photographs she'd emailed me. Our eyes met and we smiled at one another.

The priest spoke relatively slowly, but still at a pace that was too quick for me to comprehend, although I'd started night classes in Spanish a few months before and I was already capable of holding basic conversations. I found that much of it was a matter of recognising and liberating what was already buried in my subconscious.

The builders stepped forward and lifted the purple sashes, then lowered one of the coffins into the hole in the ground, an act that appeared to require little exertion, given that it contained only a few bones. They then lifted the other coffin and repeated the procedure. Father Carballo continued speaking as he dropped a handful of dirt on top of the wooden boxes.

I'd spent the past two years harrying, arguing and lobbying municipal officialdom. I'd filled in countless forms, travelled thousands of miles and spent a great deal of money to get to this point. The process had consumed much of my life, yet the burial lasted no longer than a few minutes.

The builders nodded respectfully and sloped off. The priest patted me gently on the shoulder before taking his leave. The woman walked around the graveside until she was quite near me. She had a beautiful face with a warm, intimate smile.

'*Hola, primo,*' she said as we embraced.

'*Hola*, Montserrat.'

Although we'd never met, I felt I knew her well already. In our email exchanges it had become clear that there were significant differences in our understandings of the past, and in particular of how our grandparents had died.

She'd informed me early on that Paco, her father, had survived the war and had died only the year before Papa's death. I in turn had told her everything I knew about Papa's life – what little I'd learned about his fighting for the Republic in Lerida, the small details of our grandparents' murder by a Fascist firing squad, our fathers' flight to Barcelona, the months of squalid, frozen subsistence followed by Paco's disappearance.

After Papa died, I'd convinced Mama to fill in the gaps of what I knew of his wartime experiences, and while I suspected the story she told was an abridged version, at least it had allowed me to piece together how he'd got from Barcelona to Tangier, where they met.

He and the Gypsy girl had left the city as the Fascist troops entered, staging a mass rally and victory parade in the Plaça de Sant Jaume, which housed the Generalitat, the Catalan parliament. The pair had set off on foot, cold and hungry, spending days walking along the dirt-track roads that linked the fishing villages of the Costa Brava. They slept in ditches, clinging to one another for warmth, and they begged and stole what little food they could. They passed through devastated villages lined with the hollow, bombed-out shells of buildings, whose cobbled streets were strewn with mangled masonry, abandoned possessions and rotting corpses. They couldn't risk hitching rides with passing cars and trucks because they didn't know who might stop and quiz them about their identity.

Papa had worked out a cover story for himself: he was a *Franquista*, travelling to work for his brother, a blacksmith in Almeria. But the Gypsy girl spoke only Catalan, the regional language banned by Franco, which would immediately identify her as a *rojo*.

Exhausted and close to starvation, they were eventually picked up by a party of Falangist soldiers near the town of Tarragona, less than seventy miles from Barcelona. From there they were taken to a military garrison, where they were locked in neighbouring cells. On the first night Papa heard the anguished screams of the Gypsy girl as she was repeatedly raped. In the early hours of the morning he heard a single gunshot, followed by silence.

Papa remained in the cell for several more weeks. He was given a single daily meal of soup – water flavoured with a small piece of ham and chickpeas – and he was questioned by a succession of junior officers, to whom he repeated his cover story about his brother in Almeria. But clearly they didn't believe him.

'Were they violent to him?' I had asked Mama.

She hadn't responded. My mind returned to my childhood and the discussion I'd had with Papa after I'd failed to stand up for Jorge at school, when he described the visit of the secret police to the boy's home in Chile and the abduction of his father. I realised he'd been drawing on his own experiences.

Then one morning, Mama had explained, Papa was woken early, bundled into a truck and driven to a large building in the middle of the countryside which had the appearance of a stately home, but which turned out to be an orphanage run by Jesuits.

It was to be his home for the next four years, where he was taught to love God and Franco. Every morning he was ordered to give the Fascist salute, and if he refused he was beaten and given no food. The same fate awaited him if he spoke Catalan, or if he said anything that was deemed to be critical of Franco or the Catholic Church. He soon learned what to say and what not to say and how to behave if he wanted to survive.

When he was eighteen and legally old enough to leave the orphanage, he set off alone, with no family to care for him and no desire to return to his home village. The only place he could think of to settle was Tangier, where the Gypsy girl had urged him to go four years before.

Montserrat's father had also been unwilling to discuss the war in any detail. She'd told me how, after Paco had left my father in Barcelona to look for food, he'd been arrested by the Assault Guard and thrown in jail. Many others in his position, vagrants suspected of having fought for Anarchist militias, were shot by the Communists, but with the city on the brink of invasion by Fascist troops, the senior officer had taken a lenient view and set him free after holding him in a cell for a few weeks.

From there he returned to the cave in the park where he and my father had been hiding out, but naturally his brother was gone. Paco fled the city and travelled north, on a treacherous, frozen, hungry journey over the Pyrenees and into France, where he hitched lifts along the coast until he arrived at Marseille. There he boarded a boat for Mexico.

But I had known instinctively that Montserrat was holding something back from me. Bad news.

Please, tell me, I had written. *I'd rather know.*

You said that when our fathers returned to Alguaire after the bombing of Lerida, they were told by villagers that their parents had been shot by Fascist soldiers?

She replied, *That's not what my father told me.*

What do you mean? What were you told?

I didn't heard from her for a couple of days. *Please. I want to know,* I had prompted.

She eventually wrote back. *I was told that immediately before the Fascist shelling, our grandfather was caught by another villager carrying a lantern across the village square, which was forbidden at the time. It was during a blackout, when exposing light of any kind threatened to alert the enemy. There was an accusation that he did it to provide guidance for the Fascist troops, so that they knew where to aim their shells. The suggestion was that he was a secret Franquista. A traitor. After the village was shelled, he and our grandmother were hoisted to the top of the grain store and thrown to their deaths.*

There was nothing in Collbató other than a couple of shops that were closed for the siesta, so we agreed to drive into the neighbouring town of Esparreguera a few miles away to find somewhere to talk. I followed her in my hire car into the bustling, modern town centre, and we found a bar. I thanked Montserrat for taking the trouble to come to the ceremony. I appreciated the gesture, I said. She told me she'd been at an academic conference in Paris the week before and had stayed on before flying back to Mexico City.

She placed her hands over mine and stared into my eyes, as though she was trying to draw something out. 'This is a reunion, in a sense, for both of our fathers,' she said.

I smiled and nodded.

I still felt embarrassed that my account of my father's life was so scant. She knew more, but not much.

The waiter arrived with our coffees and we sat silently while he placed them on the table before us. Now that we were in the same room, rather than on the other side of the world from one another, I felt we could get beyond the bare historical facts.

'Did you never wonder why your father refused to talk about his childhood and his upbringing?' I asked. 'Did you ever get the feeling he had something to hide?'

She frowned. 'He would sometimes answer questions that I asked, but he rarely volunteered the information, and he seldom talked about the war. I could tell he was uncomfortable with it, so I never pushed him for answers though I did learn a little from him.'

I felt comforted that I'd finally met someone who'd shared my experiences, who'd witnessed the same dark silences that had blighted my childhood and my adult relationship with my father, but I was desperate to know more, to find out what else we had in common and what set us apart, how she'd coped with the burden of living with an event that had taken place thirty years before her birth, and whether she'd dealt with it any differently. I wanted to know if she she'd suffered in the same way I had. I wanted to feel vindicated, certain that I'd done everything I could to assuage my father's anger, hurt, guilt, whatever it was that had made him so unhappy.

'Did you find that his past, his suffering in the war, had a big influence on the way he behaved towards you?'

She continued to hold her hands over mine but the smile dropped slowly from her face, replaced with a frown.

'I'm not sure what you mean.'

'I mean, did he do things that weren't entirely . . . ?'

She continued to stare, and I felt suddenly uncomfortably self-conscious, ashamed that I should be raising negative thoughts about my dead father at such a time.

'How did he treat your mother . . . I mean, did he . . . ?'

She turned her head like a confused dog, and her eyes crinkled.

'What I mean is . . . was he angry all the time?'

Her smile returned, and tears formed in the corners of her eyes. 'No, not at all. He was a loving, beautiful man.'

I'd always imagined that my father's reluctance to return to his homeland, to track down surviving members of his family, was motivated by fear. There was the fear of the enemy, but also, as he'd explained, fear of those supposedly fighting on the same side, who had turned against him and his brother. Perhaps I'd been wrong about that – perhaps he hadn't been afraid – just ashamed of the sins of his parents. I suggested this to Montserrat and she agreed.

'It doesn't matter what side you fought on. People were scared and embarrassed, and they still are, more than seventy years on,' she said. 'The elderly people in the villages still know who behaved badly, who took advantage of the war to settle feuds and scores. To this day there are thousands who don't want to talk about it, not because they can't remember or because the memory is too painful, but because they or members of their family are killers.'

She recalled the terror that had gripped her father in 1981, when he watched television pictures of the attempted coup from their home in Mexico. Despite being six thousand miles away, he was as terrified as Papa as the events unfolded.

'When that silly little general stood up in the Cortes, he shouted "*Todos, estar en silencio.*" "Everybody be quiet." He meant for everyone in the chamber to be quiet, but a whole generation of Spaniards took his words literally. It set back the cause of reconciliation by twenty years, and even now people are afraid to talk about the war.'

We talked until our coffee went cold, so we ordered some more, and then that went cold as well. She spoke enthusiastically and tenderly about her two teenage daughters and about her husband, who was a dentist in Mexico City. I told her all about Ben, how he was studying politics and history at Edinburgh University, one of the best in Britain, and how proud I was of him. I made brief mention of Cheryl, but I didn't go into detail. We'd only recently got back together, and I didn't yet feel able to talk about my marriage easily and confidently.

It was getting dark, and we decided it was time to leave. Montserrat had to drive to Barcelona to catch a flight home. I was going to take a train to Malaga, from where I would take the bus to Algeciras and then travel by ferry across to Tangier. This had been my first trip away since I'd left the paper, and although I'd only been gone for a couple of days, I missed Cheryl and Ben and I wanted to be home.

We walked slowly along the pavement in silence until we arrived at our cars. We embraced and exchanged kisses and I promised to keep in touch. As she turned to leave, I grabbed hold of her arm. I could feel tears running down my face.

'I visited that building. The grain store, where they were killed,' I said.

She drew me close to her and wrapped her arms around my neck. 'Did you?' she asked gently.

'No, I mean before I knew that's where they died. I felt drawn to it the moment I saw it. I knew there was something significant about it. Don't ask me why.'

She rubbed the back of my head soothingly until I stopped crying.

'I really need to go,' she said. 'I'll miss my flight.'

I gripped her arm again before she could pull away.

'Was our grandfather a traitor?' I asked sobbing.

'My father insisted he wasn't. He said it was untrue, a conspiracy by other villagers who had a vendetta against him. But these things happened. It was a civil war. Even if our grandparents were Fascists, our fathers fought bravely for the Republic. That is the memory that you must hold on to.'

23

The night journey to Malaga was cold and monotonous. The air-conditioning in the train was turned up high, and despite numerous requests to the guard, nothing was done about it. Outside was pitch darkness, which meant I couldn't distract myself with the passing scenery. I sat shivering in my overcoat, exhausted but unable to sleep.

It was mid-morning when the train pulled into Malaga, and as I stepped on to the platform I felt the soothing comfort of the sun's rays on my face. I walked the short distance to the bus station and bought a ticket, pleased that I had managed the entire transaction in Spanish. I had almost an hour to kill before the next bus for Algeciras left, so I went into a small cafeteria across the road. It was small and functional, sparsely furnished with a few aluminium tables and chairs and thick with cigarette smoke. A few elderly men were seated silently at the bar, eating small dishes of *chipirones a la plancha* and slices of *tortilla*. I bought a coffee and sat at one of the tables. A radio, tuned to a local music station, was playing in the background. A song came on that I recognised. I hadn't heard it for years, probably not since I was a child, but I knew the singer's voice, unmistakably, as that of Manolo Escobar.

By the time I boarded the coach I couldn't keep my eyes open, though I was frequently jolted awake as we chugged heavily over bumps in the coastal roads. It was late afternoon when we pulled into Algeciras, a functional freight port and the gateway between Europe and Africa. On the dirty streets prostitutes openly plied their trade and gangs of young Arab men stood on street corners, smoking cigarettes and offering passers-by Moroccan money at cheap exchange rates.

I made my way to the ferry terminal for the journey across the Strait of Gibraltar. It seemed like an indecently short trip for such a jarring cultural clash. Within forty minutes I'd left behind the safety and affluence of Europe and was thrust into a buzzing, cacophonous whirl of djellabas, donkeys, palm trees and mosques.

I wandered along the Boulevard Mohammed V, the unkempt main drag of Tangier that ran along the seashore. The city was crumbling and dilapidated. The few new structures that existed remained unfinished and barely serviceable. Hotels on the seafront hinted at a former grandeur, but they had not been maintained. This was not the cosmopolitan playground of the rich and cultured in which Papa had worked, and I wondered what he would have made of it all now.

The Continental Hotel, where he'd been employed as a waiter and barman, was still there, and I went in for a drink. It was late afternoon and the lounge bar was nearly empty. I chose a seat in front of a large open log fire, admiring the walls that were garnished with intricate Moorish carvings and mosaics. A waiter dressed in a burgundy suit and a white shirt sidled up to me and asked if I'd like a drink. I ordered a beer, and he smiled indulgently before shuffling away.

A large portrait window looked out on to the seafront. Dusk was closing in, but I was still able to see across the misty Mediterranean to the Andalusian coastline. The waiter returned with my bottle of cold beer. He poured a little into a chilled glass and placed the bottle on the table. I imagined Papa doing the same for Beat writers and gun-runners fifty years before.

I drank my beer slowly, almost in a trance, trying to imagine what it would have been like for my father to be here – working in a foreign country, in the shadow of his homeland, too fearful or ashamed to return.

I paid at the bar and said goodbye to the waiter, but as I turned to leave something caught my eye. The room was dimly lit, and I had to lean closer against the bar to see, hanging on the wall in a dusty frame, an old black-and-white picture of Humphrey Bogart, his signature scrawled across the bottom.

I returned along the seafront to the ferry terminal. I'd planned to stay in Tangier overnight, but I decided I'd seen enough. The trip back was calm. There was hardly anyone on board and I had the whole deck to myself. I leant against the railings and breathed in the salty evening air, watching as the lights of Spain grew closer and closer.